LOVE & WAR 2

THE BETROTHAL MELEE

SARAH EDWARDS

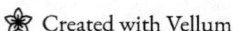 Created with Vellum

Donna and Delores are responsible for this one.
They wanted it, and they got it. Along with ketchup flavored chips.

Chapter One

Somewhere in hell, Thomas of Draycott's uncle languished, laughing his twisted bollocks off at what he'd wrought. It had taken a deplorable sort of skill to render the once prosperous vassalage of Draycott to the rotting hulk Thomas had inherited.

Flushed with drink, beady eyes glittering, Wilfred raised his goblet. "To Sir Thomas."

"Sir Thomas!" men in the hall joined Wilfred with a hearty roar.

Wilfred must have thought Thomas an unmitigated idiot. The only idiocy he'd been guilty of was trusting Leon's former bailiff with his manor while he was at war. Thomas intended to right that wrong this day. He raised his mug and added to Wilfred's toast, "And to Uncle Leon, may he burn for eternity."

"I can't drink to that." Peter mouthed piety for the sake of his priestly vestments but drank anyway. It had been a poor day for Peter two years ago when the parish had sent him to spread the word amongst the godless at Draycott.

Five years since Leon's death, and Thomas was still undoing the damage. First, he'd concentrated on making the land profitable and feeding those who looked to Draycott for protection. He had sent coin to Wilfred to keep the manor habitable.

Purse full and glad to be home, Thomas had returned to Draycott as the sun was cresting the hills this morning. It had seemed like a heartening augury at the time. The repairs to the manor were coming along. The outer walls no longer swayed with every stiff wind and the roof had been repaired, which was a good thing because the storm raging outside tonight was demanding entry into his home.

Dinner, however, told a different tale. Wilfred and his lot had taken up the best tables, leaving his fighting men crowding the two decrepit tables remaining. Those who had come to dinner late propped themselves against the walls as they ate. No one had stomach enough to sit on the noisome floor.

From the state of the hall, Wilfred had left the manor to wallow in squalor in Thomas's absence. Jesu, the rushes reeked as if they had not been changed since he'd last been in residence. Months living rough, and this was their welcome home.

Through most of the winter and spring, Thomas had been away, dissuading a southern baron from poaching his neighbor's land and riches. It had taken several skirmishes with Thomas's army to turn the ambitious lord's attentions from his neighbor's land.

A tree trunk burned in the large hearth at the far end but did little to dispel the chill. Thomas pulled his fur cape tighter around his shoulders and applied himself to his dinner, a thin gruel supplemented by the game he and his men could add to the table. The manor cook had died, and Wilfred had installed his sister.

His ass ached from the harsh wooden bench beneath him, but Thomas dared not shift lest it earned him a splinter in the balls. All their good furniture, his uncle had burned for firewood after he'd denuded the demesne's forests and made an enemy of its neighbors. Thomas had repaired relationships with his neighbors, and the forests were slowly recovering. Furniture had been on the list of items Wilfred was tasked with acquiring.

"No coin has been spent on the manor and its comforts," he said to Peter. Anger snapped and snarled at the thin chain he kept on it.

Peter looked grim. "And yet Wilfred looks hearty enough."

Wilfred looked fat and happy, as did the men about him. The rest of the manor's occupants still looked drawn, bone weary, and were still wearing the same rags they had been when he'd left.

Thomas had sent most of his coin for the outer repairs, but he had sent Wilfred enough coin to feed the manor residents and see to new clothing.

This was his fault too. He knew he should have rid himself of Wilfred from the start, but he'd allowed pity to sway him. Wilfred had a bad leg and was no longer young enough to find another home.

A rat scurried across the hall, and the manor dogs gave chase in a fury of snarling and barking. Thomas was glad his mother wasn't alive to see this. She'd died fifteen years earlier, and things had deteriorated rapidly from there.

"I look forward to our first harvest. At least then we can expect decent food." Peter grimaced at his bowl of gruel. "We eat better in camp than here."

Thomas loved Peter like a brother, but his stating the obvious grew tiresome. "There has to be a suitable cook in the village. I could do better than this."

"I shall make enquiries." Peter sipped his wine and shuddered.

Thomas empathized. The wine was horrible, but the food was worse. He had held the vague hope that he could defer dealing with the manor until he married. Bringing matters inside the manor walls to rights reeked of women's demesne to him and left him with the ballock shriveling certainty that he knew well less than nothing of how to go about it. "I erred in leaving Wilfred in charge."

"Indeed." Peter plucked at his bottom lip. A sure harbinger for Peter stewing some scheme in his head. "What you need is a wife."

Thomas laughed, couldn't stop himself. Only the worst sort of whoreson would inflict Draycott on some poor gently raised maiden. "That is impossible."

"So you say." Peter's tone was carefully devoid of expression. "There is always the invitation from Elford."

Thomas had seen the light of hope in Peter's eye on the messenger's departure. "Sir Richard loved my father and feels responsible for his death. It's nothing more than that."

"And?" Peter's sharp brown gaze bored into him. "Why does that mean you shouldn't accept his invitation?"

Thomas shrugged and forced himself to swallow a mouthful of the pigswill wine. "I need to be here and fix what Wilfred has failed to."

Peter looked at him strangely and cleared his throat. "Um... Thomas. Can it be that you've failed to grasp the import behind this invitation?"

"No." God's balls, but the contagion of believing him a simpleton had taken Peter. "This is some elaborate tourney to win the hand of Sir Richard's youngest daughter."

"Yes." Peter gave him a stare heavy with meaning. "And you're not yet wed and in need of a wealthy bride."

Thomas couldn't stop himself. The idea of Madeleine of Elford as his bride made him chuckle harder than the idea of him taking any wife. "You can't think I would wed Madeleine."

Peter flushed. "I don't see why not. One wife is as good as another, and rumor has it she's fair enough."

"Oh, she's more than fair enough." Thomas braved another sip of wine, but he wasn't much of a drinker and set his goblet aside for one of water. "I haven't seen her in a long while, but she showed every indication of growing up to be as fair as her mother."

Grinning, Peter threw open his arms. "There! You see? This is perfect."

"Yes, Peter. Other than the fact that she hates me with a heat that rivals the sun."

Peter deflated. "Eh?"

"Madeleine hates me." Thomas let his mind drift back to the time he'd been fostered at Elford. A kindness paid him due to his father. "The last time we saw each other, she bit me."

"I beg your pardon?" Peter blinked at him.

Hard pressed to hide his smile at Peter's incredulity, Thomas sipped his water. Madeleine had been half wildling, half terror. "Her older brother, Edward, is barely six months younger than me. Naturally, as youngsters, we competed."

"I'm failing to see where the biting comes in." Peter pushed his dinner away.

"I trounced Edward over some or other argument. She took exception to me shoving her brother in the midden." Thomas pushed his plate of abysmal rabbit away too.

Peter paled. "Good Lord! What did Sir Richard feel about you shoving the son and heir into the shit?"

"Not a thing. He let us fight it out amongst ourselves." To Thomas's younger self, Sir Richard had been something of an idol. "Edward and I were always getting into it about something or other. Edward resented the time and attention Sir Richard gave to me."

"Sir Richard does seem fond of you." Peter nodded and leaned his arms on the table. It creaked and rocked beneath his weight. "He has shown you much favor over the years."

"As I'm fond of him." Thomas still saw Sir Richard as his model of knightly behavior. "He has more than repaid my father for any debt owed."

Peter hummed and looked at his steepled fingers. "Your father died before you were born. I know that, but you never did tell me how."

Thomas had never met his father, and any fondness he might have had for his sire was only as a memory given to him by those who had known Hugh of Draycott. "He was a great favorite of Sir Richard's and joined with Sir Richard when he first formed a band of men at arms to save Elford. He was killed in the battle where Sir Richard and Lady Margaret parleyed peace and got married."

"Ah." Peter nodded. "You must have inherited your strength and prowess from him."

Thomas shrugged. It had certainly not come from his uncle, a weasel-faced coward of a man who had barely topped Thomas's shoulder. Yet he'd married Thomas's mother and held sway over Draycott through her. "They say my father was a skilled fighter."

Peter grunted and contemplated the hall.

A shrill giggle rose from amongst a table of oldsters, all of them what remained of Leon's former men, as a frowzy wench with red hair rose, lifted her skirts and straddled Wilfred.

"Dear Lord." Blushing, Peter looked away.

"Jesu, give me sodding strength." Not only had Wilfred pocketed his money, he now openly thwarted Thomas's authority. He had banned the whores from Draycott.

Thomas didn't care if the whores plied their trade in the village, but it was this sort of going on that reminded him how far he was from being able to offer marriage to a respectable woman of birth. His anger ignited, Thomas stood and stomped across the hall.

Around the pair, people were too busy drinking and laying bets on how long it would take Wilfred to finish.

Thomas took Martha by the arm and tugged her clear.

Silence fell. A couple of those placing wagers tried to sneak away from the table.

Shaking his head, Thomas looked at them.

The two men crept back to the table and sat.

"Out." Thomas gave Martha a nudge for the door. "You can finish your meal in the kitchen, and then you leave. Don't come back."

Martha eyed him, her cheeks flushed with drink. She must have been at the mead and not the wine. She studied him with a cunning gleam. Hand on her hip, she sashayed closer. "Are you sure I should leave?" She laid a grimy hand on his chest. "I could put a smile on your face that will last clear through the summer."

More likely she'd give him a cock itch that lasted way past the summer. "Thank you, but no. Eat and leave, and I don't want to see you back here."

She peered up at him and sucked on her lower lip. "Are you su—"

"I won't tell you again. Out." Thomas only had so much patience. Everyone had to earn a crust of bread, but he was trying to turn Draycott into a home. The sort of place respectable folk settled, with good people serving in the keep.

Martha took one look at his face and scuttled for the kitchen.

Thomas eyed Wilfred. "What did I tell you about the whores?"

"Well, but, Sir Thomas." Wilfred staggered to his feet, still fastening his braies. "A man has needs." He winked. "You should know all about that, what with your being at war so often."

Thomas did know all about needs, but his needs had to be put at the end of a long list. First came Draycott, and he poured every penny he made into it. He'd repaired cottages and improved the land for his folk. It had taken nearly everything he was worth to put drainage ditches throughout the fields and stone walls around them. This winter Draycott would survive on the fruits of her own labors for the first time since Leon's death.

Leon had corrupted Draycott. He'd spent all the coin on pleasure and surrounded himself with men who had no honor. Men like Wilfred.

"What happened to the coin I sent you for food?" Even now Thomas gave the whoreson a chance to be honest with him.

"I used it exactly like you said, but times are hard, Sir Thomas." Wilfred looked to his friends. "Prices are up and—"

"Do you think I am a fool?" Thomas stepped into Wilfred, forcing him to look up to meet his eye.

Wilfred swallowed. "No, Sir Thomas, but I—"

"You spent the coin I sent you." He fastened his hand in

Wilfred's tunic and tugged him to his toes. "You spent it on whores and drink for yourself and your friends."

Sweat slid down Wilfred's temple. "I swear, in the name of our Lord—"

"Do not, my son." Peter's smile was colder than the welcome at Draycott. "The Lord wants no part in what you've done here."

Wilfred's voice grew thinner as Thomas tightened the hold on his tunic around his throat. "I admit, we may have made free to celebrate from time to time. But we are but men, and—"

"What you are is vermin." Not wanting to touch him a moment longer, Thomas released Wilfred. "You have until sunrise to scurry away. Far, far away." Ignoring the stench of stale sweat and wine, he put his face close to Wilfred's. "From tomorrow forward, I will rid myself and my land of any vermin I see."

He turned his back on their table. He should have tossed them out after Leon had died, but he'd allowed pity to hold sway.

He prayed his mother would forgive him for the state he'd allowed Draycott to disintegrate to. At fifteen, he'd been smothered in grief over her death and had not fought Leon for his rightful inheritance. Some of the intervening years had been spent with Sir Richard at Elford, others learning his trade—death and war. He had returned to Draycott ten years after his mother's death, but Leon had robbed him of his vengeance by drunkenly falling into a river and drowning. The state of Draycott had necessitated Thomas raise coin as quickly as he could. The only way he'd known to make coin was by his sword, and so, for the past five years he'd rented it out to the highest bidder. But Draycott was a giant, hungry maw that swallowed everything he placed before her.

Draycott's voracious hunger chased him into sleep and woke starving with his belly each morning. She would swallow him whole with her hundreds of hungry mouths.

"A rich wife would help." Peter floated his suggestion gently. "Bedding a fair wench has to be easier than risking death on every field of battle."

Thomas snorted. "Clearly, you've not met Lady Madeleine."

Peter's loud laugh filled the hall. "No, indeed not."

"The girl will chew me to death."

Beneath an armload of swords, Old Saul entered the hall. Like Wilfred, Saul had served Leon. Thomas had never seen Leon mount a horse or use a sword, but Leon had kept Saul as his squire for forty years. Unlike Wilfred, Saul had switched his loyalty to Thomas.

Stumbling under the weight, Saul dropped his burden on a trestle table. An ominous creak rose from the table, and for a few heartbeats, it swayed like a newborn foal before crashing to the ground.

"Are you sure you could not woo Lady Madeleine?" Peter looked pained. "Make amends and then ingratiate yourself. You are fair enough."

Thomas smiled at Peter's optimism. "I respect Sir Richard too much to even attempt it. Sir Richard will want somebody for Madeleine who loves and cherishes her. I cannot be that man, and even if I could, look around you." Thomas gestured the hall. "How could I bring the daughter of one of the richest men in the kingdom to this?"

Peter grimaced. "Are you sure?"

"I won't deceive Sir Richard. He has my loyalty."

"Hmm." Peter plucked at his lip. "And yet you would offend him by refusing his invitation."

"You did not..." Thomas ran out of words, incredulous at the depth Peter would sink. "You are using my loyalty and affection for Sir Richard against me."

Saul picked the swords up from beneath the splintered table.

Peter looked unrepentant. "It sounds to me like Sir Richard would like nothing more than to marry his daughter to a trusted man. Perhaps he even nurses hopes as we speak." Eyes bright with his scheming, Peter leaned forward. "Should that be the case, imagine his disappointment that you did not come." He shrugged. "Disappointment that might grow to resentment after all he has done for you."

"You're a man of the cloth." Thomas stared at Peter, not able to tear his outraged gaze away. "And yet you stand here and exploit my respect and admiration for the man."

"His youngest daughter." Peter sighed and shook his head. "A tender flower to be cast up to the foul and cruel winds of fate. The beloved fruit of his loins and heart."

Thomas snorted at the idea of Madeleine as a tender flower. Despite himself, however, Peter's words slid beneath his skin and prickled. He did owe Sir Richard everything, and refusing this invitation could be construed as ungrateful, churlish even.

"Sir Richard." Peter heaved a rippling sigh. "A man who nurses the fragile hope in his bosom that a boy on whom he lavished his affection should return to the fold, as did the beloved prodigal son, and shelter his tender flower of a daughter."

"Firstly, you know Madeleine not at all." Thomas tried to harden himself, but Sir Richard would never turn down an invitation from him. "And is there no limit to how low you will bend?"

Peter shook his head. "I suppose there must be, but I have yet to find it." He clapped Thomas on the shoulder and grinned. "Come, bold and brave Sir Thomas, let us go to Elford and see how blows the wind there." He nudged Thomas with his elbow. "At the least, you could make powerful friends. Powerful friends who would need an army such as you have."

Thomas held firm. For about two heartbeats. He growled as he said, "Send a messenger to Sir Richard. Thomas of Draycott would be delighted to accept his invitation."

Chapter Two

M adeleine's "suitors" had been trickling into Elford all week. Initially she'd been horrified by the idea of Father offering her up like the fatted calf, but he had assured her that was not the case.

Mother, who had not supported the idea, had come around as well. No big surprise there, as Mother and Father always presented a united front. Mother had invited her to see the entertainments planned as an opportunity to make new friends. If one of those friends should appeal to her, well and good, but she was under no obligation to marry anyone.

Madeleine didn't know why they were bothering anyway. She had already made her choice, and she believed her choice shared her hopes for their future. Now if only she could get Robert to ask for her hand.

She had hoped the presence of so many potential suitors would spur Robert to action. Unfortunately, as the suitor ranks swelled, Robert became more and more elusive. She needed to see him and reassure him that he still held her heart. She hated the idea he might be suffering some doubt.

Sir Giles had arrived first and lost no time in trying to charm. After they'd broken their fast, he'd laid siege to her and kept her sitting with him in the hall. Frustrated in her plans to find Robert, she'd sent Heather off to find him instead.

"Now I shall tell you a thing for you to wonder at, Lady Maddy." Giles held her hand in his much larger one. Fighting-man callouses, like those adorning Father's hands, felt familiar and reassuring. Giles reminded her of her brother Simon, only less serious than Simon.

"Tell me a thing of wonder," she said, indulging him while she watched for Heather. It couldn't take that long to locate Robert.

"The true wonder here is that Giles knows a thing to tell." William of Trent winked at her. The youngest son of the Earl of Trent, William had dark soulful eyes and brown hair. He also was said to inherit a demesne on his mother's side when she passed.

Giles chuckled but shoved William with his foot, hard enough William nearly fell to the floor. "We shall see how you fare when it's more than your mouth at work."

"Indeed, we shall." A look of challenge in his eye, William adjusted his velvet doublet and returned to his bench seat.

Madeleine had four brothers and could see the challenge kindling between William and Giles. In her experience, men could keep banging their heads together endlessly. "The thing of wonder?"

"Ah." Giles took her hand again. He was the handsomest of the men who had arrived thus far. With wheaten hair and a wicked sparkle in his blue eyes, Giles already had the Elford women sighing his way. He'd kept his eyes on her, and even though her heart belonged to Robert, Madeleine couldn't say she wasn't flattered.

With one long finger, he traced the line of her palm. "I can read your future in your palm."

"You can't." His touch tingled, and it made her giggle.

"Lady!" Giles clasped a hand to his chest. "So cruel. I see I shall have to prove myself." He bent his head over her hand and traced the large line running from between her middle and fore-fingers to her wrist. "This tells me you will have a long life."

She didn't entirely believe him but was intrigued anyway. "And what else?"

"You will find your love." Giles traced the line bisecting the pad beneath her fingers. "He will win your heart completely."

"He's making this up." William leaned his elbows on the table behind him. "Either that or his mother is a witch."

"My mother is a saint." Giles glanced at William and then back at her. "But she does have a wicked temper."

Madeleine could tell them she'd already met the love of her life, but she'd promised Father and Mother she would keep an open mind. She didn't tell her parents it wasn't her mind that mattered. Her heart had already found its match. "Does it say who wins my heart?"

"Alas, it doesn't." Giles's somber expression dissolved into one of mischief. "But it does tell me you will have many stout wheaten-haired babes."

The group about her laughed, and Madeleine's cheeks warmed. Giles also had a ribald sense of humor and flirted shamelessly. Whether he was genuinely interested in her, she couldn't fathom yet. But he was pleasant company, and he did make her laugh.

"No." William took her hand. "He reads it wrong." He bent and placed a hot kiss in her palm. "Those children of yours will all be dark haired."

Madeleine thought her face might burst into flame. The men were bold in their pursuit. The man she wanted to be bold, however, had absented himself from the keep.

Heather entered the hall and looked about before locking gazes with her. Heather nodded.

Relief surged through Madeleine. With no time to waste, Madeleine retrieved her hand and stood. "I'm afraid I must leave you now."

"Say it isn't so." Giles rose with her.

William gave her a slow, sure smile. "Until later, Lady Maddy."

Trying not to be obvious, she hurried across the hall to Heather near the chapel doors.

She drew close enough for only Heather to hear. "Did you find him?"

"Yes." Heather checked behind her. "He rode out a few minutes ago, without his squire." Heather gave her a naughty grin. "His squire has a small crush on me and was more than happy to tell me where Sir Robert went."

Most men at Elford keep had a small crush on Heather. Along with her bright copper hair and ivory skin, she'd a shape both slim and curved where a girl likes most to be curved. "And?"

"The ruined church," Heather whispered. "I had your horse readied."

Heather was the very best of maids, and Madeleine pulled her into a hug. "Thank you. I must go."

"Here." Heather handed Madeleine her cloak. "You will need this as well." She jerked her chin toward the hall, where Madeleine's swains had struck up some sort of game. "You don't want any of that lot sneaking after you and trying to steal a kiss."

Madeleine pulled her cloak about her shoulders and hurried out of the hall. The bailey was full of people going about their business, and nobody thought anything of her heading for the stables.

Queen, her bay palfrey, stood saddled and ready for her. She thanked the stable lad and mounted without help of the block. Her brothers had teased her until she'd learned not to use assistance.

Having been confined by rain for the last four days, Queen danced and sidled as Madeleine walked her out of the bailey. She pretended to be alarmed by her hooves on the drawbridge, arching her neck and snorting.

Once free of the drawbridge and people, Madeleine let Queen have her head. The land around Elford sloped away from the castle and across meadows filled with summer wildflowers. From the castle parapets, she would be easily visible. She waved over her shoulder at the sentry who would be watching her departure.

Wind whipped through her hair and slapped her cloak around her legs. Riding was one of her greatest pleasures, and Adelaide had bred Queen for her.

When they reached the river, she drew Queen in. Lazy and deep green, the river lay like a thick viper winding through the land. Madeleine urged Queen into the water where the stream was most shallow. Icy water rushed over her legs and feet and Madeleine gasped.

Clambering up the opposite bank, they approached the forest that would shield them from the castle. In the forest, the deep shade made her immediately glad of her cloak. Great oaks, birches and beeches stood all around her. From somewhere in the canopy, a lark sang, and the undergrowth rustled with the escape of small creatures.

In times past, these woods had been inhabited by the old folk. As children, she and her siblings had sometimes come across strange rocks carved with runes and odd bits of bone and shiny stones.

A figure appeared out of the gloom, and Madeleine drew Queen to a halt. "Posy?"

Posy started and cleared her throat. "Madeleine."

Small, plump and dark, Posy had big blue eyes that persuaded all the men of Elford that she was helpless and fragile. Madeleine knew better. Behind that sweet face, Posy harbored the temper of a shrew and a streak of nastiness that she didn't bother to hide from other women. "What are you doing here?"

"I could ask you that question." Posy jammed a hand on her hip. "Shouldn't you be entertaining your future husband?"

Madeleine cursed the flush burning her cheeks. "They're not here for that."

"Indeed." Posy's eyes flashed. "Because if they were, one might think it meant you were unable to find a man on your own." She smoothed her gown over her round hips. "And certainly not without your father dangling his wealth and power about like a prize bauble." With that, she flounced past Queen and went on her way.

It took Madeleine until she reached the end of the woods to think of a scalding reply. Posy would never hear it however, because she'd be back at the keep by then. She'd also managed not to tell Madeleine what she'd been doing out there.

The old church, burned by Norsemen long before Duke William had come to England, stood in a small valley between the woods and the craggy ascent of the hills beyond. The front and back walls of the church still remained, but between had crumbled into a rubble of stones, rock and charred wood.

Robert's horse stood to one side cropping grass. All thoughts of everything but Robert fled.

Halting Queen, she jumped to the ground and tied the reins about a charred wooden spar. Adelaide had trained Queen for her, and she wouldn't go far even if she did come loose.

"Robert?" Her voice echoed slightly.

Robert walked around the far wall of the church, frowning. "Madeleine. What are you doing here?"

"Looking for you." Her heartbeat sped at the sight of his shoulder-length golden hair. But it was his eyes that drew her most. Such a deep, melting brown and fringed with thick, dark lashes. Only the harsh line of his jaw prevented Robert from being too pretty to be manly.

He stopped in front of her. "Why? Don't you have enough men vying for your hand?"

"Are you jealous?"

"Should I be?" Robert cocked his head and studied her. "Your father has made your choice of husband yours."

"And now he has provided more potential husbands to choose from." She was sure Robert loved her as she loved him. He had hinted so often enough. Hints and words almost spoken amounted to not enough, however, and if Robert would but assure her of his love, she would go to Father and announce their betrothal. Her heart had already chosen him, and it seemed his had chosen her, but it was hard to accept the proposal not asked. Robert kept her rushing between elation and despair, one day flirting and making her laugh, making her dizzy with his boldness, and the very next treating her as if she didn't exist. "Perhaps I have already made my choice."

"Indeed." Robert's expression softened and his eyes warmed in a way she adored. "Such a headstrong girl you are, sweet Maddy. I can't fathom what your father is thinking."

He was teasing her and her heart gladdened She was relieved he wasn't sulking about her keep full of "suitors". "He's thinking I should have a say in who I cleave to for the remainder of my days."

"Ridiculous." Robert clicked his tongue and chuckled. "Girls are not capable of making up their minds about something as important as marriage. This isn't a matter of picking your blue silk over your green velvet."

"I wonder what you would say if you knew whom I had chosen." She peered at him from beneath her lashes.

Robert wound a lock of her hair around his finger. "Perhaps I would say you know your own heart and mind." He dropped her hair and stepped back. "Of course, that would all depend on whom you had chosen."

There! A perfect example of what was driving her out of her tiny mind. First, he came over flirtatious enough to set her heart hammering, and then retreated before he said much of anything. It maddened her and kept her hanging on his words. Madeleine shifted closer to him. "You've not been in the keep."

"I've been busy." He looked down at her, tapped her nose. "I should go."

"But, Robert." Being a chaste maiden really chafed at times. If she were a more mature and experienced woman, she could close the gap between them and take matters into her own hands. "We're alone here, and it's rare we find that opportunity."

"Exactly." Robert smirked. "We shouldn't be thus. You

should make sure not to ride without an escort." He leaned close enough to whisper in her ear. "A man coming across you alone might assume you wanted his attentions."

Madeleine had been wagering on just that possibility, but Robert turned and strode away.

Helplessly, she stood there as he mounted. Not even looking at her, he called over his shoulder, "Get yourself home, Madeleine, before trouble finds you."

He mounted and spurred his horse into a gallop.

"I came here for trouble to find me," she yelled after his horse. Like with Posy, she was again too late to be heard. Her head did not come up with clever retorts fast enough. Growling her frustration, she bellowed, "There are times when a girl wants trouble to find her."

A boot scuffed on the stone behind her, and she whirled. Her heart leaped into her throat.

A tall figure, broad of shoulder and dark of hair, stepped out from behind the remains of the south wall. "That sounds like something I can help with."

Chapter Three

I t took Madeleine a moment to recognize Thomas. He'd always been tall, but he was a lot broader and more...there. It was like he demanded her attention merely by sharing space with her. She had forgotten how ruggedly appealing his features were. "You."

"Me." Thomas sketched a bow, the wind ruffling his sable hair. He wore it longer now as well. "Good to see not much has changed with you."

If she could have picked one person who she would hate to have witnessed her tantrum, Thomas of Draycott would be that person. That he'd grown even handsomer since she'd last seen him added fuel to her humiliation. "I see you're still skulking about."

It was hard to maintain one's dignity when Thomas had witnessed the scene with Robert. Dressed in his mail shirt, and armed, he might appear intimidating, if one hadn't bitten him and then shoved him into the same midden he'd shoved her brother in. Of course he'd been easier to shove and bite back then.

"Hardly skulking." He shrugged one broad shoulder. "My father's grave is near here."

Right, it was, and a twinge of remorse shot through her. "Do you visit him often?"

"As often as I can." His dark gaze locked on her, and he studied her. "You've changed."

It had sounded like criticism. "It has been some time since we saw each other."

"Yes." He grinned at her. "But you still have a temper."

"I don't have a temper." She refused to humiliate herself further. "It's those around me who take delight in provoking me."

His grin broadened and it was most disconcerting how it gave him a charming, roguish air. "What did your friend do to provoke you?"

"Nothing." She didn't have to share anything with him.

"Nothing?" He looked pensive. "And was that what made you shrewish?" His gaze strayed over her bosom and hip and returned to her face. "You issued an invitation he didn't accept?"

"No! You..." The words wouldn't come fast enough. That wasn't it at all. Nothing like it. "How dare—no!"

"It sounded to me like an invitation." He made his voice girlish. "'We are alone here, and it's rare that we find that opportunity.'"

"Is that supposed to be me?" Her cheeks were scalding hot.

He laughed, and damn him, it only made him more appealing. "A poor imitation, I admit."

He came forward, crowding her, and Madeleine stepped back before she could control it. Her voice went higher. "Get away from me."

"I was merely going to say if you're still feeling shrewish, I might oblige you by accepting your invitation."

Heat built beneath her skin. He smelled of horse and sage and —she stopped herself mid sniff. "Pig!"

"Hmm." He pressed his cheek to hers and whispered, "Am I to understand you're declining my offer?"

"Yes." She could dearly use a snappy rejoinder, but her thoughts slowed to a crawl.

He raised his brow.

"No! I'm absolutely, irrevocably, and without doubt, declining your offer. There isn't anything you have that I want."

He flashed that roguish grin again. "You sound so certain."

"I'm beyond certain."

"But Madeleine," he said in a way that made her shiver, "you've no notion of what I have to offer."

"I tell you what I do have a notion of." She stepped back before her racing heart gave her away. "I have a notion I'm tired of this conversation." She went to retrieve Queen but stopped before mounting. "I would say God be with you until we meet again, but I have no desire to meet you again."

He made an exaggerated wince. "Then I feel honor bound to inform you of your impending disappointment."

It had to be nothing more than coincidence that Thomas was there, at that time. He was merely visiting his father's grave.

Yet, in all the times she had been there, she'd never seen him. Her suspicions couldn't be true. Heaven couldn't dislike her that much. "You're not coming to Elford?"

"Yes, I am." His grin told her he noted her discomfort and loved it. "I have come to vie for your hand, fair Madeleine." He'd managed to make it sound insulting.

"Don't trouble yourself." She mounted Queen and peered down at him. "My answer is no. Now and forever more."

Laughing, he slapped Queen's rump to set her in motion. "Forever is a long time, Madeleine. Even I might grow on you in that time."

* * *

Thomas's men waited for him near the cairn marking the place his father had died. He'd been paying his respects when he'd noticed Madeleine riding toward the church. He knew of nobody else with hair that bright gold, or another woman who rode as if the beast was part of her.

Plucking his lip and probably reaching all sort of conclusions, Peter studied him as Thomas approached. "What?"

Thomas had no desire to discuss Madeleine. He had known she would grow up fair, but the reality exceeded her girlish promise. "Nothing."

"It doesn't look like nothing." Peter smirked.

They could bicker all the way to Elford, but Thomas refused to share how his response to Madeleine had been instant and visceral, a man recognizing a woman as desirable. "All right. Then it's nothing I want to talk about."

"Fair enough." Peter clucked his horse and got it moving. "Can I hazard a guess that nothing wears a bright red dress and rides like a marauder?"

"You could." Thomas motioned his men to form up. "But then I would have to punch you in the mouth, and God would damn me for punching one of his shepherds. Until he realized which shepherd, and then he would probably saint me." He made a face. "It could get messy."

Peter chuckled. "So that was Lady Madeleine?"

"Yes." A grownup Madeleine with flashing blue eyes and delicious curves.

The sound of harnesses and bits jingling and the creak of leather didn't drown out Peter's voice. More's the pity. "Does she still bite?"

A shot of lust went through him at the idea of Madeleine sinking her white teeth into his flesh. He thrust it from him. "Not on this occasion, but she's still a termagant."

"Pity." Peter grinned at him. "Because from up here it looked like you were rather partial to her...rancor."

Thomas raised his gauntleted fist. "Right in your pie hole."

"Bless you, my son." Peter grinned.

A man with no prior knowledge of Madeleine of Elford, one with a fine demesne and an elegant keep, would be a fair way to pursuing her hand in earnest. She was beautiful, but not in the way of marble effigies and far off stars, but a beauty made of silken hair and dewy skin, inviting touch. She filled out her bliaut in ways he wouldn't have imagined when he'd known her as a scrappy girl.

His reaction to her was purely animal. He wanted her, and it had taken him all of two heartbeats to know that. Which was damned inconvenient. Peter was still smugly wrapping himself in the success of his machinations, and it suited Thomas not to shine the light of truth on him.

While Peter dreamed of his taking a rich, beautiful wife, Thomas had seen instead the advantages of making himself known to men who one day would rule over their fathers' demesnes. A man who earned his bread by his sword needed influential contacts, and games of prowess could only persuade them of his skills. Peter had been right about that, but he was smitten enough with himself, so Thomas refused to give him more fodder.

Five minutes with his baser instincts clamoring for Madeleine had him reconsidering the wife option. It would be no hardship to take Madeleine into his bed. No, the hardship came with having Madeleine in the rest of his daily life.

And lest he forget and get ahead of himself, the lady had made her choice clear. For some, God alone knew what, feather-headed reason, Madeleine had chosen that pretty little peacock.

The same pretty little peacock who had been availing himself of the charms of a dark headed morsel not long before Madeleine arrived. He would find a way to let Sir Richard know what he'd seen. Her father would have a better chance of steering her clear of the peacock.

What was Sir Richard thinking? A more astute judge of a man's worth than Sir Richard, Thomas had rarely met. One only had to look at the peacock to know he wouldn't do for Madeleine. She would rip the poor sod's stones off and wear them around her neck.

No, Madeleine needed a stronger man, one who could match her fire.

"You're very quiet over there." Peter turned in his saddle and looked at him. "What are you planning?"

"Why must I be planning something?

Peter looked at him.

"I was merely considering what I saw before Madeleine arrived."

"Ah." Peter shook his head. "Will you tell her?"

"Are you mad?" He had no wish for her to rip his ears off and stuff them down his throat. "No, but if the opportunity presents itself, I'll drop a word in Sir Richard's ear."

The thick carpet of moss and fallen leaves on the forest floor muffled their horses' hooves. As a boy, he'd loved this forest. It had seemed to him full of ancient mysteries and magical creatures. It also served as a reminder that he and Edward had not always been at each other's throats.

When they were still striplings, he and Edward had set a trap for the dragon they felt sure was hiding in the woods. They had stayed out until full dark had fallen. Long enough to regret their decision.

Sir Richard had found them cowering in their makeshift shelter of branches. When they had returned to the keep, Sir Richard had said nothing of finding two scared boys but regaled the keep with how they'd built a shelter from branches and had been setting out to hunt their dinner when he'd found them. Not likely, as neither he nor Edward had fancied stepping into the forest's enveloping dark. The memory made him chuckle.

Peter glanced at him.

"A boyhood memory." Despite Edward's resentment, and Madeleine's slavish devotion to her older brother, Thomas had been happy there. Sir Richard and Lady Margaret had made him welcome in their home, and he'd learned all he needed to attain his knighthood. "I have many fond memories of Elford."

They cleared the trees and caught their first view of Elford Castle.

Peter whistled low. "She's a beauty."

"Yes, that she is." Built of warm-honey-toned stone, Elford boasted several battlements surrounding her original round tower. Positioned atop a knoll, she commanded a view from all sides. Richard had made many improvements to the castle since his marriage.

Richard's *saltire gules* flew from the round tower.

Thomas and company clattered across the drawbridge and into the lower bailey. Stables, barracks, beast pens and trades were kept to this part of the castle. As large as the whole village of Draycott, Elford castle teemed with people, full of noise and bustle. They threaded their way through the lower bailey and traversed the curtain wall into the upper bailey.

The castle watch would have seen them coming, and Richard of Elford stood tall at the entrance to the keep. Beside him stood Lady Margaret, as slim and graceful as a girl, and beside her, Edward. An inch or two taller than Sir Richard, Edward had his mother's dark hair and blue eyes.

The only of the children to inherit her father's fair coloring was Madeleine, and she wasn't here to welcome him. Let his ridiculous lust absorb the lesson.

"Thomas." Arms wide, Richard approached as Thomas dismounted. "It's good to see you."

He returned Richard's embrace and received a staggering wallop across the shoulders.

Lady Margaret caught his face between her soft hands. Her deep blue eyes studied him. "You look well, Thomas." And then she smiled and reminded everyone what had conquered Sir Richard all those years ago. "And you get handsomer every year."

Thomas blushed like a squire and cleared his throat. "Thank you, my lady."

"I had almost given up hope you would come." Richard threw an arm about his shoulders. "What took you so long to reply?"

Richard took slight to any criticism of his offspring, his

daughters especially, so Thomas needed to handle it delicately. "I didn't think to...well, I'm not in a position—"

"He's not in a position to offer a wife much more than a broken-down hovel." Peter stepped forward with his charming smile. He bowed to Margaret and then Richard. "My lady, Sir Richard, I'm Father Peter, and I keep this one collared."

Edward scoffed and then managed a stiff head tilt. "Thomas."

"Edward."

"Is that ragged lot your vaunted army?" Edward put enough sneer into his words to sting.

"Yes." Thomas refused to bleed in front of him. "My army. As in not an army that belongs to my father."

Lady Margaret sighed. "Boys! Must we begin like this?"

Thomas rather thought they must.

"You see what I must contend with." Peter appealed to them for understanding.

Richard laughed and took Peter's hand. "I'm pleased to meet you." His face hardened as he stared at Thomas. "What kept you?"

"I...er...have not long returned from the south." Thomas cursed his inability to lie smoothly. It would be best if he established his reason for being there from the start. "I understood this tourney to be in the way of a courtship. And as I am not in a position to take a wife..." He ended with a shrug.

Thomas was rather proud of how he'd handed that until he looked at Sir Richard.

Scowling at him, Sir Richard said, "Are you saying my daughter isn't good enough for you?"

"A small blessing for the rest of us." Edward sneered.

Thomas sneered back, and then tried to find the words to soothe Sir Richard.

"Fie, Richard." Margaret slapped her husband's arm. "He's teasing you."

Richard guffawed and gave him another blow to the shoulder

that would have driven Madeleine's pretty peacock to his knees. "And it's less of a courtship and more a...display of options."

Perhaps Sir Richard knew about the peacock after all, and that was the reason behind this bridegroom market. Thomas would not blame him if that were the case. He had not fingers enough to count the ways in which the peacock would make a bad match for Madeleine.

"You, however, are not one of those options," Edward said. "The only person who wants to see you wed to Madeleine less than me, is Madeleine."

Chapter Four

Strongly suspecting Thomas would be at dinner, Madeleine put on her favorite bliaut of emerald green samite. It flattered her complexion and hugged her figure. She needed to show the big lout that his earlier humiliation of her meant nothing to her.

Heather brushed her hair until it shone. "Nobody will be able to ignore you tonight."

"Why do you think Robert remains so illusive?" Madeleine had told Heather all about her afternoon. "I don't understand him."

Eyes on her task, Heather showed nothing, but Madeleine got the feeling she always hid her feelings when they spoke about Robert. "I know you don't like him."

"It's not for me to like or not like him." Heather shrugged.

They were far more than lady and maid, and Madeleine pushed. "But?"

"But I don't always trust his motives," Heather said.

That couldn't be right. Robert was so handsome and noble. He was all that a knight should be. "Robert isn't like other men. He's more reserved and gentlemanly."

Heather snorted. "A lot of good that will do you on your wedding night."

"Heather." Madeleine's cheeks heated. "You're not supposed to say such things to me." Her attempt to be proper failed as they both giggled.

Heather put the brush down. "Your mother would say much the same thing."

"True." Lady Margaret wasn't like other ladies of her kind. She spoke her mind and was honest with her daughters about men, sometimes excruciatingly so. "How should I behave if he's there?"

"Why should Robert not be at dinner?"

Madeleine's cheeks heated. "Not him, the other one."

"Thomas?" Heather peered at her. "He has all the keep girls aflutter."

Madeleine couldn't help but gape. "Whatever for?"

"Come now." Heather rolled her eyes. "Even you must see he's a handsome brute."

Handsome wasn't everything, even when combined with lovely wide shoulders and—that was enough of that. "He's still a brute."

"Some girls enjoy a brute." Heather nudged her.

Madeleine nudged her back. "How would you know? You've as much experience as I. Maybe even less."

"That would be a hard feat for anyone," Heather said, her eyes twinkling. "But Cook assures me there are lots of women who like a man who knows what he's about."

Being the cherished youngest daughter often led to a frustrating lack of information. "What does that even mean?"

"I don't know." Heather shrugged. "But perhaps that's what Thomas thought to show you."

Brave words aside, the thought of seeing him again made Madeleine want to squirm. "I suppose there is no hope that Thomas won't attend dinner."

"I think not." Heather was never one to withhold. "But you hold your head high and behave as if nothing happened."

Advice Madeleine took to heart as she entered the hall. Normally the hall was a lively place, but tonight the noise engulfed her as she entered for the evening meal.

"Ah, Lady Maddy appears at last." Sir Giles separated himself from a group of knights and approached her. Taking hold of her hand, he kissed it and laid it on his forearm. "Now, I suppose I shall have to introduce you to these oafs, but I do so only because I'm the superior man and haven't a thing to fear from them."

His flattery bolstered her confidence, and she smiled at his nonsense.

Giles proceeded to introduce her to a number of knights, whose names barely registered. Had she supported her Father's lunacy of bringing all these men here, she would have to concede he'd chosen well.

John of Warring had a handsome face and a ready smile. Sir Perregrine made up for his plainer features by the breadth of his shoulders and his height. Still another had lovely blue eyes with a bold twinkle in them. If a girl were looking for a man, she certainly had a prime crop to pick from.

None of them were a match for Robert, however.

As Giles led her to her place at the table, she cast a discreet glance around for him. Her heart gave a small leap as she saw him already seated.

Even better, he was watching her with Giles, and a slight frown marred his brow. He could be jealous, which meant he did care for her.

"The green of your gown brings to mind a slender willow." Sir William stole her hand from Giles and put it on his arm. "Good evening, Lady Maddy. You look as pretty as a spring garden this night."

"Your poetry needs work." Giles took her hand back.

Robert was watching both Giles and William, and his frown deepened.

Madeleine had never been one to employ wiles and whatnot, but she'd seen it done aplenty, and she laughed and sent William a coy glance. "What, no parry to that thrust?"

"Alas, Lady Maddy." William leaned closer and whispered, "It would be unkind of me to point out that some of us don't require poetry to impress a lady."

"God's balls, the lot of you will put me off my feed." Father pushed through her admirers and led Madeleine away from them. "You've not yet greeted our late arrival." He stopped in front of Thomas. "Maddy, you must remember Thomas."

Still tall, dark haired and handsome, and still the one knight Madeleine wanted to run and hide from. "Indeed." She tried to hold on to Heather's advice as she held out her hand to him.

Thomas took hers in his massive paw. "And I remember you so clearly." He kissed her fingers. "Almost as if I had met you again this very day."

Her fingers tingled from the contact of his mouth, and Madeleine stopped herself moments before she wiped them against her bliaut. "Perhaps we did, and I have forgotten already."

"Take that." Giles appeared at her elbow. "And thus, I shall turn you about, and Thomas is already forgotten."

As Giles led her to table, awareness of Thomas prickled between her shoulders.

Face drawn and angry, Edward took the seat beside her. It was an expression he wore all too often. Never of an open and sunny disposition, Edward seemed even broodier since his marriage. "I saw you."

"What?" Madeleine nearly choked on her sip of wine. She hadn't seen Edward at the old church.

"Yes." Edward shook his head. "Flirting with that whoreson."

"Which one?" Even as she said it, the ridiculousness made her laugh.

It also drew a rare smile from Edward. Her older brother looked so like her father, only with her mother's dark hair and deep blue eyes. As a young girl, she'd worshiped him. His smile made him even handsomer than normal. "Yes, Father has gathered a bevy of them. I meant Draycott. Don't flirt with him."

"I didn't." If Edward had been there, had he seen her and Robert as well?

"Madeleine." Edward gave her a censorious stare. "Everybody in the hall saw you blush and make eyes at him."

"Everyone in the hall." Relief swept over her. "Oh, you meant a moment ago, here in the hall."

"Yes." Edward's look turned speculative. "When did you think I meant?"

"I didn't know." She covered up her slip. "As I didn't flirt with him, I was confused as to what you could be thinking."

"Hmm." Edward raised a brow but took a sip from his wine. "Good, because I shall never consent to you and him."

This was the part of Edward she didn't worship. As she grew older, his domineering manner irked her. *Edward should concern himself less with my potential marriage and more with his very real one.* "It's not up to you to approve or disapprove of whom I marry, and as for your consent, I don't need it."

"Yes." Edward scowled at Thomas. "But you do need Father's, and I can make sure you don't get it."

Edward sometimes forgot he didn't have command of Elford and all her people yet. "Father doesn't heed every word you say, and I'm as capable of speaking to him as you." Her point made, she conceded. "It doesn't matter anyway, for I shall never consent to marrying Thomas of Draycott."

With a grunt, Edward turned and spoke to Simon on his right.

As if sensing her gaze on him, Thomas looked at her. With eyes as dark as his, it was near impossible to guess what he was thinking. He raised a brow at her.

Madeleine raised her chin in response. He needn't think he bothered her. At all. She refused to look away.

So did he.

As their gazes continued to tangle, an odd tightening sensation in her belly spread. Her insides felt as if they were melting like rich, sweet butter. Her breathing grew choppy, and her heartbeat quickened.

Madeleine tore her gaze away from him. There was no accounting for what had occurred. Odd sensation, indeed. It was more likely that her dinner disagreed with her. That was it. The beef disagreed with her.

She turned her attention to Giles. Beyond Giles, she glimpsed Robert, and he was staring at Thomas, a scowl on his handsome face.

Perhaps Thomas of Draycott had his uses after all.

* * *

As soon as it was polite to do so, Thomas excused himself to see to his men. He always took care of his men. This evening, however, it provided a plausible reason to put some distance between him and the hall. He stalked out of the keep and across the inner bailey, pounding his temper into the earth with his heels.

Not even one full day at Elford, and already his worst fears had come true. Madeleine of Elford was his curse, his cross. Watching her make eyes at that thistledown skirt chaser Giles of Fenmore had almost undone him. The way the man slathered over her hand, his gaze always stuck on the full swell of Madeleine's breast, or the enticing curve of her hip, made Thomas want to punch him.

Somebody should warn Sir Richard about that drooling dog.

That Madeleine seemed to enjoy his leering, even encourage it, made Thomas angrier than he could account for.

The barracks were well positioned, clean and spacious, certainly better than the drafty barren welcome Draycott offered. He ducked through the low door and made his way to the far end where his men were quartered.

They looked to be in high spirits and enjoying their meal and mead.

Saul creaked to his feet. "Do you need aught, Sir Thomas?"

"Don't let your meal go cold." Thomas waved him down again. Saul had it in his head that he served as a sort of aged squire to him. "I was merely checking you were all staying out of trouble."

Lowering himself as far as his old knees would allow, Saul dropped the rest of the way, rocking the bench. "We'll do our best. That we will." He winked. "But we make no vows."

"Just so you know, Sir Richard doesn't tolerate any messing about with the Elford wenches." He made it a point to bend his most severe stare on Saul. Saul was well beyond his wenching days, but the old man didn't like to admit it, and Thomas saw no harm in treating him like the lively buck he had once been. "Mind your manners. Keep your hands to yourselves and your braies laced."

Saul's raspy chuckle followed him into the bailey. The old duffer would be fast asleep before the moon had risen fully. Not ready to return to the hall, Thomas climbed the stairs to the outer walls.

Up there, the air was clear and crisp and slightly chilly even on the hottest of summer days. It cleared his head after the fog of the hall, and he breathed deep.

A clear night sky stretched cloudless and awash in stars. It made a man feel as if anything was possible. Out there, he could make sense of what had occurred in the hall, particularly that last heated glance with Madeleine. He'd met the challenge in her stare, and his blood had risen.

He would never embarrass her and tell her father about their encounter at the church ruins, but she didn't know that, and the contrariness in him enjoyed taunting her. On the morrow, he would find the opportunity to drop a word in Sir Richard's ear about Madeleine's precious Robert. Any man who would dally with another woman didn't deserve Madeleine. He'd a mind to have a word about Giles while he was at it.

A foot scuffing on stone drew his attention. A woman

stepped onto the battlements. For a moment, his blood thickened with the possibility that Madeleine had joined him. As the figure drew closer, he recognized Edward's wife, Catriona. He'd only met her tonight at dinner. It wasn't her vibrant beauty, however, that tightened his gut.

Catriona had the gleam in her eye of a woman after trouble. She'd quickly noted the tension between him and Edward. That she was here now was, Thomas would wager, for the sole purpose of exploiting her observation.

"Sir Thomas." Her raspy voice caressed his name like a naughty whisper. She drew close enough for the deep lily of her scent to encircle him. "Here I find you all alone."

"It's chilly up here. You should return to the keep."

"In a moment." Her eyes glittered up at him in the dark as she placed one delicate palm against his chest. "I thought you would enjoy the company."

Not if she were the last woman on earth. Edward and he could barely be in the same large hall together as it was. "Forgive me, my lady. It grows late."

"Stay a while." She moved into his path. Her voice quavered as she said, "Enjoy the moonlight with me." For a woman with trouble on her mind, she seemed reticent, almost fearful.

Some instinct that all wasn't as it would appear stopped him. "You should ask your husband to enjoy the moonlight with you."

"Him." She turned away and leaned against the parapet. Moonlight etched the delicate lines of her profile. "He would rather carve the moon from the sky than enjoy its light with me."

Beneath her anger, Thomas detected the hurt that he didn't think she knew she'd betrayed. "I'm sorry to hear it."

"As am I." She sighed and turned. "I came to see if perhaps you would enjoy my company more."

"Alas, my lady." Thomas didn't want to injure her further. Lady Catriona seemed far too brittle as it was. "I must decline your tempting offer."

"Offer?" She gave a jagged laugh. "What can you mean? I merely came out here for the night air and found some company."

"Exactly." Thomas bowed. "I meant no more than that."

He turned and took the far stairs off the battlement. Elford Castle, it seemed, wasn't done playing her wicked mischief on him. He'd told Peter this would happen. He should never have come, and the wisest thing for him to do would be to leave as soon as he could.

Chapter Five

Madeleine couldn't help but be excited about the activity all around the keep and even the influx of new faces, many of them handsome. Mother and Father had thrown wide Elford's doors and provided plenty of festivities to keep their guests amused.

The king had banned tourneys, so the day's entertainment would be a series of sword battles conducted with blunted swords. Quick on his feet and lethal with a strike, Robert couldn't be beaten. Even Father must expect Robert to win the contest. At Elford, Robert was second only to Edward, and Edward wouldn't be taking part. When Robert won today, Father and Edward would see how worthy of her he was.

She made sure to dress in her red bliaut with black trim, Robert's colors. In the days of tourneys, he might have asked for her favor. Maybe he still would, and she made sure to tuck a kerchief up her sleeve, just in case.

Taking extra time with her appearance meant she'd missed breaking her fast, so she settled for bread, cheese and an apple, eaten while standing in the kitchen.

"You'll make yourself sick." Cook brandished a cleaver at her. "Gobbling your meal like a suckling pig."

Madeleine grinned at Cook. Her mood this day couldn't be better, and she planned to enjoy watching Robert triumph. He would even triumph over smirking Thomas, and she relished that prospect most of all.

Noise from the bailey made her chew faster. Rising on her toes, she tried to peer past Cook's stout form out the kitchen door to see what was happening.

"Drink." Cook shoved a cup of milk at her. "Or you'll never get that bread down."

"Did you see Robert this morning? Was he in the hall?"

"Yes." Cook shook her head. "And strutting about like a bantam cock, he was. I shouldn't be surprised if he isn't looking so pleased with his plumage by dinner."

Turning to stare at Cook, Madeleine couldn't credit what she'd heard. "Everybody knows Robert is the best swordsman."

"He won't beat my Edward." Robert tended to be short with keep servants and they didn't like him. Not to mention, Cook had a soft spot for Edward. She tossed a rag at Madeleine. "Here, you've crumbs on you. A lot of those bucks out there aren't from Elford, are they? I wouldn't be counting the prize money quite yet if I was Robert."

Madeleine left the kitchen and hurried to the outer bailey. Tents had been set up to keep the watchers and the participants out of the warm sun. A cloudless azure sky with no threat of rain hung above them and restored her mood.

She joined her sister, Adelaide, beneath the shade of a red and white striped tent. The tent had been placed on the far side of the sandy combat area and faced a larger green tent shading the waiting combatants. Seen as a group, they were a stirring lot.

"Maddy, darling." Adelaide looked the very image of their mother with her crow-black hair and eyes bluer than this day's sky. "Where have you been hiding your pretty face?"

Six years her senior, Adelaide had been living back at Elford since becoming a widow four years past. It had taken this long to see the light in Adelaide's eyes once again.

"I have been about." Madeleine gestured the company. "How could I not be when this is going on?"

"Indeed." Adelaide giggled. "I can't believe Mother allowed this to happen."

Madeleine joined her sister's laughter. "I think they're done with me and want me married off."

"There are worse things." And the shadows crept into Adelaide's eyes.

To banish them, Madeleine said, "Care to place a wager on the winner?"

"I most certainly would." The twinkle returned to her sister's eyes. Adelaide tapped her chin and surveyed the combatants. "I'll place my wager on...Thomas."

"Thomas?" Madeleine wrinkled her nose in distaste and studied the men. Thomas was taller than the rest, and certainly broader, but that didn't mean he knew how to wield his steel. "I place mine on Robert, of course."

"Why of course?" Adelaide studied her face.

She could be honest with Adelaide. "Robert and I have an understanding."

"You do?" Adelaide blinked at her. "Nobody told me that."

Adelaide was mourning her husband, and Madeleine didn't like to bother her with her love trials. "We're keeping it to ourselves."

"Do Mother and Father know?" Adelaide's blue gaze sharpened.

"See." Madeleine went with distraction. "The first two are up. And one of them is yours." She nudged her sister. "We never did state our terms."

"If I win, I want that bolt of rose samite you're hiding," Adelaide said.

Madeleine would be loath to part with the beautiful fabric. She'd been hesitating to turn it into a gown, waiting for the perfect idea to come to her. But Robert deserved her faith in him. What sort of future wife would she be if she didn't place her faith in her man? "If you win, it's yours. But if I win, I'll have your amethyst girdle. It will go beautifully with the rose samite when I fashion it into a bliaut."

"Done!" Adelaide pointed. "They're about to begin."

The combatants circled each other.

Thomas locked his gaze on his opponent, his sword at the ready.

His opponent, Sir Matthias, Madeleine believed, circled the wrist of his sword arm. Although the blades were blunted practice blades, they still caught the sunlight and gleamed.

Adelaide gasped as Matthias lunged. He struck down and to Thomas's left. Metal clanged as Thomas caught him on the guard and held.

They disengaged and Matthias circled and then struck again, this time from the other side.

Once more Thomas caught him in the bind before pushing free.

"Why doesn't he fight?" Madeleine didn't like Thomas, but he hadn't struck her as a weakling or a coward.

Adelaide chuckled. "He's watching," she said and pointed. "See how he studies Matthias. He's searching for a weakness to exploit."

Or he was just a big ox without skill, but she kept that last to herself.

Twice more Matthias struck, and Thomas held the bind.

Sword and arm in perfect motion, Thomas swept left, reverse struck right, caught Matthias in the bind and wrenched his sword away. Matthias's practice sword arced through the air and thudded, point down, in the earth.

A moment of silence reigned, and then cheering, whistling and shouting broke out. With a wry grin, Matthias retrieved his sword and bowed to Thomas. Grinning, Thomas patted him on the back, and together they walked to the tent.

"Oh, my." Adelaide smoothed her long dark braid over her shoulder. "I believe I shall look very fetching in rose samite. And thank you for the idea of wearing it with the amethyst girdle. I hadn't thought to put the two together."

Madeleine gritted her teeth and swallowed her apprehension. Thomas's blinding speed and deadly skill had left her gasping. If it had been a real battle, Matthias might be missing his head. "We have yet to see Robert fight."

Sir William and another, whose name escaped Madeleine, moved into the ring. This fight lasted much longer, and William lost.

Giles won his bout amidst much crowing and smirking, and then Robert stepped onto the field.

He looked so handsome with the sun gleaming on his ripe-barley-colored hair. If he would but acknowledge her before the bout, she could be sure of his affection.

Robert got into fighting stance.

He struck before his opponent, driving the man back in a dazzling display of skill. The end was inevitable, and Madeleine smirked at her sister. "See."

"I did." Adelaide looked complacent as she clapped. "But I also saw a lot of unnecessary effort expended, and I hope he doesn't tire himself."

"Robert could go for days."

Adelaide snorted. "Always a useful quality in a man."

William strolled beneath their tent and threw himself on the blanket beside them. "Alas, Lady Maddy, I'm vanquished and in need of comfort."

Adelaide snorted a laugh and handed him a goblet of wine. "See if that helps."

"It's strange," William said, propping himself on his elbow. "But until this point, I hadn't thought being a less than competent swordsman would do me any good. But this is far better than toiling in that blistering sun."

The next pair stepped into the yard, but with Robert waiting for the next round, Madeleine's attention wavered.

The morning grew warmer, and Madeleine more lethargic as she watched the sword bouts.

Once the first round was over, squires tallied the scores and gave them to Father to announce. Serving wenches brought refreshments to the remaining swordsmen.

Thomas took a tankard from a giggling Mary Rose. He smiled politely but didn't engage her in conversation. Unlike Giles who had his arm about Ruth and was whispering in her ear.

If she had been interested in anyone other than Robert, she would have struck Giles from her list. A man who dallied openly with other women before their marriage would for certain do so once the vows were spoken.

Thomas began the second round. This time he didn't wait for the other man to show his hand but struck with the same efficient brutality as the first time and disarmed his opponent.

Madeleine had barely sipped her wine, and the entire thing was over.

"See there." William clapped and whistled. "I have never seen his like."

"His form is too blunt for me," Madeleine said. "I much prefer to see the skill behind the bout."

William gaped at her. "Lady Maddy, I would bite my tongue rather than disagree with you, but these games aside, swordsmanship is what will save your life in a battle." He pointed to Thomas, now sitting with his elbows on his knees and watching the next bout. "There is no time for games and form when somebody wants your blood."

Madeleine took his point and nodded to acknowledge it, but she still preferred watching Robert fight.

Perhaps it was because of what Adelaide had said, or even William, but on Robert's next bout, she noted that he did seem to include a number of flourishes between blows. She didn't think it quite prudent to spin in a circle and turn your back on another man's sword. Still, Robert won his bout, and she didn't know much of sword skills.

Granted she'd brothers who spoke of it often and a father whose renown spread the breadth of the kingdom, but Robert must know what he was about, or he wouldn't win.

"What a peacock." Oliver lurched into the tent and sat beside William. "He wastes time and strength that could cost him his life."

"I don't see you fighting." Madeleine gave him a look of scorn.

Oliver rolled his eyes. "Father didn't allow it. He didn't invite all these men here to parade your brothers in front of you."

Her cheeks heated, and she was hard pressed not to nudge her brother in the ribs. With her foot. Hard. Several times.

William spread his hand over his chest. "I, for one, would parade day and night in front of you."

"Give over." Oliver thumped his arm and both of them laughed.

Giles lost his next bout and joined them beneath her tent.

"Ah." He clasped his chest. "See how I am thrice slain. Once by steel and twice by beauty."

"Sit down, Giles." Adelaide smiled at him. "You're blocking my view."

Arranging himself at Adelaide's side, he sighed. "So cruel."

The next round fell awkwardly for numbers, and Father announced that each man must fight every other.

As the numbers beneath their tent grew, so did the betting. Madeleine couldn't believe how many foolishly wagered on Thomas. Did they not see Robert's dazzling skill?

Although she'd admit to a certain faltering in her faith as Thomas scythed down one man after the other with ruthless expediency. He didn't even look winded, whereas she might have caught a slight slowing in Robert's footwork.

"He's spent." Oliver gestured to Robert with his goblet. "He's wasted all his air on dancing about like a blasted trout on a hook."

Madeleine desperately wanted to remain steadfast, but in the face of the growing numbers against Robert and the evidence of her own eyes, she was struggling.

As if reading her thoughts, Adelaide reached over and took her hand. "It's not over until the last pair fight."

"I know." Madeleine forced a gay smile, but even she worried Robert was outmatched. Even thinking so made her feel disloyal.

Finally, all the bouts were done but one. Nobody was surprised to see Thomas step onto the field. A few remarked that Robert had lasted longer than they had thought he might.

With the two standing opposite each other, their differences struck her. Where Robert was slim and elegant, all long limbs and chorded strength, Thomas was like a blunt instrument, big and powerful and rough.

Both men raised their swords.

Robert struck first, and Thomas parried. Their swords clanged and held.

Thomas twisted his wrist and Robert cursed as his sword skittered over the dry ground.

Madeleine gaped. The bout was over, Robert bested. It had taken Thomas one breath, a simple air drawn in and then expelled, to dispense with her champion.

Adelaide looked at her with sympathy and said, "I believe I have changed my mind. Keep your pink samite. It will fight with my complexion."

"No." What was pink samite compared to the pride-scalding wound of Robert's loss? He barely managed a bow to her father and mother before stalking back to the keep. And that also made her uncomfortable.

The other combatants had taken their comeuppance with apparent cheer. That they might be seething beneath their smiles, she'd little doubt, but they did an excellent job of putting a good face on their losses.

Robert rarely lost, and never so convincingly. Until this day. It must have been that he wasn't accustomed to it. That must have been it. Robert had the sweetest nature and was as noble as any knight she'd met. Why, she would wager at this very minute he was berating himself for his churlishness.

Across the field, her gaze snagged on Thomas, and he raised his brow. His grin challenged her to do her worst, and Madeleine raised her brow. She'd take that challenge and gladly. For Robert.

Chapter Six

With everybody in good spirits, dinner that night was a raucous affair. Even Catriona had made a rare appearance, though she sat as far away from Edward as the table allowed.

Not for the first time, Madeleine wished she knew what went on between Edward and Catriona. They were both good people; she didn't understand what they could have done to each other to create their mutual animosity. Even her partiality for Edward couldn't overcome the way he ignored his Scottish wife, and Catriona being virtually alone at Elford without anyone to stand by her. Of course, if Catriona were a mite less prickly, she would see she had a family and she might make friends.

Catriona was not the only woman unhappy with her chosen man, and Madeleine was struggling to maintain her pretense that she was enjoying the evening. She gave Catriona a smile of solidarity, which Catriona returned with a slightly bemused expression.

As she'd predicted, Robert had rallied, and his show of temper had disappeared beneath his charming smile. The same charming smile he was bending on that sow Posy. Sitting beside her, he whispered in her ear throughout the meal. Madeleine couldn't fathom what they had to talk about and for such a long time.

Posy giggled so hard that Madeleine could almost hear her from across the hall.

The hairy, ugly jealous beast in her wanted to leap the table and yank Posy away from Robert. By the hair. Posy probably didn't even like Robert. She was merely flirting to annoy Madeleine. Although, Posy did have a dewy sparkle about her when she spoke to Robert that suggested her feelings were truly engaged. If that was the case, Robert shouldn't be encouraging Posy. He should be gently, but firmly, explaining to Posy that he was already taken. And herein lay her biggest grievance with Robert. Nothing was settled between them. In truth, anyone could flirt with Robert, and he with anyone.

Adelaide nudged her. "You're scowling."

"I was thinking." Madeleine rearranged her features. Her gaze tracked across the hall and locked on Thomas. He was polite to the women in the hall but didn't insist on giving them all of his attention. Instead, his attention remained on his priest friend.

Father Peter sat by his side, intent on their conversation. She wanted to know what held their attention so fully.

Father stood and rapped on the table.

Silence spread through the hall until all gazes were fixed on him.

"I'm glad to see so many of you at table this evening." Father had a deep, commanding voice that rolled over the assembled diners. "Particularly after your blistering humiliation of today."

Hoots and calls of protest rose from the visitors, but it was all good-natured.

"And it gives me great pleasure to announce the winner." Father beamed at Thomas across the hall.

Even Mother had a soft, pleased expression as she looked at Thomas.

Edward was the only other family member looking as grim as she felt. It must have chafed Edward not to have taken part. If Edward had fought Thomas, the outcome might have been different. She didn't like that she could not be as certain of the winner as she would like.

Father held up a leather purse. "As agreed, the victor takes your coin and mine for his trouble." Father motioned Thomas. "Sir Thomas, if you would."

Thomas rose amidst cheers. He didn't gloat or look particularly pleased but strode forward to collect his winnings.

"Forgive me, my lord." Giles lurched to his feet. His cheeks bore the flush of heavy drinking, and he swayed on his feet. "If I might suggest an additional prize for our worthy winner." He made an expansive gesture. "Given the particular nature of these proceedings."

Father pinned Sir Giles with a stare. "I know not to what particular nature you refer."

"Right." Giles was too far gone for self-preservation and winked at Father. "I get you. Not talking about the...prize."

Stiffening, Father glanced at Mother, who shrugged. "This is a course you set, Richard," she said.

"What do you suggest?" Father eyed Giles suspiciously.

Thomas had stilled beside Father and wore a similar expression.

"A kiss." Giles waved his goblet through the air, showering those beside him with wine. "A kiss from our sweet Lady Maddy." He giggled. "A kiss as extra incentive for our combatants."

The others took to his suggestion with an enthusiastic roar.

"Speaking as one of those combatants"—sprinkling more wine over his tablemates, Giles gestured himself with his goblet— "I heartily believe the big lout deserves one for his performance this day."

"Kiss, kiss, kiss!" people chanted.

If Giles had been any less drunk, the suggestion would have been an insult to her modesty. Her brothers were already looking thunderous.

And Robert?

Robert still had his mouth against Posy's ear, his arm about her waist. He was oblivious to everything happening around them. He did not even look at Madeleine or acknowledge her.

Madeleine had taken pains with her appearance and had even wound flowers in her hair because he had once said he liked it when she wore it thus.

"That's preposterous." Scowling, Edward stood and glared at Giles. "My sister isn't some fair amusement to be manhandled by whoever desires to do so." He locked gazes with Thomas. "I'll skewer the first man who tries."

"Well said, Edward." Mother tugged at his sleeve. "Now please sit down. I think Giles is the worse for wine."

Sitting, Edward continued to glare at Thomas.

Thomas neither flinched, nor looked away, but kept his expression inscrutable.

Posy looked at Madeleine from across the hall and smirked. She turned her face up to Robert and laughed.

Robert kissed her cheek.

A surge of rage shot through Madeleine. It was so intense she didn't know what to do with it, and she leaped to her feet. "I agree with Sir Giles."

All gazes swung in her direction. Finally, Robert got his face out of Posy's neck and paid attention.

Too late to regret her impetuosity now. Everyone in the entire hall had eyes on her, and she raised her chin despite her sinking belly. She should have kept in her seat with her lips closed.

Her mother gaped.

Madeleine dared not look at Father, but she could imagine the look of fury on his face. It would look a lot like the one Edward currently wore.

"What are you doing?" Adelaide hissed and plucked at her sleeve.

Her heartbeat raced so fast she could barely speak. With Robert finally looking at her, she decided to brazen it through. "It's only a bit of fun."

"Yes, Lady Maddy." Giles raised his goblet to her. "You're a game one."

The other men cheered and thumped their tables. They set up their chant once more.

Finally, Madeleine risked a look at her father.

His face bore the absolute lack of expression that his children knew meant there would be repercussions. Large, nasty repercussions. Madeleine swallowed the lump in her throat.

Mother had a similar look on her face.

She was behaving outrageously, but the devil had her by the hand now.

Then she met Thomas's stare and any desire to back down withered.

Dark eyes intent on her, he raised an eyebrow in silent challenge.

Madeleine thrust her shoulders back. "Will you collect your prize, Thomas?"

The chanting at the far end of the hall grew louder.

For a horrible, humiliating moment, Madeleine thought Thomas might refuse, and then he sauntered forward.

Stopping on the far side of the table, he held out his hand.

She couldn't falter now, but presented with him so close, she was reminded how large and male he was. Her heart pounded like a war drum and perspiration slid down her sides.

In a face as hard and hewn as Thomas's, his lips were surprisingly full.

Her mad jealousy had landed her in this predicament, and with the entire hall watching, she couldn't embarrass herself further by backing down.

Thomas cocked his head. "If the lady has changed her mind and would withdraw her favor, I'll accept her decision."

Was he challenging her? The look in his sin-dark eyes certainly suggested as much.

"No." She placed her hand in his. "You may take your prize."

Bowing over her hand, Thomas brought it to his lips and pressed a kiss on her knuckles.

Warmth tingled up her arm and coursed through her to pool in her belly.

Thomas looked at her over her hand, his gaze heating as it lingered on her mouth. Stepping back, he released her hand. "Consider my prize collected."

Cheeks burning, Madeleine took her seat again.

Thomas took his seat amidst good-natured teasing and jostling from the other men.

"What were you thinking?" Adelaide shook her head.

She didn't know what she'd been thinking. "I don't know." Robert and Posy had looked so intent on each other, and she'd wanted to flip the tables on Robert. Make him feel the uncomfortable burn of jealousy.

Across the hall, Robert scowled at Thomas. His attention was no longer on Posy.

At least she'd achieved that.

"Madeleine." Father stood beside her and motioned her to follow him. "If you would."

Despite Father's easy smile, it was not a suggestion and Madeleine trailed him from the hall, trying to keep her head up as she did so.

Mother dropped into place behind her.

This was going to be a dual attack.

Father waited until they reached her bedchamber before he spoke.

"Would you care to explain what that was about?" His voice vibrated with contained anger.

Madeleine couldn't face him, so she stared at her slippers. "I beg your pardon. I don't know what came over me."

"I can tell you what came over you." Father never raised his voice, but when he spoke thus, even the most battle-hardened man-at-arms flinched. Madeleine was no exception. "You've been panting after Robert again."

"Richard." Mother rebuked him quietly.

Father wasn't of a mind to heed her, however. "I saw you today, making a spectacle of yourself over him. And what does he do?"

"I didn't make a spectacle of myself." Madeleine winced the moment after she'd said it. Father needed no encouragement from her to flay her with words.

"Yes, you did, Madeleine," he said. "You watch him with your heart in your eyes, and I'm not the only one who sees it."

A horrible thought crossed her mind. Did Robert see, and that's why he'd chosen Posy tonight?

"He's toying with you," Father said. "One day he whispers in your ear, and the next, he whispers in another's. I see him, Madeleine, and my eyes are not clouded by infatuation."

"Richard." Mother stepped closer and tilted Madeleine's chin up so that their gazes met. "What you did tonight could have gone so much worse. You were lucky that Thomas was such a gentleman and took nowhere near the liberty you offered."

"It was just a kiss."

Father huffed and turned away.

"In front of all the kingdom's most desirable men of marriageable age," Mother said. "You wouldn't want them to consider you unchaste."

"It was just—"

"The kiss is irrelevant." Ice and steel encased Father's words. "The issue is the boldness that would cause a lady to make such an offer. It makes them wonder how bold you've been on other occasions."

"I haven't been." Madeleine wanted to cry. It had been a hideous day all around, and she needed it to be over.

"We know that, flower." Father melted and tugged her against his chest. "Within our family, we speak more freely than in others, but with all these people here, you will need to watch what you do and say."

A hug from her father always made her world a better place. "Maybe we could send them all away?"

"No." He squeezed and released her. "I gave your mother my word that I would never force you into a marriage not of your choosing, but that doesn't mean I'll consent to a man who I feel is unworthy of you."

"Robert isn't unworthy. And he did beat so many others today before that ox rolled right over him."

Mother chuckled. "Ox?"

"He's an ox." Madeleine tried not to laugh, but her mother had one of those laughs that made everyone around her want to join in. "Have you seen the size of those shoulders? And his arms? I wager they're the size of my legs."

"Mmh." Mother threw a twinkling glance at Father. "I had, indeed, noticed."

Father raised an eyebrow at her. "Don't make me kill the boy."

"I have always been partial to a strong man." Mother laughed and patted his chest. "But I already have mine."

"I find him too brutish," Madeleine said. "He looks like he could pick me up and toss me across the room."

"Indeed." Mother murmured and threw Father another sparkling look. "I fail to see the problem."

Truth be told, so did Madeleine, and she could still feel the imprint of his mouth on her hand.

Chapter Seven

Thomas couldn't fathom the spark between himself and Madeleine, but ignoring it was not working. Since he'd first come across her at the church, he'd been hoping it was his imagination, but he could no longer deny it, even to himself. He wanted Madeleine, in the manner of a man wanting a woman, and that inconvenient truth chafed at him.

The bench rocked as Edward sat beside him, slamming his shoulder into Thomas's. They were of a height and breadth, which had only made the competition between them as boys all the fiercer.

"You won today." Edward motioned a boy to fill his mead. "I expected as much."

Thomas kept his tongue. Edward wouldn't be handing him a compliment without a barb attached.

"But then you had no competition," Edward said. "It's no feat of skill to beat boys and peacocks."

"You think you could best me?"

"I know I could." Edward shrugged. "Your guard on the left is sloppy and you drag your feet."

Nothing stung quite so much as the truth. "You exclaim your strokes before you make them."

"I used to." Edward sipped his mead, but the tightening around his mouth suggested Thomas's parry had cut. And then Edward confirmed it. "Care to see if I still do?"

"I would like nothing more." Thomas would be hanged before he walked away from Edward's challenge. "On the morrow?"

"Alas, my father would have both our balls," Edward said.

"Afraid?"

"Of you? Never." Edward snorted. "Of my father? I would be stupid not to be. We will find our time and place, Draycott. Until we do, know this." Edward leaned closer. "I'll cut you down and string you up by your innards before I allow you to court my sister."

"I would cut them out for you before I went near her," Thomas said.

Edward gave him a hard look. "I have known you to be many things, Thomas of Draycott, but never a liar." He finished his mead and slammed the goblet on the table. "I see how you look at her but looking is all you'll ever do."

Rising, Edward gave him one more glare before striding away.

Thomas turned to Peter and kept his voice low. "I told you we shouldn't come here."

"Indeed." Peter's eyes sparkled with mirth. "And I beg to disagree. I have found it most entertaining to be here. It has exceeded my hopes."

"Will your hopes be satisfied when Richard's sons run me through and hang my corpse from the ramparts?"

Peter tutted. "So overwrought. I have hopes that Sir Richard would step in before that happened."

Thomas snorted into his mead. Sir Richard would have to be there to make any difference.

"If not"—Peter shrugged—"Elford looks to be a good situation for a man of my skills, should my current lord meet with a regrettable accident."

Thomas had no idea what Peter's nightly prayers must sound like, but he had a few suggestions.

The bench moved again and the second oldest, Andrew, took a seat beside him.

"Edward has already conveyed your family's feelings on my courtship," he said. He couldn't stomach another round of threats.

"Edward has conveyed Edward's feelings on the matter," Andrew said. "I'm of a rather different mind."

Thomas gaped at him. He couldn't help it. Andrew had always sided with Edward when they were boys. "Eh?"

"Edward's manner has soured since his marriage." Andrew indicated Catriona, who sat pointedly ignoring Edward standing by her seat. Both looked equally miserable and made no attempt to acknowledge each other. Lady Adelaide joined Catriona and struck up a conversation. "Edward has become more irascible of late."

"Of late?" Thomas didn't bother to hide his incredulity. "Edward has always been a miserable cur."

Andrew winced. "He is...sensitive."

Laughter burst out of Thomas, and he could barely control it. "Edward has the temperament of a badger."

Andrew almost smiled. "Yes, but a badger with delicate sensibilities."

Peter laughed along with Andrew and refilled his wine. "I enjoy a man of wit."

"Why, thank you." Andrew grinned.

Thomas tired of their budding friendship. "What do you want, Andrew?"

"You didn't take the kiss offered." Andrew studied him. "I'm not often surprised, and I find myself intrigued by this."

"I believe he feared she might bite him again." Peter smirked into his goblet.

Andrew laughed and clapped Peter on the shoulder. "Our brave Sir Thomas afeared of a mere girl? Surely not."

"And yet..." Peter raised his brows and sipped his wine, enjoying Thomas's discomfort enormously.

Thomas didn't have much of an answer for Andrew. "Madeleine acted rashly. By the time I stood before her, she was already regretting her actions." He didn't want what wasn't freely given either.

"I'll wager she's regretting it even more now." Andrew shook his head. "Our mother and father followed her from the hall."

A fierce need to protect Madeleine rose in him. A ridiculous need, because her parents adored her. "What will they do?"

"Not much." Andrew leaned his elbow on the table. "Berate her, try to correct her, but Father was never able to withstand the girls. Not when they cry."

"She'll cry?" Even that made him unhappy, and he couldn't understand it.

Andrew's gaze was on him again, assessing. "Not much. Madeleine isn't one for tears. I think we teased it out of her when she was younger."

Not as brawny as Edward or as pretty as Simon, this brother made Thomas the wariest. Andrew kept his own counsel and watched more than he spoke.

"Why do you care that I didn't accept the kiss?"

"I wanted to take your measure as a man. I only knew you as a boy."

"And why should it matter to you?"

"Why?" Andrew spread his hands wide. "I would see my sister happily married."

Thomas would believe Andrew wanted him wed to Madeleine the day his horse grew wings. "And?"

"One of us must marry." Andrew shrugged. He pointed to Edward and Catriona. "Those two have made a muddle of the entire thing and frustrate my mother's desire for grandchildren." He pointed to Adelaide. "Alas, Addy lost her man too young, and they had no children."

Thomas got an inkling of where Andrew was headed. "Which means your mother's eye has turned your way."

"Not only my way." Andrew motioned to Simon and Oliver sitting on the dais a few seats removed from Adelaide and Catriona. "They're also expected to produce offspring. Given my age, however, her efforts would most logically find their way to me."

"Unless Madeleine marries." He was right to be wary of this brother. Andrew always thought far ahead. "I regret to inform you that I won't be joining the melee for her hand."

"No?" Andrew looked disappointed. "You're by far the best prospect. My future rides on you."

"We don't suit." For reasons Andrew had witnessed when Thomas had fostered at Elford.

Andrew looked at him, gaze searching. "Are you certain of that? She's a remarkably pretty girl. Even if I do say so of my sister."

"That's not the problem."

Andrew smirked. "I thought not." With a sigh, he motioned for more wine. "I wish you would consider it further. You could derive much benefit from an alliance with my father."

Peter cleared his throat and looked arch.

"Being here and making the introductions I need will be all the benefit I require from this event." Thomas spoke to both of them then suppressed a groan as Simon stood and strode toward them.

Simon joined them on Andrew's far side. He leaned on the table and scowled past Andrew. "You should marry her."

Andrew snorted a laugh. "For once, I must agree with Simon."

"I don't want to marry her." Thomas could be no blunter without causing offense.

"Why not?" Simon pounded the table. "She's pretty. She has all her own teeth and doesn't say stupid things too often."

"How could you refuse?" Andrew's eyes gleamed as he said to Simon, "I already tried Thomas, and he says they don't suit."

"It's because she bit you, isn't it?" Simon leaned forward to maintain eye contact. "And I must say, Thomas, I thought you wouldn't be the sort to be frightened by a bite."

Peter's shoulders shook, and Thomas couldn't decide if he wanted to punch Peter or Simon more. "I'm not afraid of her."

"She has a temper." Simon shrugged. "But nothing you couldn't handle. I've seen that horse of yours. Ill-tempered brute but a real beauty."

Peter guffawed and Thomas punched him off the bench. "Your sister isn't a horse."

"But they do both have all their own teeth," Andrew said, straight-faced, but eyes dancing with humor.

Peter lay on his back and howled with laughter.

"Tell me—" Andrew turned to him. "Does your horse also bite you?"

Even Simon laughed at that one, and Thomas could see the funny side.

"It's all very well to laugh," Simon said. "But if you don't marry her, she might end up with that lily." He pointed at Robert.

"Surely she sees that?" It made no sense to Thomas. Madeleine had far too much pride to be second choice to another.

Andrew's face grew serious. "Robert plays a clever game. He gives my sister only enough rein to keep her to hand. Our darling Madeleine is spoiled, and she wants nothing more than that which she can't have."

"Look at him." Simon scowled. "Would you condemn me to sharing a table with that for the rest of my days?"

"He's a clever one," Andrew said. "He chooses the one girl at Elford to keep Madeleine's fighting spirit up. Tonight, he's punishing her for him not winning today."

Thomas had never heard such nonsense. "How is it Madeleine's fault that he can't swing a sword enough to hit a stable?"

"He failed in front of her." Andrew drained his wine. "And it can never be his fault that he did, therefore it must be her fault for putting him in such a position."

Posy giggled and pushed Robert's hand from her breast, but it was a halfhearted effort and his hand returned immediately.

"Can you not tell your father?"

"We have told him." Simon growled and drank from his tankard. "Many times, but he promised my lady mother we would all have our choice of mates."

Robert's hand was large on Posy's bosom. Madeleine had more delicate curves and the idea of that hand on Madeleine sent a bolt of rage through Thomas that had him almost reaching for his sword and cutting the infernal hand off. "I can't marry your sister," he said.

Robert squeezed Posy's breast.

"But I can ensure he doesn't emerge the victor."

Andrew watched him for a moment and then nodded. "I could settle for that."

"Could you humiliate him at the time?" Simon looked thrilled at the prospect. "I would, but we are not allowed to take part."

Robert's hand dipped inside Posy's bodice, and Thomas growled deep in his throat. "Consider it done."

Chapter Eight

At Mother's insistence, Madeleine broke her fast with the rest of the keep. A few of their visitors were nursing sore heads and the hall was much quieter than last night.

After morning prayers, Father rose and greeted everyone.

A murmur of response followed.

"This day I invite you all to the butts." He raised his tankard. "And we will see if any of you can best the finest archer of Elford."

A flutter of excitement followed his announcement. Another clear, sunny day was beckoning them all outside.

Madeleine shifted in her seat. She didn't want more attention on herself, but she loved archery. She loved firing the arrows, not so much being the one watching. Her mood dimmed slightly. After last night, she dared not test her father by asking if she might take part. For today, she intended to be the perfect daughter, meek and docile.

Father tossed a small purse on the table. "I offer the same prize as yesterday."

"Is a kiss from Lady Maddy also on offer?" Giles stood up and looked about the hall with a grin. "I assure you I wouldn't waste the opportunity as Sir Thomas did."

A smattering of laughter broke out.

Everyone stilled, all gazes locked on Father. Sobriety brought a rebirth of caution and most trod warily.

When he was your father, it was easy to forget his fearsome reputation. The man who had carried her on his shoulders when she was small and allowed her to braid ribbons in his hair was also one of the most feared warriors in the kingdom.

He looked every inch the merciless fighter as he stared at Giles. "Do you suggest, Sir Giles, my daughter is chattel to be passed from one man to another?"

Absolute silence reigned. People looked everywhere but at Sir Richard.

"No." Giles paled. "I only meant that..." He looked about for friendly face and got none. "My apologies, Sir Richard."

"And to Lady Madeleine, whose good name you've maligned."

Giles bowed low enough to touch his forehead to his knee. "I meant no slur on your name, Lady Madeleine. I got carried away by my own jest and didn't consider my words before I spoke them."

Father nodded, and Giles dropped to his seat.

"I'll see you all in the butts once you've broken your fast." Father strode from the hall.

A buzz of conversation followed him out.

Red faced, Giles sat at his table and kept to his meal.

Father had spoken against Giles, but she bore part of the responsibility. Her conduct had encouraged Giles's behavior.

"I trust you've learned your lesson." Oliver sat beside her on the bench. "Father had to humiliate a man before the entire hall to save your honor."

Madeleine wanted to shove him, but Oliver was right. She'd caused Sir Giles's humiliation, and this from the brother closest to her.

Oliver took her silence as permission to continue lecturing

her. "You're fortunate that Thomas showed his character yestereve and resisted the urge to take what you offered."

For God's sake, she hadn't tossed her virtue down as a prize. "You're not one to be lecturing me about behavior." She kept her voice low enough for only Oliver to hear. "And I'm sorry, I wasn't thinking."

"It was funny, though." Oliver never stayed stern for long. "You should have seen the look on Robert's face. It was worth it for that."

"Come along, you fallen woman." Andrew cupped her elbow and brought her to her feet. "The least you can do is watch these poor sods try to best your record."

"I didn't mean for Sir Giles to be humiliated." Of all her brothers, Andrew judged the least, and she'd hardly ever seen him angry.

Andrew pulled her hand through his arm. "I know that, and Father knows that. He needed to make an example of someone, and Giles does put his head through the noose."

"I'm sorry that happened."

Andrew patted her hand. "Giles will recover himself. See there." He pointed at Giles, who seemed to be making the best of a jug of mead and the very pretty maid serving it. "I'm sure it's not the first time his mouth has led him into trouble."

"Should I apologize to him?"

"No." Andrew shook his head. "That will only make it worse. Behave as if nothing has changed between you and let him salvage his pride."

They walked across the inner bailey and through the curtain wall. The busy outer bailey seemed barely able to contain all their visitors. The bustle lifted her spirits.

Thomas stood speaking to a group of his men. The men broke away from him and went about whatever tasks he'd set them.

"I don't know why he's still here." Madeleine glared at Thomas's back. Not that he saw it, but it made her feel better.

Andrew glanced at her. "You don't like him?"

"No." She felt certain Andrew would have felt the same. "Do you?"

"Yes." Andrew shrugged. "He's an honest man and an honorable one."

"Edward can barely stand to be in the same room as him."

Andrew chuckled. "Edward doesn't care for the competition. When Thomas is about, Edward isn't always the strongest and the fastest. They have been competing since they were boys." He shrugged. "But they were friends as well."

"Edward and Thomas?" Madeleine didn't remember anything of the sort.

Andrew nodded. "When others weren't watching them and comparing them. They're very alike."

She didn't see Thomas as Andrew did and saw no similarity between Edward and Thomas. She adored Edward. "I hope Thomas doesn't win again today."

Andrew laughed. "But he will, Madeleine. He will make the rest look as limp as he did yesterday."

"You don't know that." She couldn't let that go unchallenged. "There are plenty of men here who are good with a bow. Why, Robert—"

"Ah!" Andrew waved a hand through the air. "The estimable Robert once more raises his head."

"He's better with a bow than any man I have seen."

Andrew sighed. "No, Madeleine. Even I shoot better than Robert, and you know what Father says of my skill with the bow."

She did, indeed, and Madeleine giggled. "Too cow-handed to hit the ass end of a stable."

"Exactly. And bested by my baby sister as well." Andrew gave her a repressive look, but his eyes twinkled. Andrew may not be able to shoot a bow, but his swordsmanship was exemplary, and with a lance, he challenged even Edward. But Andrew's true gift lay in being able to get people to do what he wanted them to do. He was as smooth-tongued as a jester when he needed to be.

"Thomas is like Edward." Andrew gave her a look loaded with meaning. "He's not a man to be treated lightly or trifled with." He glanced to where Catriona stood watching the activity. "If only his wife understood as much. But then again, maybe she does, and she is placing all her hope in that."

Not sure what half of that meant, Madeleine looked at Andrew. It sounded ominously like a warning, but for her or Catriona she knew not. Perhaps both of them.

They reached the butts, the site of the archery contest, and Andrew took her to a seat beneath a pavilion. "I'll leave you here to your suitors." He winked at her. "Be a good girl and try not to besmirch the family honor."

Not that she intended to do any more besmirching.

Giles kept his distance, and Robert wasn't standing with the other combatants or readying his bow. He was also not availing himself of the refreshment tent.

When she finally spotted Robert, her blood rose hot and fierce. Posy hung on his arm, with her huge udders pressed against him. Madeleine knew not what Robert saw in her. Other than the udders, and she was pretty.

Bollocks! She knew exactly what Robert saw in Posy. With men, Posy was sweet and giggly and looked at them as if they could pull the sun from the sky. Also she had that full bosom that Madeleine envied. Her own curves were much more modest.

Fortunately, the first contestants stepped up with their bows, and she didn't have to keep watching Robert and Posy simper and smile at each other. Father's words ringing in her ears, *You watch him with your heart in your eyes, and I'm not the only one who sees it*, she kept her gaze on the contest. Posy's giggle intruded and she forced herself not to look. The other part of what Father had said took up unwelcome space in her mind. *One day he whispers in your ear, and the next, he whispers in another's. I see him, Madeleine, and my eyes are not clouded by infatuation.*

As much as she dearly wanted not to hear her father's counsel again and again, she couldn't ignore them. Not with Robert right there and doing the very thing Father accused him of. It stung and she raised her chin. She refused to be a figure of pity.

Her morning slid straight into hell and stayed there. From his first shot, it was apparent that Andrew had been right about blasted Thomas.

Like with his sword, Thomas had no showy mannerisms and took no elaborate preparations before his shot. He stepped on the mark, nocked the arrow, drew the string and raised the bow. He went still to aim, drew in a breath, and loosed.

Right into the center of the target. With all three shots.

In fairness, Madeleine had to cheer with the rest of the onlookers. One shot could be luck, but three in such proximity spoke of skill.

Unlike yesterday, the archery wasn't one man against another. The contestants all took turns shooting at the same target. Those who made the shot moved on to the next round, which was a target set further away.

Robert took his turn at the mark. His first shot went wide of the target.

Madeleine licked her finger and checked for wind. None.

Robert's second shot veered over the top.

The target was not that far away. A halfway decent archer should at least reach it.

Robert's last fell short.

Madeleine stared into her wine, not wanting to witness his embarrassment. He was the only archer to have missed on all three arrows.

"Is this bow right?" Robert yelled. His face was flushed with temper. "I'm sure the bow is warped."

Thomas stepped up to him and held his hand out for the bow. He nocked an arrow, aimed and loosed.

One, two, three arrows, and right into the target center.

"It appears the bow is sound," Thomas said and handed it back to Robert.

The men around them chuckled and smirked at Robert.

"It appears you're bested, Sir Robert," Andrew called. "Next man to the mark."

Robert gave Thomas a look of murderous rage. His hand went to the dagger at his belt, and for a horrible moment, she thought he might draw it.

Madeleine was halfway out of her seat when Thomas turned around and gave Robert a level stare.

Robert looked away first. He joined Posy, and his voice carried when he said, "It matters not. Archery is for commoners and the low born."

Madeleine's heart twisted. He must have forgotten how much she enjoyed it.

"Here." Adelaide joined her and refilled her wine. "It appears your favorite is having some black thoughts."

Madeleine sipped her wine instead of trying to formulate a response. She was bereft of words. Not only had Robert lost in spectacular fashion, but he was behaving like a child. When William had been bested easily yesterday, he had laughed and come to sit with her.

With Posy in his wake, Robert stalked to the far end of the butts and stood wearing a dark expression.

"He wouldn't have actually drawn his knife," Madeleine said, but the look on Robert's face gave her pause.

He scowled at Thomas, and even shrugged off Posy's comforting hand on his arm.

"Do you not shoot today?" Adelaide carved into the ripe flesh of a peach and popped a slice in her mouth.

"Father is angry enough with me after yesterday," she said.

Posy stood beside Robert looking uncertain. Madeleine didn't like how much attention Robert paid her, but Posy didn't deserve his furious silence.

"He will recover from it fast enough." Adelaide shaded her

eyes and watched Thomas at the second target. "He's very good, isn't he?"

"Yes." With the bow, Madeleine was unbeaten. She was Elford's best archer. Good enough to know that Thomas had near perfect form. He jerked up almost imperceptibly when he loosed. At the distance they were currently shooting, it would make no difference. But later, when the wind and the slowing speed of the arrow needed to be accounted for, that would be a different story.

Father had never balked at teaching his daughters whatever they wanted to learn.

Adelaide could wield a knife and ride the unruliest destrier in the stable. She had a way with horses that bordered on sorcery, and a skill with a dagger that nobody was foolish enough to challenge.

The morning wore on and grew hotter even than the previous day. Behind the hills, clouds gathered like big sacks of goose feathers against the pure blue sky.

Sweat slid down Madeleine's sides, and she contemplated returning to the keep. Watching wasn't nearly as much fun as taking part, and Madeleine had no doubt Thomas would win as easily as he'd won with the sword.

It was most annoying of him to be good at archery as well. Particularly as his skill with the bow insisted on her grudging respect.

Fortunately, Giles showed no sign of suffering from the morning's humiliation. However, he kept his distance from her, as did the other men. Not one of them would dare run the risk of disrespecting the daughter of the mighty Richard of Elford, which struck her as rather chicken-hearted of them.

"How did Stephen come to court you?" She turned to her sister.

Adelaide stretched out on the blanket, unmindful of her skirts spilling onto the grass. "His father approached Father."

"Ah!" That made sense. One of the disadvantages of being Sir Richard's daughter was that men didn't dare too often.

Sitting up, Adelaide studied her. "What is ah?"

"I was thinking about this morning. Yesterday, we were knee deep in men."

Adelaide wrinkled her nose. "You were knee deep in suitors."

"This morning, Father shows them all the fierce Sir Richard, and now, they cluster like a flock of hens and don't come near us."

"They don't come near me because I'm a tragic young window." Adelaide frowned. "And they're concerned they will catch my bad luck."

"What?"

This was the first Adelaide had spoken thus. Desperately in love with her husband, Adelaide had been heartbroken when Stephen died. Adelaide hadn't seemed to mind being alone with Stephen's memory.

Adelaide waved her off. "Never mind me. The sun is making my grumpy. Look, Thomas has won again."

Madeleine joined in the applause as Father handed Thomas the prize.

"There are not many who would brave our father to court you," Adelaide said. "On the one hand, it can be a long wait for a stalwart soul, but on the other, it weeds out the weaklings right from the start."

"Sir Richard, I must decline this prize," Thomas said, handing the purse back to Father.

Father laughed and studied him. "You won it by besting everyone else. The prize is yours."

"Not everyone else." Thomas turned and looked at her.

Madeleine held her breath. He wouldn't be that impudent. He wouldn't dare.

Would he?

"You said we had to beat the best Elford had to offer. If memory serves, the best archer at Elford has yet to loose a shaft."

He would! He just had!

Father would be furious.

But Father was laughing and clapping Thomas on the back. "You're prepared to be bested by a woman?"

"She's not bested me yet." Thomas grinned back at Father and then looked at her. "What do you say, Lady Madeleine? Care to accept a challenge?"

Chapter Nine

M adeleine snapped her mouth shut. Thomas must have lost his mind. He'd been in the hall and heard and seen what had happened to Giles.

Silence covered the crowd gathered in the butts.

Thomas had challenged her at archery. His dark gaze seconded his verbal challenge.

She did so love archery, and she did love a fierce competitor. "I'm not certain..." Before she said any more, she glanced at her father to gauge his reaction.

"Well?" Father raised an eyebrow. "Do you defend the honor of Elford, or do we let this braggart roam our halls."

Her smile was instantaneous. Father had forgiven her, and he was giving her a chance to regain her honor. She gave Thomas a deliberate look from his boots to his hair. "Is it fair, though? I would hate to rob him of his pride."

Behind Father, the company laughed and whistled.

"Show him Lady Maddy," William called. "Teach him a lesson."

"What say you?" Thomas raised a brow. "Do you think you could teach me a lesson?"

"I know I could." Madeleine glanced at one of the pages. "Would you fetch my bow and bracer?"

Cheers broke out as the boy rushed off.

"The participants are decided." Father stood and spread his hands for silence. "We need to establish the terms of this competition."

Thomas bowed and made an elaborate hand gesture. "Terms belong to the lady."

More cheering and whistling greeted his statement.

For the first time that day, Madeleine was enjoying herself.

"Bodkin points to our arrows." She nodded to the keep artillator, who nodded in return. "Range?" She tapped her chin and pretended to think about it. "Two hundred and eighty yards."

Raising a brow, Thomas rubbed his nape. "Is it too late to withdraw my challenge?"

"Yes." Her blood rose to the challenge.

Giles raised his goblet. "Salvage all our pride, Lady Maddy."

Father nodded, and two more pages moved the target back. Another drew the mark at their feet.

"Three shots," Father said. "Closest to the center wins."

Thomas held his hand out. "May the best archer win."

"Oh, she will." Laughing, Madeleine put her hand in his.

His warm, calloused grip engulfed her hand. Heat spread from her hand up her arm and jolted her. For a moment, the crowd and the butts melted away, and it was only him and her and their hands.

Then, she shook herself out of it and turned from him.

The day had suddenly grown a lot warmer.

Red faced and panting, the page arrived with her bow and bracer. He helped her buckle her bracer to her arm. Made of leather with beautiful stamped silver inlay, the bracer had been a gift from Father. It matched the glove she put on to protect her fingers.

Thomas wore no protection on his hands. His fingers must be made of leather.

"My eye is already in," Thomas said. "Would you like a practice shot or two?"

Madeleine tested the tension on her string. She checked the position of the sun and noted a slight breeze from the west. "No." She motioned him to go first. "After you."

Thomas went slower than he had before. He took his time on his stance, nocked his arrow and aimed. He breathed out and shot. His arrow arced through the air in a swift curve and thudded into the target a hand's span from the center.

He was very good. Nerves fluttered in Madeleine's belly, but she took a deep breath.

Left foot forward, weight balanced, she straightened her back and relaxed her shoulders. She took aim, pushing all other sounds and sights out of her mind. The bowstring creaked as she drew it back. She corrected her aim.

And loosed.

Her arrow landed half an inch closer to the center than Thomas's.

With a head shake, he joined in the applause for her and took his second arrow. "Well done, Maddy. I'll have trouble beating that." His lapse in calling her Maddy felt right and reminded her of times when he'd fostered here, when he had not been so terrible. Times like when he had shared his honey cake with her. Strange how she had forgotten the amicable times.

Muscle played across Thomas's back as he drew. He'd a perfect stance and positioned his fingers on the string closer to the fingertip than the first knuckle.

His second arrow brushed hers but rested closer to the center still.

Applause burst from the crowd.

Bowing, Thomas handed her a second arrow. Oh, he was good. Very good, but so was she.

"What was that you said?" She nearly laughed at his attempt

at modesty. "Was it something about struggling to best my last shot?"

He shrugged and chuckled. "A lucky shot."

"Hmm." She let her doubt show as she checked her arrow and nocked it.

The right side of the target grew crowded and she went left. From this distance, it was impossible to tell who was closer, and a page was dispatched to check the distance.

He came running back yelling, "They're even."

Madeleine hadn't lost at archery in years. For the first time in a long while, it looked like she might.

Not showing any tension, Thomas took his third shot. Not a soul breathed as he aimed. In silence, they all watched his arrow slice through the air and land in the center of the target.

Even as her belly plummeted, Madeleine had to concede a truly masterful shot.

Raucous yelling broke out around them. Wagers were placed on her and Thomas.

Madeleine joined in the applause. She'd one more shot, and best she make it the best shot she'd ever loosed.

Sending a quick prayer to whoever might be listening, she took her stance. The target looked farther than for her last two shots. Her palms sweat, and she had to release her bow and wipe them on her skirts.

Standing silent, and still, Thomas watched her with those steely eyes of his. For a second, she fancied herself facing him in battle, seeing that icy resolve across the field from her.

"Why does she wait?" Posy's peevish tone rose through the crowd. "It grows unbearably warm."

Was Robert watching? She could win for him, make him proud and salvage his honor.

Thomas met her gaze. He didn't look impatient. He looked as if he might wait until she was ready.

Or she could win for herself. She was ready. She could do it.

Madeleine nocked her final arrow for a second time. She

released the tension from her shoulders and drew back the string. There it was, the target, right where she wanted it to be.

She loosed.

Thomas stood beside her as they both watched the arrow.

A murmur rose from the crowd, grew into an excited chatter, and then, a great cry as her arrow landed.

Right beside Thomas's.

By unspoken agreement the group moved with her and Thomas to the target. It was impossible to tell who had won.

As they drew closer, more excited murmurs came from behind them.

Her heart was beating erratically, and competitive fever warmed her blood.

Madeleine was aware of Thomas's height and breadth beside her. His arm brushed hers, his long strides easily keeping pace with her.

They reached the target and peered at it.

Madeleine's heart dropped. It couldn't be closer. Her point shared the same hole as Thomas's but his was bedded to the left of hers, and his was the closest arrow to the center.

"Sir Thomas has it," she said, her voice not quite steady.

Thomas looked at her and then the target. "No." He pointed. "If we take the position of the tip, then we are evenly matched. And Lady Madeleine's second shot was closer than mine. She wins."

"What is this?" Edward stepped closer. "We can't have two winners." He examined the target. "I agree with my sister, Sir Thomas has carried the day."

Even knowing how childish it was, Madeleine had to force a smile on her face and acknowledge the victory. The child in her wanted to sit on the floor and cry, to stamp her feet and yell at having lost.

The grown woman, the one who would never disgrace her family with her behavior, smiled as graciously as she could and extended her hand to Thomas. "You've bested me."

"No, Madeleine." He bent over her hand and kissed it. His voice dropped low for her ears only. "I may have shot an arrow closer to the target than you, but only a stupid man would think that meant he'd bested you."

Father clapped. "Well, a good day's sport. Well done, Sir Thomas, you've earned your prize." He tossed the purse to Thomas. "I find myself in sore need of a cool drink and a cooler place to rest my arse."

Giles pushed through the crowd to her side. "Well, you lost me a tidy sum there, Lady Maddy."

"I'm sorry for that." She really hated losing, but losing to Thomas didn't seem so bad. He was an excellent archer, and he showed no propensity to crow his victory. In fact, he'd tried to hand it to her.

"Never fear." Giles waved her off and smiled. "It was worth it to watch both of you at play." He winked at her. "It becomes clearer and clearer which way the land lies."

"What?"

But Giles had disappeared into the laughing, chattering crowd.

Adelaide linked their arms. "Never mind, darling. You were quite impressive regardless of who won."

"But I do mind." She kept her smile in place.

"I know that." Adelaide patted her arm. "And you're doing a wonderful job of keeping that hidden."

Adelaide walked beside her to the keep. After the heat of the day, the cool hall was a blessed relief.

Madeleine stopped to accept a cup of ale from a serving maid.

"Madeleine." Robert strode toward her. His hair tousled from the wind made him even handsomer, but the grim expression on his face augured ill.

She smiled her welcome. "How are you, Robert?"

"How am I?" He gripped her arm and tugged her out of the hall and into the dim passage beyond. He glanced left and right, and then scowled down at her. "How can you ask me that when you humiliated me in front of everyone?"

"What?" Shaking spilled ale from her fingers, Madeleine rather thought the humiliation was on her. She had lost the contest.

"You saw how I was cheated in the first round." His eyes blazed at her. "I had to accept that with good grace or look like a sore loser. But I don't have to accept how you then made it clear how lacking my skills were."

"But Robert..." She didn't know what else to say. Telling him that she'd not even thought of him when accepting the challenge wouldn't assuage him. Nor would her not having any idea what he was so angry about. "He challenged me."

"Then the right thing to do would have been to refuse." Robert sneered. "Like you should have refused before you made a spectacle of yourself last night."

Heat flooded her cheeks. The events of the night crept up on her and made her want to crawl away and hide. "I acted rashly last night. My father has already spoken to me about it."

"As well he might." Robert gave her a censorious look. "First, to allow your name to be tossed around in such a fashion and then to accept a kiss from the lout."

"He didn't kiss me. He kissed my hand." And just a moment. Her memory served up another bit of truth. She hadn't been the one crawling over Posy last night. "Which is a lot less than happened with you and Posy."

Robert reared back. "I beg your pardon."

"You stand here and accuse me of making a spectacle of myself." She leaned forward to keep her voice down, but she was angry enough to bellow at him. "I saw you with Posy. You near enough mounted her in the hall."

Cheeks flushed, Robert glared at her. "That you speak that way only makes me reconsider my attachment to you." He gave his doublet a fussy jerk and stepped back. "I won't stand here and exchange words with you like a peasant." He smoothed his hair into place. "But know this, Madeleine, no wife of mine will speak and behave thus, and I'll certainly never tolerate my wife humiliating me."

He stormed off down the passage.

Picking up her skirts, Madeleine ran for her chamber before anyone could stop her. Tears threatened, and she barely shut her chamber door behind her before they spilled.

"I have your silver silk ready." Heather's smile of welcome dropped. "What is it? I know you hate to lose."

"It's not that." Not only that. "I had the most fearful fight with Robert just now."

"Robert?" Heather put her arm about her shoulders. "What did you fight with him about?"

"He said I had humiliated him because I accepted Thomas's challenge. He also rebuked me about my behavior last night." Now that she was safe in her chamber, her tears once more dried up, and she grew angry again. "I didn't humiliate him, and I may have behaved badly last night, but it's not his place to correct me."

"No, it's not." Heather turned Madeleine and worked on her lacings. "And what happened last night wasn't so very bad."

Madeleine gave her ever-loyal friend a hug. "It wasn't that good either." She wriggled out of her bliaut and then her chemise. "I don't think I want to go to the hall tonight."

"They'll say you are a bad loser." Heather grimaced.

Madeleine didn't care. "I'd rather that than spend another evening watching Robert drool all over Posy."

Heather looked like she might say something but shook her head and brought Madeleine her dressing robe instead. "Then again, those that know you will know better."

"But Robert did say that no wife of his would behave in such a way." Feeling cheered, Madeleine threaded her arms through the robe sleeves. "Which I take to mean he thinks of me as his future wife."

Heather nudged her to sit on the dressing stool so she could do her hair. "Oh, joyful day."

Chapter Ten

W hile Heather tidied up, Madeleine opened her casement to the sweet night air. Conversation and laugher drifted up from the hall, but she was glad for her solitude.

Robert had upset her, and the harsh sting of it lingered. Flirting with Posy, behaving badly after losing at archery, even treating her as if she didn't exist she might have stomached, but his unprovoked anger made her want to march up to him and set him straight. Also, the more she thought about the other things he'd done, the less she felt inclined to accept those either.

"Madeleine?" Adelaide poked her head around the door. "How fierce you look."

"She's sulking." Heather jerked her head at Madeleine.

There were times, and this was one of them, when having an outspoken maid was irksome.

Not bothering to hide her scowl, Madeleine spoke to Adelaide. "I'm not sulking. I'm thinking."

"About losing today?" Adelaide carried a jug and three goblets with her. She poured one and handed it to Heather. "I came to check you were not too upset, and here I find you brooding."

"I'm not happy about losing." Madeleine closed her eyes and

leaned her head against the stone embrasure. "But that's not why I'm angry. Robert and I had a horrid row."

"Oh, dear." Adelaide poured two more goblets and handed one to Madeleine before she took one for herself and perched on the end of the bed. "Now, tell me what happened."

The more time passed since her argument with Robert, the more aggrieved Madeleine felt. "Robert was angry because I accepted Thomas's challenge. He said it made him look foolish."

"How?" Adelaide gaped.

Heather hummed her agreement and sipped her wine. "That's what I said."

Adelaide said, "And I don't know how he can claim she made him look foolish after his petulance when he lost."

"He lost badly?" Heather leaned forward.

Adelaide nodded and grimaced. "He did everything except throw his toys at us."

Robert had been petulant, but her instinct to defend him rose before she could quell it. "He was upset."

"He was a big baby." Adelaide sipped her wine.

Heather pointed at her and said to Adelaide, "Ask her what he said about last night."

"What did he say about last night?" Adelaide turned, her eyes already bright with outrage.

"He rebuked me for my behavior last night." Madeleine didn't want Addy and Heather hating Robert like her brothers did. These two weren't Robert's biggest supporters. For the most part, they kept their peace about him out of respect for her, but this would set spark to kindling.

"Now that's going too far." Adelaide ruffled up like a mother hen. "It's not his place to correct you about anything."

Madeleine agreed with her sister, but of all her siblings, Adelaide was the most likely to side with her. Even if Addy didn't side with her, she would not stand in opposition, and Madeleine was starting to need all the ayes she could get. "It might be his place to correct me. He did mention something about me being his future wife."

"Ah." A pained expression crossed Adelaide's face. She took a careful sip of wine and glanced at Heather before speaking. "Maddy? Are you certain he's the one you want to wed?"

Humming her agreement, Heather said, "I ask her that all the time."

Apparently, Adelaide would side with the rest of her family, and Madeleine was so tired of them all asking this question. It was like they didn't believe she knew her own mind. "Of course I am. I've been in love with Robert since I was barely more than a girl."

"You're still barely more than a girl." Adelaide gave her a fond smile. "I know you believe yourself to be in love with him, but have you ever asked yourself if you like him?"

"Of course I like him. I love him." Adelaide's question caused a queer stirring inside her.

"Love and like are not the same thing." Adelaide watched her with serious eyes. "Liking is about spending time with someone, having conversations with that person, sharing a comparable interest. Like is the foundation of friendship."

"True." Heather nodded.

Madeleine wasn't sure why Adelaide's reasoning perturbed her as much as it did. "Did you like Stephen?"

"Immensely." Adelaide smiled. "He could and did make me laugh all the time."

"Robert makes me laugh." Madeleine said it without thinking. Robert did make her laugh. Why, just the other day he'd made her laugh. She couldn't quite recall about what and it had been more of a smile than a laugh, but she found him very funny. She did.

"Before you make up your mind absolutely to have him, consider if you like him." Adelaide stood and shook out her skirts. "Father will ask you that if it ever gets to a betrothal."

"It will get to a betrothal." Madeleine would make sure of it.

She had dreamed of hundreds of ways in which Robert could ask her to be his. All he had to do was the asking. "And I do like him."

Adelaide shrugged. "If you say so, and now, I'll leave you and join the hall." She gave a tendril of Madeleine's hair a gentle yank. "Don't spend too long up here pouting."

"I'm not pouting," she called to the door as Adelaide left.

Heather put her nightclothes near the fire to warm. "To be fair, you are pouting a bit."

And this was her maid. How fortunate she was.

After making sure Madeleine didn't need her for the rest of the night, Heather left.

From the sounds still drifting up, merriment in the hall continued without her. But that didn't tempt her to join them. Robert's current distance had started with visitors coming to Elford. Other than the day at the church, that was, and now she thought on it, maybe he'd known Thomas was nearby enough to see them.

Could that be it?

She'd like to think so. She'd like to think Robert had known Thomas could hear them and had acted to protect her modesty. Maybe if Thomas hadn't been there, Robert would have kissed her.

Except, as much as she wanted to traipse along that thought path—and she really did—Robert had been cold with her before. Some days, he took it into his head to treat her with icy disdain. Flirting so outrageously with Posy had also happened before, but not as obviously. If his aim was to make her jealous, then he'd succeeded. She was pea green all the way to her soul.

Outside her casement, a bright half-moon rode a cloudless sky. The cooler evening breeze was a welcome respite from the day's heat. Only the soft tramp of the night watchman on the ramparts broke the silence.

By stages, the castle fell silent around her. Footsteps passed her door. Chatter from the hall died to a murmur and then quiet. Perhaps she should have gone to the hall after all. Then she would know if Robert had spent the evening with Posy. She would also know if Thomas had found a warm body to celebrate his victories with. Not that she cared who Thomas spent his time with. As long as it wasn't her.

Giving up on sleep, she opened her door and peered out. Braziers stayed lit along the hall to help visitors find their way.

She and Heather had shared dinner in her room, but Madeleine was hungry again.

Wrapping her shawl around her, she found her slippers and put them on to ward against the chill of the stones. Even in high summer, the stones stayed cold beneath your feet.

She crept down silent corridors. Snores and sleep murmurs rose from the hall as she slipped past it and into the kitchen.

A fire burned low in the hearth and cast an orange glow in the gloom. Two keep dogs raised their heads and looked at her. Their tails thumped the ground as Madeleine crouched to greet them.

Cook always left something for hungry souls in the back pantry, and Madeleine went in search of it. Ever hopeful she'd share, the dogs followed.

A large game pie, a fresh loaf, a bowl of pears, and a pitcher of ale sat on a large shelf to the left of the pantry entrance.

Madeleine poured herself a cup of ale and selected a ripe pear.

"I see we had the same idea," Thomas said.

Madeleine almost dropped her pear as she whirled toward him.

Dressed in his chemise and chausses, his hair sleep ruffled, Thomas stood at the pantry entrance. The dogs squirmed and wagged in greeting.

"Um...yes." Madeleine had no idea how such a large man could move so silently. She sipped her ale to ease her suddenly dry mouth. "I couldn't sleep."

"Neither could I." Thomas cut a wedge of the game pie and motioned the ale pitcher. "May I?"

"Yes." Madeleine took up the pitcher, poured him a cup and handed it to him.

The low light from the kitchen hearth barely touched the back pantry. They seemed to be the only two people awake.

Thomas leaned his shoulder against the wall as he ate. "Are you still angry with me about besting you?"

"No." Every word out of this man's mouth seemed to be for the sole purpose of annoying her. She shot a glare at him.

His eyes gleamed with barely suppressed amusement.

He was teasing her, and it took the sting out of his gloating. "You didn't beat me by much."

She broke off some cheese and handed it to the dogs.

"True." He toasted her with his ale cup. "You were a formidable opponent. I wasn't sure I could win."

"Well, you did." She cut a slice of pear and ate it. The next piece she held out to Thomas, and he took it and thanked her. In the quiet night, it was hard to remember what she disliked about him.

"I had forgotten how good you were," he said with a wry smile. "Otherwise, I wouldn't have challenged you."

He'd caught her with a mouthful of ale, and she nearly spat it across the pantry as he surprised a laugh out of her.

With difficulty, she swallowed, and he patted her on the back.

Her shawl slipped from her shoulders and sighed to the floor.

Thomas bent and picked it up for her. His gaze roamed her night rail to her slippers and up again, leaving a curious warmth in its wake.

The still night, the muted hearth in the kitchen, and their seclusion in the small pantry wrapped them in a curious intimacy that Madeleine didn't want to pierce.

His eyes, so much darker even than the night, gleamed down at her, and his voice was soft as he said, "You were abed."

"Yes." A strange breathiness beset her voice. He filled the small back pantry, and not only by the breadth of his shoulders and his height. There was a stillness to Thomas, a calm assurance which spread from him and enfolded her. It was the same quality her father had, but her father didn't make her pulse skip and heat prickle beneath her skin.

Thomas laid her shawl on the shelf beside the pitcher. He stroked the fine wool with his large hand and Madeleine shivered. What would that stroke feel like on her skin? Madeleine resisted the urge to snatch the shawl up and hide in it. She didn't want him to know the effect he had on her.

The air between them shifted as they stood in the dark, silent pantry. It grew heavy and laden like before a summer storm.

Seeking to dispel it, she made conversation. "You seem to be winning everything."

"Two things." He shrugged and sipped his ale. "Tomorrow will likely see me get my comeuppance."

Somehow she doubted that. "You're just saying that."

"You're right." His grin flashed white in the dark. "But I can't have you disliking me for being a braggart as well."

His honesty chastised her. It made her dislike of him seem petty and childish, which it was. She finished her pear and wiped her hands on a cloth lying on a lower shelf. "I don't dislike you. Not anymore."

One of his dark brows shot up, and he crossed his arms. "Now who is just saying words?"

"I mean it." She couldn't honestly say she liked him. Although standing there with him, she couldn't recall her reasons so clearly. He smelled of sage and leather. "I didn't like you before. When you fostered here."

"You bit me." He chuckled.

Madeleine's cheeks heated. She'd been a wild one as a child. "I was protecting my brother."

"He didn't need it." He took a tendril of her hair between his long fingers and studied it. "Only you are fair like your father."

"Yes." Her hair seemed to absorb his attention as he played it through his fingers. Madeleine hunted for distraction. "How did you get to be so good?"

"Your father." Thomas laid the lock of hair on her chest, his hand perilously close to her breast. His attention remained on that lock, or was it the swell of flesh it lay upon? "He taught me well."

Her nipples hardened and pushed at the thin linen of her night rail. Mortified that he might be able to see, she reached for her shawl. "And since then?"

Thomas took the shawl before she could and stepped closer to her. He wrapped it around her, cupping her shoulders and holding it in place.

Madeleine was forced to look up to maintain eye contact.

He'd always been taller, but he hadn't been this broad and muscular when he'd lived at Elford. She wanted to touch the thick brawn of his arm and feel if it was as solid as it looked.

"When you hire your sword out, you had best be better with it than anyone else." His deep, raspy voice demanded her attention, caressing her skin like velvet.

Madeleine had nearly forgotten her question. His hands on her shoulders felt hot and hard. "I think you are...better." She spoke in a laden whisper. Her voice caught in her throat. "Better than everyone else."

"Hmm." His grip on her shoulders firmed as he drew her closer. "Shall we see if I am?"

Madeleine couldn't remember what they were speaking of. "What?"

The roughness increased in his voice as he drew her closer. "Shall we see if I'm better than everyone else?"

"What are you doing?"

His lips touched hers, lighter than a butterfly wing and withdrew. "Claiming my reward."

His gentle touch set off a cascade of sensation that stole her breath. "I thought you didn't want your prize."

He came back with a firmer touch and lingered longer. "Oh, I wanted it." He caught her bottom lip between his and drew it into his mouth. Then let go. "But not like that. In the hall with everyone watching."

"No?" She had no will to move or do anything but stand and let him kiss her.

His breath was hot on her wet bottom lip. He paused with a whisper between their mouths. "I merely wanted to choose the time and place of claiming."

He caught her quiet exclamation in his mouth. His hands left her shoulders, and he cupped her head and held it still.

Madeleine lost herself in the sweet pressure of his mouth on hers.

He touched his tongue to the seam of her lips.

Madeleine had seen others kiss that way, only she'd never understood the desire to do so. She did now as she parted her lips for him.

His tongue stroked into her mouth as his deep, guttural moan rippled through her.

Sensation coursed from where he tangled his tongue with hers. It swept over her sensitive breasts and made them ache. It shivered over her belly to pool between her thighs. His kiss laid claim to her, branded him on her senses.

Thomas broke the kiss, long before she was ready, and she murmured a protest.

"I'm going to bed, Maddy." He kissed her forehead. "Before I forget how much I owe your father."

Chapter Eleven

S ir Richard would beat him to a bloody pulp if he knew Thomas had put his hands on Sir Richard's youngest daughter, and he deserved whatever the man wanted to hand out. Hellfire, Thomas would help him deliver the beating. His mind had gotten stuck on how good she felt and tasted and smelled, and any hope of restraint had vanished.

It was a sobering how quickly his honor had surrendered to desire.

Thomas stalked the quiet corridors to the bedchamber he'd been given. With the keep so crowded, only a few had been gifted chambers within the keep. Many of the rest had to make do in the barracks or find a comfortable spot in the hall.

He'd been given a chamber because Margaret and Richard esteemed and trusted him. They didn't expect him to stick his tongue down their youngest daughter's throat.

God's balls, he didn't even like Madeleine. She was a prickly, impetuous vixen with a devil's temper. Not the sort of woman he favored at all.

Rounding the corner to his chamber, he dodged a sleeping page.

She had stood in the pantry with the linen of her night rail caressing her curves. A good man would have replaced her shawl or moved so he couldn't see so clearly. But no, not him. He'd stood there with his cock growing harder and leered.

He thrust open his chamber door.

He had no decency and no control. A man not in charge of his baser urges was a beast, an animal.

"Thomas." Catriona rose from her place by his hearth. "Where have you been?"

Thomas bit back a groan. Edward's young wife in his chamber was the last thing he needed. He didn't even bother being polite. "What are you doing here?"

"Looking for you." She walked closer to him, her hips swaying suggestively, her gaze eating every inch of him. "I didn't know you had already found a friend to warm the night."

"I was in the kitchen." He caught himself before he explained further. Conversation with Catriona in his chamber in the middle of the night was an even worse idea than kissing Madeleine in the pantry. He strode to his door and opened it. "You need to leave."

She blinked at him. "I beg your pardon."

"Leave." He jerked his head at the door. "You're not welcome here."

"But..." She looked a lot younger in her uncertainty. "I came—"

"Don't finish that statement." Thomas didn't want to embarrass them both. "It matters not why you came, only that you leave."

Catriona stood and gaped at him. "You're sending me away?"

"I'm sending you back to your husband. Edward. The same husband who needs no reason to hate me more than he does already." Thomas knew her game. "Which is probably why you're here in the first place."

She tossed her head. "I think you underrate yourself."

"I think you're looking for trouble," he said. "But you won't find it here."

Giving him a look of pure venom, Catriona stalked for the door.

As she reached it, Madeleine stormed through.

They met in the doorway and both of them stopped.

"What are you doing here?" Catriona scowled at Madeleine.

"I could ask the same of you," Madeleine said. And then her scathing gaze found him. "But I suspect I already know."

"Madeleine." Thomas went after her. She knew nothing.

Leaping over the page, who now blinked sleepily awake, he caught her arm. "Just wait. It's not what you think."

"You don't know what I think." She tugged her arm from his grasp.

"You think I had Catriona in my chamber for...base purposes." He sounded like a sheltered nun.

She stepped closer to him and jabbed him in the chest with her finger. "There is nothing else to think when you go about this keep kissing unwilling women."

"Unwilling?" He snorted. As misguided as their kiss had been, she'd been a willing partner.

Catriona's throaty laugh came from behind him. "Kissing, Thomas?" She slid around him and looked between him and Madeleine. "What have you two been doing?"

"Nothing." Madeleine folded her arms. "And anyway, you're in no position to question me." She gave Catriona a scathing look. "What were you doing in Thomas's chamber?"

"I had to speak to him about...something." Catriona almost managed to look innocent.

Adelaide's chamber door opened, and she peeped out. "What's going on here?"

Dear God, no. Thomas's night was going from bad to worse.

Madeleine and Catriona started guiltily, and Thomas swore.

Agog, Adelaide stepped into the hall and looked at them. "What are you all doing?"

"Speaking," Catriona said. "We were having a conversation."

Adelaide snorted. "In the dark, in the middle of the night."

"I wasn't having a conversation." Madeleine raised her chin and threw him a scornful glance. "I was hungry and went to the kitchen for something to eat."

"Really?" Adelaide sneered. "The kitchen is the other way."

"I know that." Madeleine cleared her throat. "I was on my way back to bed."

"When she met me," Catriona said. "I was also hungry, and we bumped into each other in the dark." She waved her hand at Thomas. "Madeleine screamed and Thomas came to see if everything was all right."

"I see." Adelaide tapped her chin. "I didn't hear a scream."

"It was a more of a gasp," Catriona said. "Like this."

The sound that came out of her was like a chicken having its neck wrung.

Adelaide blinked at her before recovering her poise. "I find it interesting that Madeleine is gasping over here when her bedchamber is the other side of the kitchen."

Madeleine whimpered and cleared her throat. "I ate too much and thought to walk off my full belly."

"Right." Adelaide raised an eyebrow. "I don't know what any of you are doing out here." When Catriona tried to speak, she held up her hand. "Nor do I care. Get yourselves to bed and stay there for the rest of the night." She gave them all a menacing look. "And every other night, for that matter."

Sir Richard's voice came out of the dark. "What a splendid idea, Adelaide."

And Thomas wanted to sit on the floor and howl. This was what came of his stupid decision to come to Elford. The last time he'd left here sporting a bite and a black eye.

All three women grew wide-eyed as Sir Richard appeared out of the gloom. Hair mussed and barefoot, he looked to have tugged on his clothing in a hurry He folded his arms and waited.

Catriona broke first. "I feel sure Edward must be looking for me."

From what Thomas had heard, that was as unlikely as Madeleine's excuse to Adelaide.

Catriona scurried off and Sir Richard turned his hard gaze on Madeleine.

"Well, I'm tired." She gave a huge yawn and scuttled off.

"They woke me up." Adelaide held her father's gaze for a breath and then vanished inside her room.

Richard turned to him and raised an eyebrow. "Thomas?"

"Yes, Sir Richard."

"I love you like a son, Thomas, but if I ever catch you taking liberties with my daughters, I'll break every bone in your body."

In his youth, Sir Richard could have done it too. He could still inflict a punishing amount of damage now. "Understood." Thomas bowed and went back into his chamber. None of this would happen again, because he cared not what Peter said or thought, they were leaving in the morning.

* * *

Peter, it turned out, had plenty to say on the subject, prattling on and on while Thomas packed. "You came here to save your crumbling manor. Need I remind you of the scene in the manor before we came here?"

"I came here to meet those of influence." Thomas didn't need reminding of any of Draycott's weighty needs. He folded his one and only velvet doublet and jammed it in his bag. As a fighting man, he had no need to lavishly adorn himself. On a battlefield, his metal spoke for itself. "I have done that. They will all go back home and tell their fathers of me."

Peter regrouped and took his doublet out of the bag. "What about the prize purses you're winning?"

"I didn't come here to profit off Sir Richard." He snatched his doublet back and refolded it. Picking up his bag, he headed for the door.

"They will say you're not giving the other men a sporting chance to best you at something else." Peter followed in his wake.

"They're right." Thomas strode down the corridor. "Because none of them will best me at anything."

Peter's habit flapped around his ankles as he trotted to keep up. "They will call you conceited."

"It's only conceit if it's not true." Thomas descended the stairs to the hall. Even for Peter, he was being particularly insistent. "Why are you so intent on me staying?" Their conversation over the invitation had set the tone. "Why were you so determined we come here in the first place?"

"For you." Peter plucked at his lip and stared past Thomas's shoulder. "You needed the money and you needed the connections."

"And I saw the wisdom in that, which is why I came here." Thomas wanted out of Elford. He felt like he'd fallen into a hostile badger sett, and he wanted out before they all attacked. "But I told you nothing good ever comes of me being in this place."

Peter made a dismissive snort. "Come now, Thomas. Last night was...a mere nothing. A misunderstanding."

Catriona in his chamber was a mere nothing? And this from a man of God. "Did you hear nothing I told you?"

"I heard it all." Peter leaned into him. "But I still don't know why you're making such a fuss over this. You fostered here, so although it might have been difficult at times, you cannot truthfully say no good came of you being here."

Thomas spoke each word slowly and carefully, to be sure Peter understood this time. Whatever good had happened in the past had been worn to a stump last night. "Catriona came to my chamber in the middle of the night."

He might have left a few salient details out of his recitation of last night's happenings.

"Catriona is a troubled wife seeking her husband's attention." Peter replied as slowly and carefully.

"Well, she won't find her husband's attention in another man's chamber." Done with arguing with Peter, he sidestepped him. "We leave within the hour. With you or without you."

Peter got to the door before him and barred it with his chest. "What about Lady Madeleine? If you leave here, she will accept one of the others."

"Lady Madeleine has made her choice." He refused to feel anything but relief about that. Robert was wholly unworthy of her esteem, but Thomas didn't care. It was nothing to him that she favored that peacock over the rest of them. It mattered not one whit that she could give Robert the right to kiss her tempting mouth or put his hands and mouth on her beautiful curves. "Get out of my way or I'll make you."

"Thomas." Peter hopped out of the way before Thomas could lay hands on him. "I can't tell you how strongly I feel you must stay."

"Peter." Thomas brushed past him. "I can't tell you how strongly I feel I must go."

"All because of last night?" Peter followed him down the staircase to the bailey level. "It was nothing."

"What if Edward had found his wife there?" Thomas couldn't believe Peter needed the risk spelling out for him. "What if Sir Richard had discovered Madeleine and me in the kitchen."

Peter's gaze grew shrewd. "You never did tell me what happened in the kitchen."

"Nothing." And he cursed the heat climbing his cheeks. "We shared a meal and went to bed."

Peter gave him a knowing glance. "Indeed?"

"Yes. That's what happened." Thomas needed to impress it on Peter, or he would never hear the end of it. "And that's all that happened."

With that, he threw open the bailey doors stopped.

Rain fell in great sheets from a leaden sky. It turned the earthen bailey floor to a huge mud puddle. "Jesu on the flaming cross."

"See." Peter smirked. "It's a sign you must stay."

A tremendous bolt of lightning flickered across the sky.

"You're a priest; you only believe in signs from God." Thomas stared into the sodden day. He could stick to his plan and leave. It would, however, be a long, miserable, wet and cold ride, and he hated to subject men or beasts to that without good reason.

Thunder pealed and made them both jump.

"Indeed." Peter made no attempt to hide his gloating. "Therefore, this is a sign from God that you must stay."

"This." Thomas jabbed his finger at the rain. "Is weather."

"God works with the tools at hand." Peter smirked. "In this case, sufficient weather to make you remain?"

Thomas turned and uttered his response on a growl. "Yes."

"Splendid." Peter almost capered about him. "Let us return to the hall and the fire. I feel sure Lady Margaret will plan something for us to sit out the weather."

"You may go back to the hall." Thomas loaded his bags about Peter's neck. "After you take this back to my chamber."

Peter staggered a bit beneath the weight. "What of you?"

Thomas stepped into the soaking morning. "I'm going to make sure the men and animals are well cared for and dry."

Running across the bailey, he was still soaked to the skin by the time he made the stables. The dim quiet smelled of horses and hay.

Inside, the horses stirred as another crack of thunder sounded. But they were warm and dry and well fed.

At his approach Brute looked out from his stall and blew a soft welcome. They'd been through much together and Thomas stopped to greet him.

A woman giggled, followed by a man's murmur.

Dear Lord, did nobody rut in their own bed anymore?

"This place is a den of sin," he whispered to Brute. "I apologize for putting you in this embarrassing position."

The animal lipped his sleeve and blew.

Straw rustled and the woman giggled again.

Brute whickered.

"You're right. It's an awkward position to be in." Thomas scratched beneath his forelock. "Does one announce one's presence or hide?"

Footsteps pattered from deeper within the stable and Thomas slipped into Brute's stall. He was firmly in the hide versus announcing one's presence camp.

Posy sauntered into view, picking hay from her hair, her cheeks flushed and her bliaut crooked.

Thomas's gut tightened, and he prayed to whomever was listening that he wasn't about to see what he suspected he would. God had given up on him today because Robert sauntered out after Posy. He caught her about the waist and kissed her soundly.

Dog's bollocks! Now what was he to do?

Brute nudged his shoulder and dipped his head.

"I know." Thomas hooked an arm over Brute's neck. "It would be so much easier to pretend I had seen nothing, though, don't you think?"

Brute stamped and nipped him.

Thomas shook his head. "Blight on it, but you're right. It's not my way to turn aside."

Chapter Twelve

It took Madeleine a moment to realize her name was being called and that it was Robert doing the calling. She'd been on her way to the hall for dinner, deep in her own thoughts.

About Thomas and him kissing her, and then Catriona being in his room. Then about how Robert's anger at her was so misplaced. And back to Thomas and him kissing her. Round and round went her head, like a spinning top.

"Madeleine," Robert called, quickening his steps to catch up to her. "I've been waiting for you to come down so I could speak with you."

"Indeed." If Robert thought she would stand there and be chastised again, she'd some choice words for him. "You were waiting for me?"

"To speak to you." Dimples appeared in both Robert's cheeks, and he looked abashed as he reached for her hand. "Although if you never spoke to me again, I would thoroughly deserve it."

He'd caught her wrong-footed and she could do nothing more than stare as he raised her hand to his lips.

"I had no right to speak to you as I did yesterday." He ghosted his lips over her knuckles. "You've always been high spirited, and it's what makes you so enchanting."

She liked enchanting, and her irritation with him eased. "I, too, am sorry that we fought. I don't like it when we do."

"Then we should make a pact never to do so again." He kissed her hand again before placing it on his arm.

Madeleine had to chuckle at his optimism. "I'm not sure I can swear to that."

"Then it's a good thing I'll be around to remind you of it." He gazed down at her with such tenderness that her heart missed a beat. Robert did care for her; it was right there in his eyes.

She'd wager he had never called Posy enchanting. Or maybe he had, and that put a cloud in her sunny mood. She shoved it away again and walked by Robert's side into the hall.

The noise of so many folks staying out of the miserable weather rushed to meet them.

"Lady Maddy," Giles yelled out a greeting, "you're pretty enough to make a man regret he'd sworn off marrying."

"You devastate me," Madeleine called back. "And here I was embroidering our names on a doublet for you."

"In that case." Giles stood and took her hand. "I shall see your father immediately, and we can send the rest of these curs home."

"Some of us were here long before." Robert returned her hand to his sleeve.

Giles slid around to her other side and took that hand. "Like a faithful old hound, no doubt."

"Come." Robert quickened his pace and took her away from Giles. "The hall is busy tonight. Let me take you to your place."

Madeleine turned and waved to Giles, who winked at her as he returned to his place.

Robert helped her on the dais and took her to her seat. Instead of leaving to find his place, he took the seat beside her. "That fool trails you like a puppy. You should not give him false hope." He shot a baleful look at Giles.

"Giles?" The idea was laughable, also because she was equally certain Giles was here for the festivities and had no thought to marrying her. "Of course not."

Robert's thunderous expression relaxed. "Or any other of these dogs sniffing at your skirts."

His rudeness startled her, and she couldn't think what to say. Robert had no call to be angry with the other men. Surely he knew he already had her heart. All he needed to do was take it. Then the most delicious idea twirled through her mind. Could Robert be jealous of the other men?

For so long, she'd been his and his alone for the asking. Madeleine had believed she had made her interest in him obvious, obvious until almost the point of humiliation.

A new possibility teased her. Perhaps Robert wasn't as sure of her as he seemed.

"Wine?"

Madeleine nodded.

He took the jug from the serving man and filled her goblet himself. "Giles is right about one thing," he said. His gaze ran over her. She was almost certain he lingered on her breasts. "You do look very pretty tonight."

"Oh." Her cheeks warmed. She couldn't remember the last time Robert had looked at her thus. It could even mean Robert was looking at her with desire.

Unbidden, another pair of eyes flashed through her mind. Darker than pitch, Thomas's gaze had blazed down at her. There had been no doubt as to whether he lusted for her or not. His unadulterated ardor had gone to her head like strong mead.

Despite the crowds in the hall, she spotted Thomas immediately. He stood taller and broader than most, and more present in that still, sure manner he had. There was just more of him, taking up more space and demanding more attention.

Over by the hearth, he stood beside Father Peter. They had their heads together and spoke earnestly. They did a lot of that, and she'd no idea what had Thomas looking intense, even angry, this time.

He glanced up and trapped her gaze in his.

She couldn't seem to drag her gaze away from the harsh beauty of his face. Not pretty or elegant, but a man's rugged looks. He glanced at Robert, and his face hardened further.

Like his lust, his anger showed clearly on his face. He didn't disguise what he felt.

His anger stung, and Madeleine raised her chin. He needn't look at her as if she'd done something wrong. Last night, he'd gone straight from kissing her to Catriona in his bedchamber. Yes, she suspected that had been more Catriona's doing than his, but he had no reason to look at her accusingly either.

Two seats down, Catriona sat beside Edward. Neither of them looked at each other. The tension between them kept a clear space between the couple and the next person. Madeleine couldn't think what Catriona had been about going to Thomas's room last night. Thank the Lord, Edward had not witnessed Catriona's nighttime visit.

She should speak to Mother about what had happened and let Mother talk to Catriona.

"What are you looking at so fiercely?" Robert's breath was warm on her ear. "Tell me what fascinates you so that you no longer pay any attention to me?"

She couldn't tell him that, so she plastered a smile on her face. "Nothing. I was merely deep in thought."

"Would you tell me your thoughts?" Robert twirled a lock of her hair around his fingers. When Thomas had touched her hair, the breath had left her body and taken her good sense with it.

Robert pressed closer to her. "I would love to understand what happens behind that pretty face of yours."

Madeleine had to snap her mouth shut. This wasn't Robert as she'd become accustomed to him. The Robert she knew noticed her when it suited him, sometimes outright ignored her, and never showered compliments on her. Getting him to declare his intentions was like trying to hold water. Some days he was with her, and others he kept a harsh distance between them. For months, she had kept believing they had an understanding, but he had remained elusive. It must have been having men there who might offer for her. Or perhaps at last he was finally seeing her.

Robert leaned closer and spoke but as if she had no say, her gaze hunted and found Thomas.

The look he gave her was loaded with scorn and it cut her to the quick. What right had he to judge her?

Madeleine yanked her gaze away.

Robert whispered in her ear, "Will you?"

"Will I what?" She'd heard nothing of what he said.

"Come, pup." Andrew's hand landed on Robert's shoulder. "You're in my seat."

Suddenly Madeleine dearly wanted to know what Robert had said.

Flushing, he stumbled to his feet. "I was merely keeping Lady Madeleine company."

"Of course you were." Andrew's smile stayed clear of his eyes. "This is the family table, pup, and you're not family...yet."

Robert's flush deepened as he tugged his doublet and walked stiffly away.

"Must you be so nasty to him?" Madeleine wanted to thump Andrew. For the first time in so long, Robert had looked at her as if he desired her. And then he'd whispered something, and she'd been too busy gawping at Thomas to hear him.

Andrew sipped from her goblet and grinned. "I think I must. At least one member of this family must make him work for their esteem."

"Give me that." She snatched her wine back. Heat rose in her cheeks. "I know nothing of what you speak."

Andrew sat back and motioned for wine. "Really? That pup thinks all he has to do is lift a finger and you'll come running."

"That's not true." But it was. The mortifying scene at the church came back to haunt her. The scene Thomas had witnessed. Yesterday Robert could barely be parted from Posy, and now he was at her side.

As Robert strolled through the hall, Thomas watched him like a wolf would its prey.

Madeleine couldn't think what he held against Robert. Except Robert's manners at the contests had been sorely lacking. Love him as she did, even she could see that.

"All these young men are here for you." Andrew's hand swept the hall. "They might not all intend to marry you, but merely the lure of you brought the greatest houses and families to our hearth."

That idea stroked her conceit, but she kept a lid on it. Andrew wouldn't be telling her this to make her boastful. "Giles is here for the fun."

"Yes." Andrew chuckled. "I'll grant you that, but the rest are here because of who you are."

"What does this have to do with Robert?" She grew impatient for him to get to the point.

"You're Lady Madeleine, daughter to Sir Richard of Elford and Lady Margaret des Guilles. You've wealth, influence, and don't let this go to your flighty head, but beauty." He sipped his wine. "They're here because you command that level of consideration."

"Oh." Her face heated. Andrew didn't often say complimentary things.

"Yet you're tossing all that away on some mangy runt who has his nose up every welcoming keep skirt."

Madeleine choked on her wine and came up spluttering. That was far more like what she expected from Andrew. And also extremely offensive.

"Robert's bloodline is at least as good as..." Robert's partiality for Posy had been noticed, and she felt on too shaky ground to address that. Instead, she searched the hall to rebut Andrew's insult, and locked on Thomas. "At least as good as Thomas's, and yet you don't call him a mangy runt."

"Yes, their bloodlines are alike." Andrew cleaned his fingers in the bowl held by a serving man. "But their honor isn't. Come now." Andrew raised a brow. "You glare at me, yet you were right there when Robert lost at swords, and when he sulked over the archery. You were right there, Maddy, and you can't tell me you condone such behavior."

"I..." But she couldn't, and Andrew knew it. "I agree he didn't behave well, but Robert isn't used to losing."

"Robert is a child, Maddy." Andrew helped himself to several slices of succulent roasted pig. "And you're a woman who will need a strong man."

Her gaze went to Thomas.

He was laughing at something Peter had said to him. Certainly, not as pretty as Robert, but there was something about Thomas that drew her back for a second and a third look. His shoulders, even she conceded, were enough to make any girl stare. Broad, and heavy with muscle, the velvet of his doublet clung to every dip and swell. Most of the time when she saw Thomas, he was in armor, but tonight his doublet showed what his chainmail concealed.

He kept his hair close-cropped, probably because he spent much of his life in a coif and helm, but she rather thought it accentuated the decisive jut of his cheekbones, and the hewn line of his jaw. The only soft thing in his face was his mouth, and it was easy to overlook beneath the intense scrutiny of those dark eyes.

They didn't need to be enemies, she didn't want to be, and Madeleine smiled.

There was the tiniest softening in Thomas's features that if she hadn't been looking, she would have missed.

The hall and the chattering folk faded to a hazy murmur. Once more they were in the dark pantry together. His gaze heated, and he looked at her like he wanted to possess her, own her, put his mark on her and declare she was his.

Yes, a tiny voice whispered deep inside her, *we should like to know what that was like.*

Chapter Thirteen

Needing air, Madeleine slipped out of the hall. She couldn't credit her thoughts on Thomas. She was in love with Robert, and they were exact opposites. Nothing about Thomas should appeal to her.

Except, his skill at everything was effortlessly impressive. And his shoulders filled his tunic like the men's she'd sighed over as a younger girl. And the way he'd kissed her in the pantry had left her craving more.

She leaned against the corridor wall for support. The cold stone against her back rooted her and helped her regain her composure. What was happening to her had nothing to do with Thomas himself; it had to do with the situation. Her father had created this most unnatural and awkward gathering, and it had her all disordered.

"Madeleine." Thomas strode down the passage toward her. His thick, powerful legs ate up the distance between them.

Her belly tightened and her skin heated.

No, she wouldn't have this. She got her wayward thoughts under control and held up her hand. "Stop."

He did, cocking his head and looking at her.

"Don't." She motioned between them. "No more grabbing and kissing me whenever you feel like it."

"I see." His eyes gleamed with amusement.

"No, you don't." He scattered her good sense by breathing the same air. "But it can't go on."

Thomas's brow shot up. "And you're certain I'm here for... grabbing and kissing?"

"You followed me out of the hall." A mortifying suspicion wiggled into her head that she may have spoken too hastily. "For what other reason would you do so?"

"I could think of a few." His gaze raked her. "You're comely, Madeleine, but I believe I can keep myself and my kisses under control."

Heat flooded her face. As he stared at her, several responses bloomed and died before she could utter them. There really was no recovering from what she'd said. "I understand." She forced her stiff neck to nod. "I was mistaken. Why did you seek me out then?"

"I need to speak with you." He clasped his hands behind his back and cleared his throat. "On a rather delicate matter."

That didn't sound good. It also made her think about kissing again, so she kept her lips buttoned and put on a listening face.

"I believe you're mistaken in your esteem of Sir Robert."

"Eh?" That would be one of the last things she had expected him to say. "I think it's you who are making assumptions now."

"You deny that you esteem him?" Up went that dark eyebrow again, in a most annoying and knowing manner.

He had her there. She raised her chin, refusing to give him the satisfaction of pressing his advantage. "I make no claim as to whether I do or not."

"Madeleine." He grimaced. "You don't need to speak it for the entire keep to know it. We see how you are with him."

Madeleine opened her mouth to deny him, but the words got stuck in her throat. She'd made her feelings clear to Robert, but the idea that the entire keep was aware of her love made her want to find a hole and hide in it. "I don't have to stand here and listen to this."

"That's where you're wrong." He grabbed her arm and prevented her escape. "There is something about Robert you need to know."

"What can you possibly tell me about Robert?"

"He's playing you false." Thomas's face grew stern. "The first time I saw him with Posy was at the church ruin that day. They were there before you, and then this morning, I saw them again in the stable."

His accusations robbed her breath, and Madeleine pushed her back against the wall to keep standing there. Images rushed through her mind in rapid succession. Posy in the forest that day she'd ridden out to find Robert. Posy and Robert, heads together all through dinner the other night. Posy, flushed and giggling, adoring eyes on Robert.

But today Robert had been by Madeleine's side. He'd apologized and been most attentive. "You must be mistaken."

"Madeleine." His expression gentled, and he stroked his thumb over her arm. "I wouldn't tell you this if I wasn't certain."

He couldn't be right. Robert was hers. He'd always been hers. She would be damned before she lost him to Posy. "No. Posy and Robert have known each other since they were children. There isn't anything to be thought from seeing them together."

"I'm not wrong about this, sweeting."

His endearment felt like a lash against her lacerated heart. "I'm not your sweeting." She yanked her arm away. "I'm not your anything." Her mouth once opened wouldn't stop, and she spoke before her mind had a moment to temper her words. "And that's what this is all about, is it not? If you were honest, you would admit that you're jealous of Robert. He has what you want."

Color rode Thomas's cheeks and he scowled at her. "By this, you mean you? That it's you I want, and that I want you so much I would malign another to get you?"

It sounded ridiculous when he said it, but pride wouldn't

allow her to back down. "Why else would you have done what you did in the pantry?"

"You're the most infuriating girl I've ever had the misfortune to meet." He closed the gap between them and loomed over her. "I came out here to save you from making a foolish mistake, and this is how you repay me."

"Repay you!" She straightened from the wall and met his gaze. "You try to break my heart, destroying my faith in the man I love, and you expect me to repay you."

"Hearts and love." He scoffed. "I would suggest that your heart is far less engaged than your pride. You've decided on Robert, and you're so pig-headed as to be unable to accept that he doesn't feel the same."

"He does feel the same." His derision stung. "Did you not see him tonight? He couldn't have been more attentive." Her anger rose, and she jabbed a finger into his chest. "He even apologized for not behaving well by me over the last few days." For his arrogance, she gave him another jab. And another because she felt like it.

"Did he now?" He grabbed her hand. "Stop that, before you hurt yourself." Trapping her hand between them, he leaned close enough that his nose almost touched hers. Darker brown rings surrounding the lighter brown of his eyes. "Or is he one of those men who like to keep their choices open?"

"You would think like that." Her blood rose to the challenge. "A man such as you."

"A man such as I?" Jaw clenched, eyes like flint, he all but dared her to go further.

She feared nothing from him. Nothing. "A cur, a hound, a knave."

"Knave?" Up went that accursed eyebrow again. His voice grew silky quiet. "If I were the man you accused me of being, I would have taken what you freely offered."

"Argh!" Words escaped her and she shoved at his chest. "You kissed me."

"You kissed me back."

Madeleine couldn't say who moved first but suddenly he was kissing her. Again. And she was kissing him back. Again.

Only there was nothing tentative or tender about this kiss. It was an all-out rout of tangling tongues, and lips scraped by teeth.

She speared her hands in his hair and kept him her captive.

He grabbed her hips and yanked her against him.

The size of the man made her feel delicate and cradled against his bulk. Yet she knew he would never hurt her. The arms that held her tensed with controlled strength, and he could withstand what she gave him. This was a man she could break over like a wave, and he would stand.

Dear God, the thought went to her head like mead. She wanted to push the limits of his strength and his control. She wanted to drive him wild and see him abandon himself to her. Her breasts were sensitive against his chest, and she pressed them into him.

His groan rumbled through her as he hoisted her off her feet.

Her back hit the wall, he pressed deeper into her, his hips parting her legs.

Anybody could come across them at any moment, but Madeleine wanted one more moment, one more taste.

He drew her leg around his waist. Big and calloused, his palm slid over her knee.

The heat of his touch made her gasp.

Halfway up her thigh, his hand stopped, and his fingers dug into the muscle.

With a hiss, he broke the kiss and rested his forehead against hers. They remained like that for a long moment, both of them breathing hard.

As if it cost him to do so, he released her thigh one finger at a time.

Madeleine dropped her legs from his waist, and he lowered her back to the floor.

The silence grew weighty between them as their breath mingled in the small space between their mouths.

His voice sounded rough. "This madness must stop."

"Yes," she whispered, but she wasn't sure she meant it.

Thomas stepped back. A flush rode the harsh line of his cheekbones, and his eyes still held the fever that had raged between them.

"Madeleine." Edward strode toward them, his gaze moving between her and Thomas.

"God's balls," Thomas murmured. Turning on his heel, he stalked away.

Edward stepped into his path and their shoulders slammed.

"Watch yourself." Edward took a step toward Thomas.

"Don't." Thomas shook his head. "Not now."

Then he turned and strode away.

"What was that about?" Edward turned to her with suspicious eyes. "Has he upset you, threatened you in any way?"

Upset her? Nearly every time their paths crossed, but Thomas would never threaten her. "No." She dug deep for a semblance of composure. "We had harsh words."

"About?" Edward glared at Thomas's retreating back.

"Robert." She told the truth, her senses too scattered to manage a lie. "Thomas doesn't like him. He believes Robert untrustworthy and playing me false."

"Huh!" Edward stared at the corner behind which Thomas had vanished from view. "I never would have thought he and I would agree on anything."

Andrew, Oliver, Heather, Adelaide, Thomas and now Edward spoke ill of Robert, and suddenly Madeleine wanted to cry. Instead she aimed her ire at her oldest brother. "Why do you all hate him so?"

"Maddy." Edward looked back at her with a frown. "He's not worthy of you, and the only one who can't see that is you."

Chapter Fourteen

Enough! Thomas cared not what new reasoning Peter invented, he was leaving Elford this morning. He had managed to avoid Madeleine for the remainder of yesterday, but he didn't intend to press his luck, so he rose at dawn before most of the keep was awake.

Fortunately, the rain had passed, and the morning dawned cloudy but dry.

His bag was still packed, and he grabbed it up and strapped his sword to his hip. Last night's scene with Madeleine had made his leaving a necessity. God alone knew what it was about her that got to him so. He'd only to share space with her and his blood boiled. The heat between them was like smoking oil, and he needed distance before the entire mess spilled over and burned them both.

His restraint was threadbare, and he no longer trusted himself to withstand her. Therefore, he needed to remove himself from temptation.

He owed Richard of Elford a debt that could never be repaid. After his father's death, Richard had made sure he and Mother were cared for. Even when his uncle had moved into his father's place, Richard had hovered. He had insisted Thomas foster at Elford and then stayed nearby if Thomas should ever need him.

For that reason, Thomas had made it a point of pride not to need him.

Slaking his lust on Sir Richard's daughter was a betrayal of a man to whom he owed everything.

He sent a page with a message for Peter and strode out of the keep toward the barracks. Getting trapped in the detail of getting the men ready to travel would cool him down.

"Thomas." With a face like thunder, Edward strode out of the keep toward him. He looked at Thomas's bag. "You're leaving?"

"Yes." He wouldn't get into it with Edward. In a short while, he could quit Elford without putting his hands on either of Richard's children again.

"Good." Edward glared. "I never wanted you here." He stepped closer to Thomas. Of a height and breadth, they locked gazes and held. If it came to it, he and Edward would be evenly matched. "But in case you get any ambitious ideas, let me warn you not to come near my sister."

Thomas had no trouble agreeing to that. "Fine."

He sidestepped Edward and continued to the barracks.

Like the finely trained army they were, his men responded to his commands to make ready. He had handpicked every last one of them, and he expected no less. He would not put it past Wilfred and that lot to sneak back to Draycott in his absence. He had accepted Sir Richard's invitation; no offence could be caused by him leaving now.

"Thomas!" Sir Richard strode across the bailey toward him. "You've a fine group of men here."

It was as if his thoughts had summoned the man. Had Peter been causing mischief behind his back?

"That I do." Thomas gave Saul a nod, and he limped off to bring Brute. "I didn't wish to disturb you this early. I intended to catch you when you broke your fast."

Sir Richard shrugged. "I heard a rumor you were leaving."

A rumor he'd wager his sword arm had begun with Peter.

"Yes." He forced himself to meet Richard's gaze. The closest thing he had to a father was this man. "I think it best that I do."

"Why?" Sir Richard's pale blue gaze held his.

There was no way Thomas could answer truthfully without insulting a member of Richard's family. "I'm needed elsewhere."

"Indeed?" Richard folded his arms and raised a brow at Thomas. "And where would that be?"

Nothing, not one single place came to mind. "Not here?"

Richard threw back his head and guffawed. "Like your father, you're the worst liar. Never wager on games, Thomas. You've not the face or the heart for it." Sir Richard clapped a hand on his shoulder. "Now that we've stopped wooing each other, we can get to the real reason you're leaving."

Thomas sent a quick prayer heavenward for some inspiration or deliverance. Draycott! He should have said he was needed at Draycott.

"Actually." He tried to recover lost ground. "I need to return to Draycott. Matters there are unsettled. Some of Leon's old folk might cause havoc in my absence."

Richard nodded. "You should have gotten rid of them."

"I know." Thomas knew as much. "But they're old and I took pity on them."

"You're a good man, Thomas. Your father had the same sense of fair play that you do." Walking him away from his men, Richard led the way out the castle gates. "Above all Hugh valued peace."

Their boots rang hollow on the bridge and Richard stopped at the edge. Leaning his elbows on the bridge, he peered over at the water.

Unlike other keeps, Elford didn't befoul its moat with stinking matter.

"However, I don't think you're leaving because of Draycott." Richard smirked. "I can guess what drives you away."

Thomas wanted to squirm like a youngling. "All right."

"Then, let me see where I shall begin." Richard turned and leaned on the stone post. "Let us start with the most obvious. Edward and you can't be in the same keep without drawing each other's blood."

Thomas tried to find a polite way to tell a man his heir was a whoreson. "It has always been thus with us."

"Yes." Richard nodded. "You're too similar in nature and too evenly matched in ability. I have always believed there will come a day when the two of you are no longer facing each other like rutting bucks that you will find much in common."

That was about as likely as Thomas flying, so he kept his tongue.

As if reading his thoughts, Richard chuckled. "I also believe my daughter-in-law has been casting her lures in your direction."

Heat climbed Thomas's cheeks. He couldn't fathom how Sir Richard knew that, but he was neither going to deny nor confirm.

"Catriona is...unsettled." Richard grimaced. "She feels lost amongst strangers, and my idiot son doesn't see that. You're a fine-looking man, Thomas, but Catriona's advances are more about Edward than they are you."

"I thought as much." The less he said about Catriona the better.

The day was overcast, but heat caught beneath the heavy cloud blanket and sweat slid down his sides beneath his gambeson. Or perhaps Sir Richard excelled at interrogation. He needed to end their chat. "I thank you for your invitation." He held his hand out. "I have made a number of useful acquaintances. Your continued friendship is dear to me."

"Yes, and yours to me." Richard took his hand. "And I'm going to stretch that friendship now when I ask you to stay."

"Stay?" This is what he'd feared when he'd seen Richard approaching.

"I know being here is like sitting with your arse in nettles for you," Richard said. "Not the least of which is my youngest daughter."

Thomas dared not breathe, dared not move. "What of Madeleine?"

"She's...spirited." Richard laughed. "I raised both my daughters to speak their minds and remain true to themselves. That doesn't always make them amiable and biddable women."

Thomas laughed. He couldn't stop himself. The idea of Madeleine as biddable stretched credulity too far. "She has never liked me."

"No." Richard stroked his cheek and contemplated the water beneath the bridge. "I suspect what Madeleine feels when she's with you is much stronger than like. Like is such a tepid emotion, and my Maddy is many things, but never tepid."

"No." The less said on that matter, the better. It brought a disturbing thought, however. Not many men would enjoy Madeleine's fire and vigor. Some would be challenged by it and seek to obliterate it. The idea of a lessened, diminished Madeleine sat like a bad bit of fish within him. She might madden and frustrate him. Indeed, she most certainly did madden and frustrate him, but she sparkled like a prized gem, her facets many, and all of them brilliant and liable to cut you, but her beauty and fire undeniable. "She's a rare girl."

"She is." Richard clapped him on the shoulder. "And not to be given to that prevaricating pudding whom she has convinced herself she's in love with." Richard sighed and stared at the water. "I find myself in a bind, Thomas. I promised their mother I would never force our girls to marry where they didn't choose. But that promise bites my arse at times."

Unusual as the notion was, it didn't surprise him. Lady Margaret was a strong-willed woman, who led from beside her husband. Sir Richard adored her and would do blasted near anything to ensure his lady's happiness. "Adelaide chose well."

"Did she?" Richard glanced at him and then returned to his water study. "Stephen was a nice enough fellow, affable, and for certain pretty enough, but Adelaide ran him in circles."

Thomas could barely remember Adelaide's husband. He'd attended the wedding but hadn't lingered long after the feast.

"Madeleine is my blood and bone. She comes at you head on, like a battering ram. No subtlety or trickery. She wants what she wants and will thrash anyone in her way." A fond smile flit over Richard's face. "But Adelaide is more like her mother. She hides the dagger in her skirts and leads you astray with that beautiful smile."

Thomas didn't know if Richard meant Lady Margaret or Adelaide, and his discomfort grew.

Richard laughed and looked at him. "I love my wife, Thomas. I don't have to tell you this for you to know it's truth, but that woman is a fiendishly clever wench. She keeps me on my toes, and I adore her for it." His cheerful expression dimmed. "But it takes a certain man to handle a woman like that, and Stephen wasn't that man." He sighed and straightened. "The young man is dead now, and I don't want to speak ill of him. Let us speak of you instead."

"Me?"

"Will you stay?" Richard thumped his shoulder. "Or will you betray my trust and faith in you all these years and leave me in the lurch?"

Apparently Lady Margaret had taught her husband much about hiding the dagger, and there really was only one answer. "I'll stay."

* * *

Mounted, Thomas waited with the other knights in the training yards. Once Sir Richard had returned to the keep, Thomas had realized he still didn't know why Sir Richard wanted him to stay.

Today's event was the quintain, and Thomas had no intention of losing. The king had outlawed tourneys, melee in particular, soon after his reign started, and this was a mild replacement.

Still, a couple of the younger knights tittered and chattered like girls at their first feast. The rules were simple. The knight with the most hits to the four-inch target won. Any run resulting in you missing the target meant you were out.

Lady Margaret arrived from the keep and took her place on the hastily erected pavilion. Adelaide sat beside her, and beside her, Madeleine took a seat.

Madeleine's gown, the exact blue of her eyes, clung to the full jut of her breasts and caressed the flare of her hips. Both girls were built like their mother, and Lady Margaret still looked as slim and lovely as a girl.

Sir Richard was a very lucky man, as would be the men who married his daughters. Thomas eyed his competitors and turned back with a sour taste in his mouth. Not one of them would do. They were a pleasant enough bunch, but Sir Giles was attending for the mead and wenches. William seemed more serious, but rumor had it his father had emptied the estate coffers and William sought to plump them up through marriage. The ginger whose name he forgot had a weak chin, and too many freckles. Tristan was a pretty fellow, and he danced well, but he didn't know the arse end of a sword from the business end. Madeleine would skewer him within hours of their vows. And so, he went from one to the other.

Had Richard asked him to stay because he saw the same thing?

Thomas's own conceit surprised him. They might be looking at him and finding him wanting.

Then he looked at Robert, and his lip curled. Of all her potential suitors, this one made him sick to his stomach. Richard was right to call him a prevaricating pudding. As he watched, Robert nudged his mount forward and approached the pavilion.

He lowered his lance to Madeleine. His voice rang over the yards. "Lady, would you honor me with your colors."

Madeleine blushed and looked startled, but she tied her kerchief to the end of the whoreson's lance.

Behind Madeleine, Posy paled. She cast stricken eyes at Robert, but he turned and rode back to the waiting jousters.

Thomas didn't miss the gloating look Robert tossed in his direction.

Had that duckling sought to challenge him?

It was time to give Sir Robert a lesson in humility, and Thomas was looking forward to it.

Chapter Fifteen

Robert took his turn at the quintain and scored a neat hit that sent the arm prancing around. Cheers rose from the pavilion, and Robert saluted them as he rode past.

Already most of the field had gone, and three had missed in the first round.

Thomas took his starting position. With this not being a battle, he left his helm off. Always eager to engage, Brute danced beneath him, loving the excitement in the air.

Madeleine's gaze met his over the distance, and she raised that stubborn chin of hers, daring him to beat her precious Robert.

Thomas raised his lance. Challenge accepted. He dug his heels into Brute and set off. Hitting a quintain target was a lot easier than hitting a moving mounted knight. Thomas hit the target and sent it soaring around. He made a point of looking at Madeleine as he rode past.

She should know better than to challenge him.

Another four men dropped out before he rode again.

Robert went before him again, and again scored his hit. He wasn't quite as useless as Sir Tristan, but Robert fought like one who'd never engaged a living enemy. Form and beauty were quickly set aside in the rough, raw ugliness of battle.

Thomas took his place again.

Again, Madeleine raised that chin at him. Her pretty eyes glittered and heated his blood.

He kicked Brute into movement.

The saddle felt strange beneath him and Thomas firmed his thigh grip.

The saddle slipped to the left. The quintain loomed ahead of him, but if Thomas stopped now he forfeited. He'd be dead and buried before he did that.

The saddle slipped some more, and he nearly lost his seat.

His sudden weight shift disconcerted Brute, and Brute shied.

Gasps rose around him, but Thomas righted himself. As he rode past Madeleine, she smirked at him. Yes, she would love to see him land on his arse in the sand and see her pretty favorite win.

His saddle slid again, and Brute threw his weight to his left. Thomas reined him in, but it was too late. Unbalanced, Brute faltered and stumbled. Like the well-trained destrier he was, Brute lurched back into motion.

Thomas hit the ground hard enough to rob his breath. His hip and arse ached from their impact with the hard ground, but he was still breathing. Sharp pain lanced through his side, but his concern was for Brute.

Brute had stopped six feet away from him, his right front leg cocked and held gingerly.

Saul hobbled forward, pale and shaken. "Sir Thomas, I tightened the girth. I know I did."

Saul was getting on, but he didn't make stupid mistakes. There was always a first time, however, and any injury to Brute, he would extract from the old man's hide. As angry as he was, though, he wouldn't bellow and humiliate Saul in front of Elford keep. He would save his anger for when they were alone.

"I must see to Brute." Thomas stepped over his fallen saddle and approached Brute. "He's favoring his leg."

Running a hand down the horse's right foreleg, Saul shook his head. "I don't like it, my lord."

Thomas trusted Saul's way with horses and bit back a curse. Perhaps if he'd trusted Saul less, Brute would be hale and well. He crouched and touched Brute's fetlock. "Is that bothering you, my big fellow?"

Brute shifted away from him.

"Blight on it." Thomas had taken Brute from an older knight who had deemed him unrideable. Brute wasn't unridable at all. He just needed a rider who respected him. Thomas wouldn't risk hurting him further. "Withdraw me."

"My lord?" Saul frowned.

"He may be fine, but I won't take that chance."

Saul stood and walked to the arms tree. Glancing back at Thomas, he sighed and took Thomas's shield from the board. "Sir Thomas withdraws from the lists."

For the first time since Leon had ousted him at fifteen, Thomas was refusing to fight. It scored his pride and fanned his anger to fury, but Brute was worth the price of his conceit. A mistake had been made, however, and somebody would pay for that.

Chatter arose in the wake of Saul's announcement.

Oliver crouched beside Thomas's saddle where it had fallen into the dirt. Holding up the girth, he showed it to Thomas. "The cut is clean," he said, frowning. "It was cut on purpose."

"I told you, Sir Thomas." Saul looked like he might weep at any moment. "I don't let nobody else near your horse. I saddled him myself, and his girth was tight. I know because he puffed his belly out and tried to nip me." Saul swallowed and his hands shook as he gesticulated. "You know how he does that, Sir Thomas. And you need to give him a nudge to make him let all the air out. And I remember it this morning because Jem in the stables and I share a jug at night, and Jem was laughing at his tricks."

"Indeed." A murderous rage rose in Thomas. He hated to

lose, and withdrawing was a bitter potion, but he hated to risk a good animal even more. Relief that Saul was innocent didn't allay his rage. Somebody had cut his girth, and he could think of one man who hated being bested. "Who would want me out of the list most?"

As he stood, Oliver followed the direction of his gaze to Robert. "I don't like the piece of thistledown any more than you do, but this is deliberate sabotage."

"Or worse." Thomas picked up his saddle and shouldered it. "My girth was cut, and I mean to discover by whom."

Somebody who wanted to see his pride, along with his arse, ground into the dust.

Robert rode past him and smirked. "What a pity you must withdraw."

Thomas breathed deep. It didn't help. He went after the sod, but Oliver stepped into his path. "Don't do it. Let's first find out for certain, and then I'll hold him while you pummel him into the dust."

"I'd offer to help." Sir Giles stared at the cut girth. "Whoreson! But as much as I'd like it to be that preening princess, he was in the hall making me want to punch him all morning."

"You're sure?" Oliver stared after Robert. "Because it would make me so happy if it were him."

William snorted. "You and me both, but I saw him too. He didn't leave table until we came for our horses."

"Would he have had a chance then?" Oliver asked the questions and Thomas let him. His anger almost choked him. He might have lost Brute, and all because of some pointless games.

"No." Giles shook his head. "His horse is stabled right beside mine."

At the far end of the stable from where Brute had been kept.

Robert had stopped his horse in front of Madeleine, making it do some asinine bow over its left leg to her. And Madeleine ate it up with a spoon. She giggled and smiled and blushed at the lying turd eater.

As much as Thomas disliked the sod, it was not his place to deal with his advances toward Madeleine. And apparently, he had no grounds to lay the cutting of his girth at Robert's feet either.

Which made it imperative he find who had done it. It had been an underhanded trick, a trick by someone who wanted to see him lose more than anyone else here.

Madeleine watched Robert lining up for his next bout at the quintain. Eyes shining with delight, she clapped and cheered her favorite.

Even had Thomas carried the day, he would not have gotten one crumb of the praise she lavished on Robert. He was acceptable for kisses in secret, good enough for incendiary trysts in darkened halls and pantries, but not once had she smiled at him with the approval and delight she was presently bending on that sodding wastrel. She hadn't even considered that Thomas might be telling the truth about Robert and Posy.

While he followed Saul and Brute to the stable, his mind turned to his fall. Dislike of Robert was clouding his reasoning. It could have been any of the knights. They would all stand to gain through his withdrawal.

A young stablehand rushed out to meet them. "Is it his fetlock?"

"We think so." Saul scratched Brute's mane. "He's a brave lad though, and he wouldn't show it if he were hurt."

"Jem!" The stablehand called.

"What ails ya?" The grizzled old veteran in charge of the stables stumped out of their gloom toward Brute. With a groan, he crouched down and examined the fetlock. "I got a poultice to take the heat off the joint."

"I'm obliged to you," Thomas said.

Brute looked at him, trust and love in his huge limpid eyes. For Thomas, he would bear them looking at his injury, and for Thomas, he would take a thousand more injuries. Other than Peter, Brute was the closest creature to him. Indeed, when Peter was at his most vexing, Thomas preferred Brute's company. They were a pair, their minds working as one with their bodies. A stupid spiteful act had almost cost him this fine friend. He tucked his face into Brute's neck. "You rest up, and I'll make sure whoever did this to you pays."

Brute whickered and nudged his pockets.

"You're a game one, aren't you?" Thomas almost laughed. "But yes, you can have extra oats in your feed." He looked at Saul. "See to it."

"Yes, Sir Thomas."

Thomas followed Jem into the stables and put Brute in the stall Jem indicated.

Jem sent the young stablehand running for his herbs. He crouched at Brute's feet muttering to himself and murmuring soothing words.

Brute looked at Thomas over Jem's head, and Thomas was ready to swear Brute rolled his eyes.

When the lad returned, Jem selected the herbs he wanted and chewed them. He spat the chewed up mess into a cloth of rough linen and selected another herb. The entire process turned the stomach to watch, but Brute stood quietly while Jem worked.

After the poultice was in place, Thomas led Brute back to his stall. "Well, that's you for the day." He patted Brute's glossy shoulder. "You stay here, court the mares, fill your belly and get yourself better."

Brute blew hard and grunted.

"That's a good horse, that is. As finer beast as I've seen in a long time." Jem leaned against a stable upright. "Got a good solid heart, and that and my poultice will see him fixed."

"I pray you're right." Thomas had to clear his throat past the lump in it. Brute had seen him through many a battle. "We have traveled long roads together, and I would see us go on a few more."

"Cut girth is what I heard. All kinds of new faces in the stables with these tourney goings on." Jem shook his head. "That's a foul trick to play on man and beast."

"Yes." Thomas's anger simmered beneath his skin. "I would know who was in the stable this morning before the jousters came for their horses."

Jem scratched his shrunken pate. "I can't rightly say, my aching knees kept me abed this morning, but you should ask Lady Madeleine. She was in here first light."

* * *

Seeing Thomas lose didn't feel as satisfying as Madeleine thought it would. Alone in her chamber, Madeleine eased into the steaming water of her bath. She was hot and sticky after watching the joust, and she'd asked Heather to have a bath prepared for her.

Robert had won the contest with the quintain, followed by William, which should have made her feel happier than it did.

The way Thomas had left the lists hadn't been fair, and even from the little they had seen of him, it had been clear he would have won had he been able to continue.

She slid further into her bath until the water lapped at her chin. Thomas had hit the ground hard, yet his immediate concern had been for his horse. He'd even withdrawn and suffered the loss rather than risk his horse further. She had to admire that about him. Father always said you could tell a man's heart by the way he treated animals and servants.

Thomas had been gentle with both his horse and his aged squire.

Her chamber door flew open and crashed into the wall behind it.

Madeleine jerked up in her bath.

Thomas stormed through her door and slammed it shut behind him.

Taken aback, Madeleine was speechless, and she stared at the large intruder.

"You've gone too far this time." He stalked into the room.

It occurred to her, slower than it should have, that he was furious. It then occurred to her, also slower than it should have, that she was sitting naked in a tub of water. "You shouldn't be here."

"I never thought a daughter of Sir Richard's would let her malice drive her to endanger a beautiful animal." In his anger, he seemed oblivious to her nudity.

And then the other part of what he'd said penetrated her shocked mind. "What are you talking about? Endangering an animal?" That he could think such a thing of her made her angry enough to spit. "I would have—have never—nor will I ever— what in God's name are you blathering about?"

"You cut my girth strap." He clenched his fists, color riding high on his cheekbones.

For the second time in as many minutes, he rendered her speechless. "I did what?"

"You cut the girth on my saddle." He stalked closer. "Causing my weight to unbalance my horse, and he stumbled." He loomed over her. "A stumble that has sprained his fetlock."

"Stand back." Madeleine pulled her knees up to her chest to cover herself. He cast a shadow over her and would be able to see through the clear water. "Stand back and we can discuss this like sensible people."

"There is nothing to discuss." He scowled at her.

She returned his scowl. An injured horse left much to be discussed, and his assumption of her guilt rankled. "When you barge into my chamber and catch me like this, and then accuse me of damaging your horse, I would say there is plenty to discuss."

His jaw clenched.

"Or are you in the habit of tossing about accusations, and then not giving the other person a chance to respond?"

He paused and some of the tension drained from his shoulders.

Madeleine motioned him back from her bath. "Turn around."

"Why?"

Now he was being idiotic, and she sneered at him. "So I can make myself presentable."

"Oh." More color stained his cheeks, and then his gaze sharpened on her as if seeing her predicament for the first time. He ran a slow gaze over her shoulders and cleared his throat.

"Turn around." Madeleine's face felt hot enough to burst into flame.

Thomas turned his back.

Not chancing him changing his mind, she snatched up her robe and wriggled into it. It was no easy feat considering how wet her skin was and how much the linen enjoyed adhering to it.

Eventually she was done, and she bound her wet hair atop her head.

Thomas wore only a chemise, and it accentuated the breadth of his shoulders. A chemise currently stained rust red on his left side.

"Thomas." Such a large stain could mean a deep injury. "You're hurt."

"Eh?" He peered over his shoulder. "Oh, that. It's nothing."

"It doesn't look like nothing." Madeleine stopped behind him and peered at his back. "What did you do?"

He tried to turn, but she caught his arm and held him still.

With an impatient growl, he said, "It must have happened when I fell." He gathered himself with a frown. "And if you didn't cut the girth then why did you look so smug when I was unseated."

"I didn't look smug." Perhaps she'd felt a tiny bit satisfied to see him rendered a mere mortal. Mostly, however, she'd been impressed by the way he'd handled his fall. Not that she intended to tell him so and give him an even fatter head. "I didn't realize you had hurt yourself."

"I'm more concerned for my horse." He crossed his arm.

Madeleine plucked at his chemise. It stuck to his injury, and he hissed. She gave it a tug. "You need to take this off." Then she fetched a washing rag. "But first, let me dampen it so it comes free easier."

"I don't care about my back." He glared over his shoulder at her. "Brute is injured."

"And I would wager my life that Jem is dealing with your horse. How does you bleeding to death benefit the situation?"

He muttered and subsided into a grudging silence.

"Brute?"

Color climbed his cheeks. "It's what his previous owner used to curse at him. It's become a joke between us."

Adelaide spoke to her horses, and swore they understood her. The bond between Thomas and Brute was obvious to anyone watching them ride together.

Madeleine damped the russet stained area and carefully eased linen from his wound. "Am I to infer from your bluster that my smirk was the reason you blamed me for cutting your girth?"

His low opinion of her cut deep.

"Not merely that." He grunted as a section of chemise stuck and she had to pull. "You never lose an opportunity to let me know how much you dislike me, and how much you dislike me winning."

She'd done that, and Madeleine winced behind his back. In any other man, his prowess would have been something she celebrated and applauded. "I don't dislike you...completely, and you make others look inferior with your skill."

"Be careful, Madeleine, you drift perilously close to praising me."

"A vicious lie." But she giggled anyway. "I can possibly see how I would appear guilty, but I didn't cut your girth."

"No?" He glanced over his shoulder. "What are you doing back there?"

"Freeing your wound." She stepped back. "Remove your chemise. And I didn't cut your girth because I am, as you pointed out, my father's daughter, and he has impressed upon all of us a sense of fairness and also a respect for animals. You know that. You spent years amongst us."

He tugged his chemise over his head and clasped it in his fist. "Jem said you were in the stables this morning."

"Yes." She shoved his uninjured shoulder. "Sit! I'm in the stables most mornings for my ride. Jem knows this, and he also saw me when I returned. He waits for me."

"Ah." He lowered his bulk to a dressing stool.

The gash on his side was deep but wouldn't need stitching. "Ah? Is that an ah that you believe me, or one that means you've yet to be convinced?"

He chuckled. "I believe you."

"It's an honest miracle, to be sure." She fetched her basket of medicaments.

Thomas chuckled and shook his head. "You're more like Richard than some of your brothers, and he would never resort to such a low trick."

"No, he wouldn't." Madeleine cleaned his wound. "And neither would I."

He tensed as she touched the deepest part of the wound. "Then who do you think would do it?"

Immediately Robert leaped into her mind, but she clamped her jaw shut around his name. She smeared a honey and herb ointment over his wound. "There are any number who could be jealous," she said. "Any of the men you've defeated might feel slighted."

He grunted.

"We need to speak to my father, regardless. If someone is cheating, he will want to know." She nudged his arm. "Lift."

"You've a soft touch, Maddy." Warmth infused his deep voice. "I thank you."

"Now you try to wheedle your way back into my good graces." She wrapped healing strips around his torso. His hot to the touch, muscular, broad torso. Heat prickled beneath her skin and rendered her fingers clumsy as she tied the bandage. "All done."

"My thanks." His face was alarmingly close to hers and she sensed his gaze on her. He caught a tendril of her hair between his thumb and forefinger. "Your hair is wet."

"I was washing it." Her heart pounded against her chest, and heat blossomed through her muscles and made them fluid and languorous.

"When you were in your bath?" He wove his spell around her with his deep, raspy voice. A voice that promised her more of the passion that flared whenever they were together.

This time, they were alone, in her chamber, and both of them wearing less than they normally did.

The rich male scent of him sunk deep into her senses.

His thick finger smoothed her hair against her shoulder and then traced the line of her collar bone to the edge of her robe. "You smell of roses."

"It's an oil Heather puts in my bath." Madeleine's breath hitched. She should stop him, but she didn't want to. She wanted his touch on every part of her. Her nipples puckered and chafed against the fabric of her robe.

He slid a finger beneath her robe, down over her chest and over the slope of her breast. "Maddy," he rasped. "What spell do you cast over me?"

Spell she cast over him? Madeleine rather thought it the other way around. "Thomas?"

"Yes." He dipped his head. Hot and wet, his mouth branded her neck.

"I can't think when you touch me."

He groaned and sucked her neck. He slid his entire hand inside her robe and cupped her bare breast. "Sweet Mother of God, I want you."

She wanted him too. Desire pooled between her thighs, making her damp with need. Adelaide had told her how her body would respond when she desired a man. Adelaide hadn't exaggerated the strength of the emotion that rampaged through her.

Her nipple pushed against his palm, demanding more attention.

His other hand slid over her knee, pushing her robe aside.

Madeleine inched her thighs open. Her entire being focused on the hand squeezing her breast. His thumb strumming her nipple. And also on the warm, rough clasp sliding over her knee and between her thighs. "Please."

"Please what?" His breath was hot against her neck.

She'd no more articulate words than "More."

The door opened and Heather strode in. "Are you done yet?"

Thomas leaped to his feet.

Grabbing the edges of her robe, Madeleine tugged them about her.

Not fast enough by the look on Heather's face. She drew herself straight and gave Thomas a cold look. "Sir Thomas, you seem to have strayed into the wrong bedchamber."

"Forgive me." He blushed and executed a clumsy bow. Turning back to her, a look of frustration crossed his face. "Maddy—"

"Go." She wanted to sink into the floor and disappear. Heather had caught them, well and true, and now, she would hear about it from her outspoken maid. "We will speak later. Of the girth. And other matters."

For a moment, it looked like he might refuse to go, and then he bowed stiffly, snatched up his chemise and stalked from the room. He shut the door behind him.

Madeleine couldn't look at Heather. Her face felt hot enough to boil water.

"It seems your night for trouble." Heather cleared her throat. "Sir Robert has asked you to meet him in the armory."

Chapter Sixteen

It would be too much good fortune for Heather to hold her tongue for much longer than two heartbeats. Robert's message delivered, she jammed her hands on her hips. "Have you lost your wits?"

"Did Robert say what he wanted?" Madeleine turned her back and tried for a nonchalant tone.

"Never you mind Robert." Heather strode over to her dressing tree and selected a gold bliaut. "What were you thinking letting Thomas into your chamber?"

"I didn't invite him in." Avoiding the issue with Heather never worked. Madeleine wriggled into her white silk chemise. "He came here because he thought I cut his girth."

"But you didn't." Heather glared and tugged her fastenings closed.

"Of course I didn't."

Frowning, Heather dropped the gold samite over her head and tugged it into place. "It could be any one of the men he's competing with or any of their people." Heather groaned. "There are so many possibilities."

"I know." Madeleine stood still while Heather laced her. "I need to speak to Father."

"That you do." Heather nudged her to the dressing stool. The same one Thomas had sat on. "But I suggest you don't tell him about Thomas with his hands up your skirt and down your bodice."

Fresh heat flamed over her face. "Saw all that, did you?"

"Yes." Heather snorted and grabbed a comb. "And you're lucky it was me and not one of your family who came through that door."

The idea of her mother, or worse one of her brothers or her father seeing what Heather had seen made her shudder. "I have no idea why I can't think when he's around."

"Madeleine?" Heather stopped midstroke through her hair. "Are you saying this has happened before?"

"Not as much." Damn her continued blushes. "But we have kissed."

"How many times?" Heather tugged through a stubborn snarl.

Confession was meant to save your soul, right? "Twice."

"Including today?"

Heather could jaw a thing to death. "Excluding today."

"By the rood, you take a huge risk." Heather yanked her hair. "What do you think your future husband will have to say when he finds his bride is no longer a virgin?"

"It won't come to that." Heather's assumption annoyed her. She wasn't that beyond control when Thomas touched her.

Heather gave her hair another tug, and this time it was no accident. "Where do you think touching and kissing leads?"

"I know that." She hated when Heather took it upon herself to lecture. Like she knew any better. "I won't let it come to that."

With a snort, Heather went back to combing. "That's not what I saw when I walked into this chamber."

"It won't happen again." And she meant it, despite the pang of disappointment. Robert was her future husband, and she wouldn't give to Thomas what was Robert's by right.

"How will you make sure of that?" Heather peered at her over her shoulder.

There was only one way to ensure Thomas kept his hands to himself, and as much as it rankled to admit it, her mastery of her desire for him was not it. "I shall ensure not to be alone with him again."

After a pause, Heather nodded. "I think that would be for the best."

After she was dressed, Madeleine hurried to the armory. The only person about was Posy, and they passed in the corridor.

Posy didn't greet her but ducked her head and hurried away.

There was nothing she wanted to hear from Posy. Then something about the other woman stopped her. She had been so intent on not speaking with Posy, that she hadn't immediately registered what she had seen. Had she caught the glint of tears on Posy's face? It didn't matter. Posy would rather eat rats than confide in her, and it suited Madeleine that way.

Hands clasped behind his back, Robert waited in the armory. He turned as she approached and smiled at her, looking so handsome in a doublet that matched the blue of his eyes. "Madeleine. Thank you for meeting me."

"As if I could stay away." Madeleine took his outstretched hands. The oddest thing happened at Robert's touch. Odd in that nothing happened. Her pulse didn't pound. Her skin didn't heat. She didn't get that delicious melty feeling that always happened around Thomas.

Robert raised her hands to his beautiful mouth and kissed them. "I couldn't wait another moment. I had to speak to you."

"You did?" How long had she yearned to hear such words from Robert? Perhaps her endless wait was the reason for only a small tendril of pleasure snaking through her. That must be it. She didn't want to entertain false hope. She kept her response playful. "I saw you this morning."

"But not alone." Robert slid his arm about her waist and drew her against him. "Every day I must share you with all these other men."

"Robert?" It was so unlike him to speak to her thus that surprise kept her joy at bay.

"I'm jealous, my love." His free hand cupped her cheek and he gazed at her tenderly. "All this time, I have gotten used to having you all to myself. And now I must share you, and I don't like it."

Madeleine could barely credit the words coming out of his mouth or the warm look in his pretty eyes. If she'd known all it would take was some rivalry to get Robert to act, she would have encouraged her father to invite possible suitors years ago. Or not, because she didn't like the idea of using them to bring Robert to her side. "You're jealous?"

"Hmmm." Robert dipped his head and feathered her lips with his. "I asked you here so I could remind you who loved you first."

Robert had admitted that he loved her. The news rippled through her and struck her dumb, which was why it took a moment to react to Robert's kiss becoming more earnest.

He touched his tongue to her lip, asking permission.

Madeleine opened her mouth to him. She'd wanted Robert's kiss for so long that it felt impossible that he was kissing her now. She closed her eyes and opened her senses to his kiss.

Robert had her in his arms. Her breasts pressed to his chest, as he kissed her like a man who desired her.

His tongue thrust in and out of her mouth, tangling with hers. It wasn't entirely...unpleasant, but it also didn't engender in her any desire to kiss him back.

The shock of Robert's hand on her breast made her lurch away from him. "What are you about?"

Robert ran a hand through his hair. "I would apologize, but it would be a lie." He held out a hand in entreaty. "I lose my wits around you, Madeleine. I can't control my desire to make you mine."

"Since when?" she blurted, but now the words were uttered,

she didn't regret them. Suddenly Robert had discovered unbridled passion for her where there had been no sign of any before. At the church, she had all but begged him to kiss her, and he had refused. Thomas needed no pleas to kiss her.

Looking chagrinned, Robert shoved his hands behind his back. "It's my fault that you doubt me now." He sighed and stared past her shoulder. "I have fought what I felt for you for so long. I have done such a good job of it that now you doubt my passion."

The almost irrepressible desire to laugh bubbled through her, and Madeleine had to study her feet to regain her composure. His claim struck her as nonsensical. The reason she thought he didn't desire her was because he desired her too much and was too good at hiding it?

Robert dropped to his knees in front of her. "Say I haven't smote your desire for me." He grabbed her hand and pressed it to his cheek. "Please tell me there is hope."

"Get up, Robert." She wasn't much of one for having men falling at her feet, and it made her feel awkward that he had. This entire encounter made her twitch, but she had wanted to marry Robert for so long. She still did. "Of course it's not too late."

"Thank God." He pressed a feverish kiss to her hand. "You professed your love to me before." He gave her a coy smile. "Will you not do so now?"

Madeleine opened her mouth with every intention of doing so, but instead she said, "We should go before we are late for dinner."

* * *

In the hall, Madeleine took the seat beside Adelaide. This conversation needed an older sister's opinion. Not for her life would she ask her mother.

Adelaide glanced her way and went back to her grim study of the hall.

Taking a moment to spot what had earned Adelaide's ire, she came up empty. The hall looked as it usually did, with a few more faces than normal. "What are you scowling at?"

"Nothing." Adelaide huffed. "A vast bloody nothing."

"Addy?" Her sister's mood threw her off topic. "Is something the matter?"

"No." Adelaide's smile looked forced. "Nothing any of us can do anything about."

Other than the months following the death of her husband when she had isolated herself in her grief, Adelaide had always been her older sister, all knowing and full of wisdom. "Tell me anyway."

Adelaide gave her an assessing look and then nodded. "There are times when I feel I died along with Stephen."

"As in your heart being broken." Madeleine would never forget the sound of Adelaide's choking sobs in those terrible months.

Adelaide grimaced. "No. In the beginning it was that, but now I feel as if I've been shoved in the ground with him."

"Addy?" She didn't understand.

Adelaide growled. "It's the way people see me, Mads. It's like widowhood is a disease that everyone fears is contagious."

"You want to get married again?"

With a loud laugh, Adelaide shook her head. "Dear God, no. But there's a lot of being a woman between the dusty relic I am now and being married again."

Before Thomas had turned her passion into her enemy, Madeleine might have been baffled by Adelaide's statement. "You want a love affair."

"I'm not sure how much love has to do with it." Adelaide gave her a sparkling mischievous look. "But a passionate affair. Now that, I would dearly like."

Up until very recently, Madeleine wouldn't have known the difference. "Can you have one without the other?"

"I'd like to try." Adelaide laughed and sipped her wine.

Their discussion led so near to what she needed to discuss. "Can all women do that? Have passion without love? Mother had both and—"

"Madeleine." Adelaide shifted closer and scrutinized her. "Why are you asking me this? Have you done anything you shouldn't have?"

Her sister knew her too well, and color heated her cheeks. "No. Not really. Not that much."

"Madeleine!" Adelaide shrieked her name loud enough to have heads turn their way. She lowered her voice to a whisper. "What have you been doing, and with whom?"

At no time would she give Addy any names. She spread a smile on her face and kept it there for anyone watching them. "Who isn't really relevant, but say there were two people, men, in my life."

"Two?" Addy raised her brows. "Little sister, you're a bolder woman than I."

"It's not like that." Her face grew hotter. "I haven't done anything...irreparable."

"I'm glad to hear it." Addy snorted. "I need to hear what you have done."

"I'm confused." Madeleine stared at the hall rather than meet Addy's eye. Across the hall Thomas looked up suddenly. It was like he had a sense for where she was, and she for him. "Can you desire a man but not love him? And can you love a man and not desire him...much?"

Adelaide followed her gaze. "Are we at the moment staring at the one you desire?"

"We might be." That look Thomas gave her awoke her senses to him. Merely by looking at him, she could recall the smell and taste of him. Her skin still retained his touch.

"And might Robert be the man you love but don't desire?"

Madeleine wanted to squirm in her seat. "It's not that I don't desire him. It's more that I mightn't desire him as much as Th— the other one."

"Mm-hmm." Adelaide chuckled. "You know Father would be delighted to know his plan had worked so well."

Addy's declaration surprised her so much it dragged her attention from Thomas. "He planned this?"

"Of course he did." Adelaide rolled her eyes and gestured the hall. "This entire tournament was organized to turn your head from Robert."

"I still love Robert." She didn't want her sister getting the wrong idea. But her utterance lacked her usual heat.

"But you want to tangle with Thomas." Adelaide nudged her. "Although he would never admit it, Father would love it if you picked Thomas."

This conversation was tying her in knots. "I'm not going to choose Thomas. Just because I can't think when he's close to me, doesn't mean I'm going to marry the man."

"Madeleine." Addy fixed her with a stern look. "As much as you believe you love Robert, if matters progress beyond a certain point with Thomas, make no mistake, Thomas is the man you will marry."

Chapter Seventeen

Knowing all his men were avoiding him only worsened Thomas's mood. He'd woken this morning ready to thump his own arse, and robbed of that, had made it a point to terrorize his men with his temper. Yes, he was well aware he was being a whoreson, but that only increased his self-loathing.

He had his men strip all their gear, clean and oil it, and put it away again. He followed by insisting they do a thorough cleaning of their portion of the Elford barracks. If they completed that before his ire had blown itself out, he knew plenty of practice yard activities to keep them busy.

Peter strode across the yard toward him. "Dear God, Thomas, your men surrender."

He suspected his men had sent Peter in desperation.

"Clean them." Thomas yelled at Saul attempting to sneak by with an arm full of swords. "I want to see my face in them."

Saul flinched and hobbled to the table, leaving Thomas feeling like a nasty brute, which soured his mood further.

Peter turned and watched Saul. "Are we sure seeing one's visage is the most important matter here?"

"A dirty weapon could be a flawed weapon." Thomas could

barely contain his growl. "And a flawed weapon could mean your death."

"Right you are, Sir Thomas." Saul nodded sagely from behind his table full of swords.

Humming, Peter turned back to him. "Most alarming, I'm sure."

"What do you want, Peter?" The only man who wasn't afraid of his temper and here to vex him for certain.

Turning, Peter surveyed him. "I have been tasked with dealing with you."

Thomas laughed. Peter never minced words. "I thought as much."

"Care to explain what has put you in the devil's own temper?"

Not at all, but Peter could be persistent. "Somebody endangered Brute, and I'm no closer to finding who."

"Ah." Peter gave him a knowing glance.

"What?"

"Is that all?" Peter raised a brow.

The temerity of the man still amazed him. "Is it not enough that I'm angry someone is trying to kill me?"

"Thomas." Peter chuckled and clapped him on his shoulder. "People have been trying to kill you for most of your adulthood." He winced. "And your childhood, if one must count your uncle."

Thomas's ire simmered into a grim amusement. "Yes, but nearly all of those were in war and not by sneaking about. Except in my uncle's case, but as he's been dead a number of years. I feel we can acquit him of this."

"True." Peter frowned. "But how is it that you make the jump in reasoning from someone trying to make you lose to trying to kill you."

"It makes a more plausible reason for my temper."

Peter laughed and clapped his hands. "That it does." He grew serious again. "But someone is out to do you mischief, and I shall nose about a bit and see if I can catch anything."

His loyalty was part of the reason Peter could speak to

Thomas as freely as he did. "I appreciate that. I'm not that partial to seeing my arse."

"No." Peter winced. "None of us are partial to seeing your arse."

"Enough." Thomas nodded to Saul. "Tell the others to stop this needless make-work, and those swords are fine. I'll have some mead and food sent to them."

Saul scurried off, and his men relaxed. One or two shot him a wary glance before believing they could stop.

He really shouldn't have taken his temper out on them. "Let's go and chat to Jem about who was in the stable that morning. Doing something will help."

"Let me do that." Peter put a hand to his chest. "Whoever did this has to know you will be trying to find them out. And your manner is less...subtle."

Thomas gave him a look that stated Peter's attempt at tact was a waste. "You mean you don't want me charging through the stable banging heads together."

"Exactly." Peter winked and sauntered away in the direction of the stable.

Both because of his priest robes and his manner, Peter had a way of getting information out of people. He would find out who had been able to cut his girth that morning without anyone being any wiser. Which left him with nothing more to stew over on that front, and no distraction to prevent his next irritant from pushing forward.

Madeleine. Infuriating, beautiful, impertinent, sultry, impetuous, desirable, tempting...irresistible Madeleine.

The mead and food arrived for his men, and Thomas took himself off. They deserved the rest of the day free of him. On the far side of the bailey, he went through the wooden door to Lady Margaret's pleasure gardens. Here they had often played as children while she watched and laughed.

He took a sandy path to a small pond filled with bright fish.

He and Edward had lain on their bellies and spent hours trying to catch those fish. The garden's peace soothed him.

Lying to himself would no longer suffice. Jesu, but wanting her had become a deep ache in him. If her maid hadn't interrupted them yesterday, he would have pushed that flimsy robe from her glorious body and explored her with his hands and then his mouth.

He thanked God for chainmail hiding his reaction to merely the thought of her.

She was woven into his senses. The taste of her skin and mouth lingered on his tongue.

He needed to stay away from her.

As if to mock his decision, her laughter drifted in the still air and he turned, like a scenting dog, in that direction.

Madeleine was walking with Robert, her arm through his, her lovely face turned up to him as she laughed. Neither of them had seen him. Robert was playing her false, and she didn't believe it. His jaw ached he clamped it so tight around the desire to swear long and hard. Instead, she accused him of being jealous.

Robert lowered his head to hear what Madeleine said. They made a pretty couple with their flaxen hair shining in the sunlight.

He was jealous, horribly so, and he wanted to march over and rip Robert away from her, stomp his pretty, lying face into the sandy path.

Thomas liked her. The truth stared him in the face. He liked her a lot and it was tugging apart his reason for being here. He could no longer pretend he was here only to form bonds.

Madeleine smiled up at Robert, her laughter taunting Thomas in the quiet of the garden. Enough prevaricating. He most assuredly did like her, but she did not feel the same.

"There you are." Peter hurried toward him. "Saul said he saw you come this way.

Thomas shook his head to clear it. "Did you discover anything?"

Looking about him, Peter caught sight of Madeleine and Robert and stilled. "Ah."

Thomas refused to ask because he could guess what Peter would say, and Peter would probably be right. Blast him! "Tell me what you discovered."

Too near the swell of Madeleine's arse rested Robert's hand. The same hand Thomas itched to remove from Robert's arm. He pulled his gaze to Peter.

"Everything and nothing." Peter sighed. "That lanky ginger, and the one with the crooked nose were in the stables that morning. As were ladies Madeleine, Adelaide, and Catriona."

Frustration welled up, and his attention wandered back to the pair now idling near the well. "We are back to knowing nothing."

"Not quite." Peter shrugged. "Because who wasn't in the stables that morning was the man you're presently searing with your gaze."

"No?" Disappointment tasted bitter in his mouth. He would have liked nothing more than to rearrange Robert's pretty face for him.

"No." Peter shook his head. "Saul did mention he might have seen a familiar face."

Bringing Madeleine's hand to his mouth, Robert kissed it.

She withdrew her hand immediately and put some distance between them.

It wasn't nearly enough distance to satisfy Thomas. "Who?"

"Wilfred." Peter's look was loaded with meaning.

All of which escaped Thomas. What didn't escape him was how Robert closed the distance between him and Madeleine. "Who?"

"Wilfred." Peter cleared his throat. "Burly, used to reside at Elford. You recently unearthed him from beneath the whore, Martha."

"Wilfred?" Robert had his head nearly on Madeleine's shoulder. It wouldn't be there if Thomas got hold of it and twisted. "Wilfred has no business here."

"Exactly." Peter nodded. "But Saul's eyesight is going, so before you launch an all-out rampage throughout Elford, let me discover more."

"Do it."

Robert and Madeleine wandered under the shade of an oak.

"You know." Peter leaned into his shoulder. "Instead of standing about glowering. You might consider entering the fray."

"Eh?" Madeleine's pale green bliaut clung to the full swell of her breasts and hips. Her waist was tiny enough for him to span with his hands. And, dear God, he wanted nothing more. To grip her by that tiny waist and lift her onto his lap. Put those long legs on either side of his hips and have her straddle him.

"You could woo her for yourself," Peter murmured.

His response was pure reflex. "Don't be ridiculous."

"My mistake." Peter grinned.

"But just because I won't woo her, doesn't mean I intend to let that knave have her. He's up to something with Posy and playing her against Madeleine. I feel sure of it."

"What can you do?" Peter shook her head. "You've told her, and she didn't believe you."

That didn't make him powerless. "I can grind his shiny, lying face into the dust."

Chapter Eighteen

The hall was festive, but Madeleine couldn't find the cheer within herself. As much as she hated to admit it, part of the blame lay with Robert. He'd sat beside her once the meal was concluded and insisted on all her attention. Nobody else came near them, and she was running out of conversation.

He took possession of her hand and played with her fingers. She wanted her hand back, but he would likely be offended if she took it back, so she gritted her teeth.

Giving her a melting look, he bent over her hands. "Such delicate fingers. So pretty." He kissed each one in turn.

"Really, Robert. Someone might see." Feeling like every eye was on them, she tugged her hand back. "Even I can't believe that. I ride too much, and I have the callouses to prove it."

Robert clasped her hand to his chest, his eyes gleaming in a way that made her fidget. "Your hands are perfect, and I'll allow nobody to tell me otherwise."

Madeleine gave up. Her hands were perfect, her hair shone like moonlight, her skin rivaled the cream they had eaten with dessert, and her eyes were bluer than a summer sky. "Fine. But can we stop with the flattery now."

It came out tarter than she'd intended, and Robert's wounded expression rebuked her.

She gentled her tone. "I mean I love that you think of me this way, but it makes me feel like an imposter."

His expression cleared, and that troublesome gleam returned. "Because you're so meek and modest."

"Meek?" It came out in a squeak, and she was hard put not to laugh. Meek and modest! Jesu give her strength. Not on her best day. Nor would she want to be. "I think you're confusing me with someone else."

He edged closer. "As if I could, when you torment me night and day."

"How very uncomfortable for you." She tried to lighten the atmosphere. There must have been something amiss with her. For so long, she'd dreamed of Robert as he was now, yet his attention felt cloying.

Minstrels struck up a lively tune and the tables were cleared for dancing. She did love to dance. The dancers formed for the first dance, and she dearly wanted to be one of them.

Thomas stood between three of her mother's women. May stood far too close to him with her overblown bosom pressed against his arm. She would have a word with Mother about having trulls in the keep.

What was she doing?

She liked May. They had spent many a boring winter day laughing and entertaining each other.

God in heaven, but Thomas was changing the way she thought of people. It might have been his fault she couldn't enjoy Robert's attentions. Even as she thought it, she knew that wasn't the reason, but her heart veered away from examining the true reason for her tepid response to Robert.

Robert got hold of her hand again and rubbed his thumb in circles on her palm. He was also looking at her like she was a ripe peach. It made her uncomfortable.

She pulled her hand back and barely stopped herself in time

from wiping the odd sensation in her palm against her thigh. "My father is watching us."

Immediately, Robert blanched and looked about for her father.

Madeleine had last seen Father swapping battle tales with a group of knights, unashamedly embellishing. Perhaps Father would think more of Robert if he wasn't always sneaking away in fear. Thomas faced Father eye to eye, like over the archery challenge. However, Father had always favored Thomas, and she was not being fair to Robert. Larger, more powerful men than Robert quailed before her father.

The minstrels were playing one of her favorites, and dancers moved into the clear space. Under the table, her feet tapped out the tune.

Catriona was dancing with William and laughing up at him. It was nice to see her happy and carefree, even if it was only for a few moments.

When Giles headed in her direction, hope swept through her, and she gave him her most encouraging smile.

Momentarily taken aback, he stopped and blinked at her. Then a wicked grin spread over his face, and he strolled toward her. "Lady Maddy—"

"Yes, I would love to dance." She leaped to her feet.

Robert started and stared at her. "If you had wanted to dance, you should have said. I would gladly have danced with you."

"I know that, Robert." She gripped Giles's arm in a death hold. Even the most loving of couples needed time apart. "But I lost a wager to Sir Giles, and I must now pay up."

Giles's laughing gaze mocked her, but he murmured, "So true. I'm most diligent in collecting my bets."

Madeleine put iron into her voice. "Shall we?"

Giles bowed and led her away from Robert.

Madeleine's head whirled. It made no sense. How often she'd dreamed of Robert behaving as he had tonight. Only, in her

147

dreams she wallowed in his attention. She didn't get restless enough to make a man dance with her.

Giles leaned close enough to whisper in her ear. "Are we escaping, or are we making him jealous?"

"One of us is shutting our pie hole." She gave him a stern look. "And the other loves to dance."

Throwing his head back and laughing, Giles led her into the dance.

Giles was a wonderful dancer, strong and sure, he led her through the forms, twirling her until her head spun. Her dull mood vanished as the music and motion swept her along.

She danced with Giles until William interrupted and swept her into an even livelier dance. Tristan followed shortly after, and she forgot Robert and his irksome gleam and her own inconstancy.

Madeleine abandoned herself to fun.

Around them, people laughed and bumped into each other. Men laughed and clapped, girls giggled and shrieked, and the minstrels drifted from one lively tune into another.

A pause in the dance allowed her to catch her breath. Her gaze tracked left and locked on Thomas's.

Standing beside the dancers, he had a half smile tilting the corners of his mouth, and his pale eyes warmed with approval. He was watching her and enjoying what he saw.

Hardly knowing where the impulse came from, Madeleine crooked her finger at him.

Thomas laughed, his teeth flashing white in his face, and raised an eyebrow.

Madeleine stood her ground, her challenge out there for him to accept. She lifted her chin and squared her shoulders.

His grin broadened, and he pushed his way into the throng of dancers toward her.

Her pulse sped, and heat flooded her. The raw challenge of woman to man thrilled her, and she waited for him to reach her.

When he did, he hooked an arm about her waist and tugged her flush against him.

Mine, roared the look in his eyes as he said, "Good luck to you, Maddy. I'm a horrible dancer."

And Madeleine laughed. It came from a part of her, free and wild, that recognized a kindred soul.

Time blurred as she and Thomas danced, but one thing became startlingly clear; he really was a horrible dancer. All the grace and control he exhibited on the battlefield wasn't present on the dance floor.

He more charged than promenaded, plowed down than side-stepped, and hefted her over his head instead of a controlled lift. Madeleine loved it, because along with his ineptitude, Thomas laughed at himself and became even clumsier.

After Thomas had nearly flattened another couple for the eighteenth time, Robert appeared behind him, weaving his way through the dancers with purpose.

As ever sensitive to her slightest change in mood, Thomas glanced down at her, flushed and smiling. "What is it?"

"Robert."

Thomas glanced over his shoulder and then back at her. He hoisted her in the air and romped to the other side of the hall. "I think not."

* * *

Madeleine woke the next morning to Heather banging around her chamber. She slammed the top of Madeleine's dressing chest shut and looked up with an innocent expression that fooled neither of them. "Oh, are you awake?"

"Apparently." She stretched muscles aching from all the dancing she'd done the night before.

Heather dropped a bowl of pottage on the stool beside her bed. "The keep has already broken their fast. I managed to talk Cook into giving me this for you."

"My thanks." Madeleine gave her a sympathetic wince. Cook ruled the keep kitchens, and she didn't like people interfering with her ways. "She even allowed you honey and butter."

"You've Sir Thomas to thank for that." Heather pinned her with a heavy stare. "He was in the kitchens when I went for your pottage. Seems Cook is no more immune to his charm than someone else we know."

It took some resolve steeling, but Madeleine held her stare. "Whoever could you mean?"

"You're a cool one, you." Heather pointed a finger at her. "But I saw you last night, laughing and dancing and giving him looks."

Laughing and dancing she would admit to but—"Looks?"

"Yes, looks." Heather fetched the split skirt bliaut and breeches she used for riding. Only the grander one and not the one she wore each day. "Am I riding?"

"Yes." Heather dangled her boots. "Today's entertainment is falconry, which you would have known if you had broken your fast with the rest of the keep." She dug out a fresh chemise. "Which you didn't because of the aforementioned revelry of last night."

With Heather, she could be honest. "Thomas is...good company."

"And Robert isn't." Heather's grave stare dared her to disagree. "I also noted the way you ran away from him last night and stayed away."

"Robert has changed." Her confusion clouded her good morning mood.

Heather snorted. "Not from my view."

"You saw him last night." Madeleine needed to protest. "He's most solicitous and attentive to me. If he has not changed, then how do you explain that?"

For a long moment, Heather fussed with her wash water. Finally, she looked up. "I don't want to hurt you, Maddy. Not for anything would I wound you, but Robert cares for nobody but

Robert. You don't see this about him because you think you're in love with him."

"I am in love with him." She'd thought of no other since Robert had returned to Elford as a knight and served in her father's household. Until recently, that was.

Heather threw up a hand. "And for as long as you stay constant to that, nothing I say will gain any ground."

"I'll stay constant." She filled her mouth with pottage before it said something stupid. Her love for Robert was of the forever kind. The sort of love that existed between her mother and father.

Except, Father adored Mother, but he didn't use smooth words or practiced phrases. Indeed, at times things might have gone better for them if he had. No, her parents were well acquainted with each other—the good and the bad—and loved each other all the more for it.

After eating, she washed and dressed for a day of falconry.

The keep bustled with horses and people when she arrived. She saw neither Robert nor Thomas, but Giles joined her and helped her mount.

"You look fresh and lovely, Lady Maddy." His admiring gaze followed her as she gathered her reins.

Giles was a charmer and said the same sort of things Robert did, but she never felt uncomfortable with Giles. Perhaps because she knew he meant only one word in ten that he spoke and didn't mind who knew that.

He mounted and moved his horse beside hers. "Do you enjoy falconry?"

"Not really," she said. Giles's honesty with her made it easy to reply in kind. "But I always enjoy a good ride."

"I can see why." Giles ran his admiring gaze over her mount. "She's lovely. Was she bred at Elford?"

"Yes, Adelaide bred her for me."

Giles raised an eyebrow. "The widow."

"Yes." What Addy had said at dinner came back to Madeleine. "She's more than a widow."

Giving her a strange look, Giles nodded. "Yes, but she has never recovered from her husband's death."

Never was a very long time, and Madeleine couldn't agree. "She will always miss him, that's true, but they didn't put her in the ground along with Stephen."

"Lady Maddy? I'm not sure I understand. I meant no disrespect to your sister." Giles frowned and looked over to where Adelaide rode a spirited bay with a white blaze on his face. "There is something sad about a woman who lost a love so young."

She smiled to let him know she took no offense. "But there is something even sadder about a young woman condemned to being seen as no more than a widow for the rest of her life."

"You're right." Giles nodded, his gaze still on Adelaide. "I'll do my best to seduce her at the earliest opportunity."

"Stop." Madeleine laughed and smacked his arm. "And if I catch you near my sister, I'll have to tell Father."

Giles cast a meaningful glance at Edward. "It's not your father who concerns me most." He cocked his head and studied Edward. Behind him rode Oliver, Andrew and Thomas.

Thomas wore a leather jerkin and rode one of their horses. His dress was as plain and practical as his manner. Everything about him one could glean at first glance, and he made no attempt to apologize or disguise that. Not that he should. Even though his forthrightness bothered her at times, she knew she could trust in the honesty of his blunt statements.

Giles cleared his throat. "Actually, Lady Maddy, I hung back this morning to speak with you."

"You did?" She dragged her attention away from Thomas. Even looking at him tangled her up inside, and she ignored the yearning to ride close to him and capture his attention.

"Yes." Giles gave her a sweet smile. "I want to take this opportunity to quietly bid you God be with you."

"You're leaving?" Madeleine would miss him. Despite his outrageous statements, she'd enjoyed getting to know him.

"Yes." He pulled a face. "I didn't come here to find a wife, but I was open to the possibility."

If he was leaving, did that mean he found her wanting? A sting of hurt made her blink. "And now the possibility is closed to you?"

"Yes." He leaned across and took her hand. "You're everything my father said you were, Lady Maddy. You're lovely, spirited and damn fine company. You also have that tempting dowry, and I would be foolish not to want to count your father as family, but despite all that, I suspect you've already made your choice."

Maddy started. She hated the idea that everyone might have seen her feelings for Robert and whispered about them behind her back. Embarrassment stiffened her voice. "I'm not sure what you mean."

"Come now, Lady Maddy." Giles kissed her knuckles and dropped her hand. "There needn't be any maidenly blushes between us. The way you look at each other fair set flame to my chausses."

"I beg your pardon." Heat blossomed over her cheeks and she wanted to end the conversation. Her father wouldn't be happy to hear her partiality for Robert was so clear to everyone else."

"For what it's worth." Giles winked at her. "I think you've made a good choice, and Sir Thomas is a very lucky man."

It took a moment for that to sink in, and the implications rattled around her head. "Thomas? What does any of this have to do with Thomas?"

Giles gaped at her. "Of course, Thomas—"

"Arrow!" Madeleine froze as an arrow lanced through the air. Straight for Thomas.

Chapter Nineteen

"Beware!" Andrew shouted.

Pulse spiking, Thomas spun in the direction of the threat.

An arrow sliced through the air, right for him. Thomas stared at it.

A tremendous weight hit him as Andrew tumbled him from his horse.

The arrow hit the tree behind him and embedded in the trunk.

Time caught up with him and things moved at the right speed again. His horse danced away from him, not wanting to trample its rider.

Oliver leaped from his horse and caught Thomas's.

Crouching beside him, Andrew gripped his shoulder. "Are you well?"

"Yes." Thomas went through all his moving parts. Legs and arms, fine. Chest, unpunctured. Head, whole. Arse, aching. Fighting blood pumped in his veins, and he stood. Someone had shot an arrow at him and damn near skewered his head to the tree.

Still quivering in the tree, the arrow could have belonged to anyone. A normal hunting arrow, with no distinguishing colors on the flight. Thomas wiggled it out of the tree.

"Anything?" Edward breathed down his neck.

Thomas shook his head. The arrow had come from the thicket to his right.

Having reached the same conclusion, Andrew stomped ahead of him to the thicket. From the angle of the shaft in the tree it was possible to locate the position of the shooter.

"Here." Oliver pointed to a broken branch and a depression in the thicket floor. "Somebody must have been crouching here for a while."

"But they're gone now." Thomas cast about for signs of the fleeing archer. His blood boiled for vengeance. Some coward had lay concealed in the foliage and shot at him. A direct challenge was one thing, but this man deserved to be hunted down like the cowardly cur he'd shown himself to be.

Oliver kept his gaze on the floor, looking for signs. He grunted. "Here." He touched the edges of a boot shaped depression in the soft ground. "He went this way."

Not having any great tracking skills, Thomas followed Oliver as he hunted for and found small signs of the passage of someone through the trees and bushes.

"He'd a horse tethered there," Oliver said and indicated an area. "And they took off to the west."

Richard strode over. "Someone has dared to attack my guest on my land. This won't go unanswered."

"I'll take care of it." Edward nodded to his father. "You take our guests back to the keep."

Leveling him with a sharp stare, Richard raised an eyebrow. "Careful, son, that sounded close to an order."

"Only expediency." Edward held his father's stare, and in that moment, the similarities between them were potent and clear. Richard had raised a man in his image. Thomas wouldn't like to get between them if they fought.

Thomas ran back to his horse and mounted. Immediately,

Edward, Andrew and Oliver surrounded him. Even Madeleine nudged her mount into the group.

"Where are you going?" Thomas thought of forbidding her on the grounds it might prove dangerous.

She raised her chin and the determination in her gaze dared him to contradict her. "With you."

"Keep up, then." Thomas shrugged at Edward's incredulous stare. Madeleine couldn't be better protected than surrounded by him and her three brothers. Besides, if he'd learned one thing about Madeleine, it was to pick his battles. If Edward wanted to take it up with her, let him have at it.

As they rode in pursuit, Oliver demonstrated an uncanny skill at tracking. He read the smallest signs of the archer's passage as if they were writ across the land. The archer had made good speed and must have been prepared.

They pushed their horses faster. Time was critical in trying to intercept his attacker.

Rounding a knoll, Oliver held up his hand and they all drew rein. He waited for them to draw closer before he spoke in a hoarse whisper. "Up ahead. He hides beneath that oak tree."

By what means Oliver knew this, Thomas knew not, but he was also not about to question.

Edward looked to him. "This is your battle. How would you like to proceed?"

"Someone wants to put a hole in me, and I want to know why?" Anger surged within him. If he counted the saddle girth being cut, then somebody wanted to damage him, and he wasn't inclined to let them. He dug his heels into his horse and rode hard for the oak. "Don't let him slip away."

The archer must have seen him coming, because he broke from behind the tree and tried to run for it. Triumph coursed through Thomas. Let the bastard run, he would mow him down.

The horse he'd borrowed from Sir Richard was a beautiful creature, and although it didn't know him as well as Brute, it leaped at his command, great legs eating the ground in furious strides and closing the distance between Thomas and his quarry.

The archer glanced over his shoulder, fear widening his eyes and urged his horse to greater speeds. It was a doomed effort as Thomas closed the distance between them. Edward and Oliver were closing from either side.

He prayed Andrew had Madeleine close to hand, and he wished the man strength if he did.

The distance between him and the archer narrowed. Thomas tightened his thighs about his mount and dropped rein. Someone had trained the horse well. It obeyed his feet and drew closer to the other rider.

Thomas kicked off his stirrups and leaped. He caught the man about the waist and bore him to the ground.

His teeth clacked together as they landed, the ground hard against his shoulder.

The archer yelped and lay still and winded.

Thomas rose above him.

The archer's eyes dominated his face as he stared at Thomas in terror. He caught his breath and wheezed out a litany that made no sense and spoke more of fear than sense.

Thomas caught a whiff of her roses as Madeleine knelt beside him. She put her hand on the archer's shoulder and spoke firmly. "Hush and breathe."

The man gulped and stared at her. "My lady."

"Yes. You tried to kill my friend, and I want to know why."

Thomas stared at her, lost for words. She'd taken his question from his mouth and spoke it.

Also his mind locked on her calling him her friend and wouldn't budge.

Then, before his astonished gaze, she drew a knife and pressed it to the archer's neck. "I suggest you speak."

"No, my lady, spare me." Sweat beaded on his forehead and top lip. "Mercy, lady, mercy."

She pressed the dagger to his skin. "Do you think because I'm a woman I'll show mercy?"

Her eyes sparkled, and tendrils of hair stuck to her neck and cheeks. Dear Lord, what a magnificent woman. She looked like an avenging battle maiden.

"I did it for the coin." Tears sprang into the archer's eyes. He threw a desperate glance at Thomas. "Honest, my lord, it was nothing against you, but my smallest one is sickly, and my woman cries all the time."

"That's very sad." Baring her straight, white, teeth, Madeleine leaned over him. "Imagine how sad she would be if I slit your throat."

This was the strong warrior woman a man needed by his side. Thomas might need to seduce her, right this second. If he dared, that was.

The archer blanched. "I can tell you who paid me."

"That might help," Madeleine said. The knife didn't move. "But it would depend on how well your memory works."

Could a woman be more perfect? Thomas backed her with a menacing glower at the archer.

"I hadn't met him before. He's not from these parts." The archer kept his eyes on the knife. "He gave me a purse and said he'd have double that after the job was done. But I swear on my woman's life I weren't going to kill the big knight."

"Why should we believe you?" Her voice could have cut steel. It stroked warm fingers over Thomas's flesh. This was the sort of woman to stand toe to toe and shoulder to shoulder with her mate.

"I'm not a killer, my lady. I'm the best shot in my parish. If I'd wanted him dead, he'd be meeting his maker instead of talking to me. The man only said he wanted the big knight taken care of. He didn't say exactly what he wanted."

"Taken care of?" Thomas could think of any number of interpretations to that vague phrase. "What does that mean?"

"He didn't say." The archer glanced at him. For once Thomas

wasn't the scariest person in the fray. Blast, but she reminded him of her father with that steely look on her face, that feral glint in her eyes. Except being around Sir Richard didn't make him ache to touch, to stroke, to pleasure.

"My arm grows weary of holding the knife at this angle." Madeleine smiled.

The man yelped. "Taken care of, that's all he said."

Andrew frowned and turned down the corners of his mouth as he thought. "Taken care of? That speaks to a certain lack of resolve."

"Resolve being the outright desire to end my life." Thomas couldn't stop his sardonic snort.

Andrew flashed a grin. "Exactly. You're so perceptive, Thomas. It's one of the things I like about you."

Madeleine chuckled, and the knife moved. It nicked the archer, who screamed as if she'd disemboweled him. She watched the small trickle of blood snake down his neck and disappear beneath his tunic. "Oops."

"Let me help you, friend." Andrew crouched at the archer's side. "I suggest you describe the man who hired you. Only do it soon. My sister has...moods."

Sweat poured down the archer's face. His eyes grew rounder and rounder. "Thick set, bald."

"Hmm." Madeleine beamed a smile of pure sunshine at the man. "I think you can improve on that."

The archer thought. Really, really hard. Thomas was surprised no wheels turned behind his eyes. "I've never seen him here abouts." The archer produced that detail like a salvation. "He was an oldster, heavy like I said, but going to fat." Feverish hope gleamed in his eyes. "He had a limp."

A memory tickled the back of his mind.

"Is that all?" Andrew watched the archer like a hawk would a dormouse. Thomas was relieved all the family intensity wasn't aimed at him. Other than Madeleine's. He wouldn't be at all opposed to Madeleine's intensity. Except perhaps at a more auspicious time, and not when they were trying to ascertain who had attempted to damage him. Still, she was glorious to watch.

"Yes." The archer jerked as if he would nod his head, and then thought better of the idea and said louder, "I never spoke to him longer than it took to finish my ale."

Andrew hummed and looked up at Thomas. "Sound familiar to you?"

"Perhaps." He would need to consult with Peter.

"Do you know anyone who wants you taken care of?" Madeleine blinked at him.

Raising a brow, Andrew glanced at Edward. "Other than Edward that is."

"If I wanted him dead, I'd kill him myself." Edward held up his hands. "And I don't hate him enough to kill him. I merely dislike having my glory tarnished when he's in my vicinity."

Madeleine giggled, and Andrew and Oliver guffawed. Thomas admired Edward's honesty and didn't know if he could be quite as brutally frank with himself. "I'll describe him to Peter. We already have an idea and this could confirm it."

"I'm glad he did not succeed," she whispered.

The soft smile she gave him was worth any price. To catch that moment of vulnerability and sweetness again, he would do nigh anything. "Thank you."

Edward's stare, in frigid contrast, said he read Thomas's thoughts and saw all there was to see. Also, Edward didn't like what he saw.

"It was two days ago," the archer said. "I haven't seen him since."

Andrew growled. "When news gets out that Thomas is well, if he's got any wits, he'll disappear."

"To try again another day," Edward said. "If we put this together with your cut girth, you have someone who would like to see you with your toes up."

"Thomas is annoying." Madeleine's mischievous smile all but

begged him to kiss it off her face. "But he doesn't annoy me enough to make me want to kill him."

Bugger Edward and his hostile gaze. He flirted back with her. "Why, thank you. Your admiration renders me speechless."

"One can but hope," Edward drawled.

Everyone laughed, and it felt more like the times when he had fostered there, and they had all been friends. Those times had been few and far between, but they had happened.

"Um...my lady?" The archer wet his lips. Thomas had almost forgotten about the wretch.

Madeleine turned to him. "What?"

"Might you take the knife from my throat?"

She thought about that. Huffing, she tucked her knife back into her boot. Dear God, but she got better and better. He wanted to conduct a body search for other places she might hide a knife.

His imagination went awry with that train of thought, and he had to tightly rein it. Someone wanted his blood and he needed to get his head out of his chausses.

"Your decision." Edward raised a brow. "What would you like to do with him?"

Thomas looked at the fearful man at their feet. A man who had made a very stupid decision, but a man with children relying on him. "You tried to kill me."

"I'm the best with a bow for leagues about here, and I wasn't shooting to kill," the archer said. "It's why I wasn't going to take the second purse he promised. I'm not a killer."

"You are either a very good liar or a very good archer." Edward stared down at the man. "Fortunately for you, it is Thomas and not me who will decide which."

Madeleine snorted. "Or a remarkable poor archer. You missed."

"I missed on purpose," the archer said indignantly.

"I could still have been injured," Thomas said. "And that

means you owe me recompense. Killing you now would benefit me nothing."

Edward cocked his head, waiting to hear what Thomas said next.

Unless the wretch was lying, he could shoot and do it well. If Andrew hadn't dived for him, he might be wearing a new head piece right this moment. Thomas stared at the archer and then obeyed his instinct.

"You will report to my army first thing in the morning. I never pass up a good archer, but you will work harder than you've ever worked, and no shirking or rebellion will be tolerated." Thomas motioned the archer to silence when he would speak. "We will leave your life in God's hands. If you fight for me and survive, you can go free once your debt is paid."

Tears streamed down the archer's face. "Thank you, my lord."

"Don't thank me yet. Your family will reside at Draycott and be my assurance of not getting an arrow in the back." Thomas knew the story would get out, and the archer's time with his men wouldn't be easy. He would have to win their trust and his place in their ranks. "You will curse me before your time with me is done."

"Thomas." The gentle warmth in Madeleine's eyes made it all worth it. She filled his name with approval that made him want to strut. "That was so well done."

Chapter Twenty

Madeleine, Thomas, Oliver, Edward and Andrew rejoined the main party traveling back to the keep.

While Edward and Thomas rode ahead to apprise her father what had occurred, Madeline kept to the back of the party, her head too full for idle chatter and gossip. People looked her way, eager to question her, but she didn't feel like satisfying their curiosity.

Giles rode back to join her and matched his mount's pace to hers. He stared at her. "You're quiet."

"Merely lost in thought."

"There is some speculation about what happened." Giles studied her face.

Madeleine affected a casual shrug. "We caught the archer. He says someone paid him to hurt or kill Thomas."

Giles whistled between his teeth. "Thomas has an enemy."

A cold shiver snaked down her spine. "But who would want Thomas dead?"

"Verily." Giles laughed. "I could think of any one of us who have been shown up by his prowess."

"But those are just games." Madeleine looked around the main party with newly opened eyes.

"Games, yes, but the prize is a rich one." Giles scoffed. "Nobody has dared to suggest something so crass, but we are all aware of why we are here, Lady Maddy." He gave her an appreciative look. "And while I wasn't looking to put my head in the marriage noose, I considered it when you were the offered bride."

Her blush heated her cheeks. "You're a terrible flirt."

"No, lady." He looked affronted. "I'm a good flirt. It's my intentions that are terrible."

That made her laugh and drew her out of her solemn thoughts. "And now you're leaving."

"I'm retreating with my pride intact," he said and winked. "But I'm not the only man here who would welcome an advance from you, sweeting. Everyone here has their reasons for coming, and some of those reasons might compel men to do many things, desperate things."

"I hadn't thought of that." Any of her suitors might have decided her father's wealth and influence were worth any price. "Who do you think would have done it?"

Giles raised a brow and mulled his words before he spoke. "There are a number here who thought you."

Shock ripped through her. "Who thinks that?"

"One or two. Not many." He reached for her hand and kissed it. "And not enough to concern you. I merely mention it so that you might be prepared."

"Thank you." But she wasn't sure how grateful she was. She might have felt a lot better never knowing that.

Giles turned to her with a wicked twinkle. "I pointed out to all who even entertained such a nonsensical idea, that your plans for our Thomas depended on him being very much alive."

Madeleine managed a giggle for him, and pretended outrage, but even Giles's banter couldn't cheer her. She'd made no effort to conceal her dislike of Thomas. Indeed, it might be said that she had demonstrated her feelings clearly, too clearly even.

Thomas knew she didn't really feel that way. He had experienced the flames that leaped to life between them at every opportunity. But lust wasn't love, or even like, and she'd given Thomas many reasons to believe she disliked him.

In truth, her dislike was based more on the way he had bested Robert. Had Robert not been involved, she would have been as impressed by Thomas's skill as every other person there. It did not speak well of her that she had been so set in her opinions.

In fact, had anybody else behaved as she had, she would have accused them of being petty and childish, of looking for a way to drag Thomas down, of acting on incidents from their childhood. Her parents would be ashamed of her. Indeed, she was ashamed of herself. It wasn't like her to be so unfair, and she owed Thomas an apology.

He rode beside Andrew, deep in conversation with her father, Edward, Oliver and Simon. Edward spoke to Thomas. Thomas replied, and both of them laughed. The threat to Thomas had united them, even if only temporarily.

Even Edward was being fairer than her. She had been raised better than her behavior suggested, and it was about time she started showing that.

Her path resolved, she'd wait for an opportunity to catch him alone. She needed but five minutes, certainly no more than ten.

Executing her plan, however, proved difficult. People constantly surrounded him on the ride back to the keep. Everyone wanted to hear of the incident firsthand and discuss what he intended to do about it.

When they arrived back at the keep, more women flocked to him, all whispering and clucking and sighing in a way that made her want to punch her way through them.

Then her mother hugged him and commandeered all his attention.

There were better ways to get a man to notice you than bobbing along like a cork at the back of a flock of other corks.

She left the hall and took the stairs two at a time. Mother would scold her for striding like a man, but she'd a plan to set in motion.

Heather waited in her chamber with her bath water ready. It was as if Heather read her mind at times. "Tonight"—she paused in the door to increase the weight of the moment—"will require the red velvet."

Heather gasped and pressed her fingers to her chest. "The red velvet?"

"The red velvet." Madeleine slammed her chamber door behind her.

Course set, she disrobed quickly and stepped into the bath.

In every girl's armory, was a dress designed to make people stare, and the red velvet was such a dress. Cut low across the breast, it had three sets of laces to mold it tight to her trunk and hips. The skirt flared to the floor in a sparkle of beads sewn into the fabric. The sleeves fit so tight it was hard to eat, but then flared over her hands and belled all the way to the floor. A garnet and gold girdle would hug her hips and almost brush her gold beaded slippers.

Heather held up a gold stoppered vial. "The jasmine oil?"

A perfect choice, the jasmine oil was a sultrier, more sensual aroma than her normal rose oil. It would pair perfectly with the red velvet. "Yes. And I'll wear my hair loose tonight."

"Loose?" Heather's eyes gleamed. Then her delight vanished. "Please tell me we are not wasting red velvet and jasmine oil on Robert."

For a moment Madeleine almost protested, and then she let it be. "No, we are luring a different prey tonight."

"Who?" Heather grew breathless with excitement.

"Thomas."

Heather squealed and clapped her hands. "I knew you liked him. I knew it."

"I owe him an apology." She hated to crush Heather's hopes, but it would never do to let her believe in air bubbles. "I need to look my best."

"Uh-hmm." Heather looked not at all convinced.

"I mean it."

Heather pointed downward. "Dunk your head."

With Heather, doing as she was told was a good idea, so Madeleine wet her hair. As Heather helped her bathe, Madeleine told her what had happened with the archer. "My brothers think this is linked to whoever cut his girth."

"I have been nosing around about that." Heather lathered her hair with the sweet-smelling jasmine. "But I haven't wanted to draw notice to myself so I moved slowly."

She could trust in Heather's discretion. The woman was like a buried chamber beneath a castle. "Anything?"

"Opinions are split between Robert, Edward and the ghost of Thomas's uncle."

"Eh?" She'd nothing better. "Ghost?"

"They never got on." Heather tipped warm water over her head to rinse. "Whispers tell that his uncle forced Thomas's mother to marry him after Hugh died." She lathered Madeleine's hair a second time. Heather swore it made her hair shiny. "They say he had to fight his uncle for his inheritance, and now the ghost is bitter and wants revenge."

"Only half of that is true." Madeleine had always known Thomas's father, Hugh, had died the night her parents got married, and had been a great favorite with Father. It was why Father had always made a place for Thomas in their lives. For the first time, and she was ashamed it was the first time, she thought of Thomas as a lonely young boy, needing the direction of man in his life, and living with that awful uncle.

Father had done what he could to help, and fear of him had kept the worst of Thomas's uncle reined in, but it couldn't have been easy for Thomas.

She and Edward had never thought of that when they made him their enemy. It seemed the apologies owed Thomas grew.

"What?" Heather glared at her.

She glanced away. "What what?"

"You sighed, and that means you're chewing something over in your head." Heather held a towel up for her.

And blight on it if she didn't sigh again. "I was thinking about Thomas as a young boy, and how cruel Edward and I were to him."

"Hmm." Heather wrapped a second drying cloth around her head. "We don't always have the wisdom as children that we gain later on." She gave Madeleine's hair a vigorous rub. "We don't always know what we need to know as children."

Heather's face had grown grave as if her thoughts saddened her, and Madeleine wagered they were not speaking only of Thomas now.

Like she often did, Heather disappeared inside herself, lost in thoughts that however close they got, she never shared. Heather had arrived at Elford eight years prior, a young woman with nothing but the clothes on her back and a story in her eyes that she still hadn't told.

"Heather?"

"It's nothing." Heather nudged her to sit before the fire. "We need to ready you for battle."

Madeleine laughed. "And here I thought I was offering an apology."

"When will you learn?" Heather shook her head. "Every encounter with a man is a battle."

Chapter Twenty-One

Preparing for battle took longer than normal dressing, so the evening meal was drawing close by the time Madeleine left her room.

She was, however, looking and feeling her best, and Thomas had better beware. The thought made her giggle as she threaded through the corridors toward his chamber. She was prepared to enter the den to best her dragon.

Knocking on his door, she waited for permission to enter before pushing the door open.

Thomas sat on a dressing stool, naked from the waist up, with Peter hovering nearby.

"Good evening." Peter gave her his charming smile. "I was admiring your earlier work." He indicated the wound on Thomas's side that she'd patched two days ago.

Distracted by all that naked and muscular Thomas, she tried not to show it as she eased farther into the room. It helped that his wound reminded her someone wished him ill. "How does it look?"

"It's fine." Thomas glared at Peter.

Peter motioned her forward. "Come and see for yourself."

The wound was healing, but the sides were still raised and red. "Cook makes a salve for healing."

"I don't need it." Thomas stood.

Madeleine hid her grin at his peevishness. "Yes, you do, or you won't be so pretty anymore."

"That's what I said." Peter smirked. He looked between them and nodded. "I shall get the salve from Cook, if you will keep him busy whilst I do."

"I don't need it." Thomas called to Peter's back.

Madeleine tried to look stern. "Yes, you do, and you will get it."

Turning his glare her way, Thomas stilled. His gaze touched her hair, the swell of her breasts above the red velvet. It caressed the dip of her waist and tracked the girdle over the flat plane of her belly. He cleared his throat. "You look beautiful."

"Thank you." Her voice wasn't so steady now. The appreciation in his eyes warmed her from within. "I dressed for you."

His eyebrow shot up and his gaze blazed. "For me?"

Dear Lord, that had sounded wrong. "I mean, to apologize to you."

"Apologize?" Confusion warred with desire in his face.

"I have not been fair to you since you came here." The way he looked at her scrambled her thoughts and made words difficult. He looked as if he were starving and she a banquet. And she liked it, craved it in the times they were not together. "I let Edward's resentment flavor my opinion of you and let our childhood differences spill into our adulthood."

He stood as if carved from stone.

"You deserved neither my childish peevishness nor my disgraceful behavior since you came here." The way he looked robbed her of breath and made her words sigh from her. "You've been nothing but noble and honorable since you came here."

"Madeleine," he rasped. "You owe me nothing." As he stepped closer, his heat enveloped her. He raised one large hand

and stroked her hair, then slid it around her neck and cupped her nape. "As for nobility and honor, I deserve neither claim."

"You do." She couldn't think with him so close. Couldn't breathe. Her knees felt like water. "You're—"

"I'm a miserable cur." Tilting his head, he pressed his forehead to hers. "Is it noble to put my hands on my mentor's daughter behind his back? Is it honorable to ache with wanting her?"

He spoke as if he was the only one who wanted these things, as if she had been an innocent to their every encounter. "Thomas." Needing to touch, she lifted her hands to the strong swell of muscle on his arms. "You can't blame yourself."

"No, Maddy?" He cupped her face and stroked her cheek with his thumbs. "Why is that?"

She didn't know what happened when he was about, but reason deserted her. "Because you did not do those things, feel those things, alone."

"What are you saying, Maddy?" His eyes blazed at her.

Madeleine felt breathless, as if she stood on the edge of a precipice. "I am saying that whatever wanting you have felt, you haven't felt it alone."

"Jesu, Maddy." He pressed a soft kiss to her mouth. "You shouldn't come here, looking so beautiful and say these things to me. I haven't the strength to resist you."

Stroking his arms, she found a boldness within and whispered, "Then stop resisting."

He made a sound half groan and half laugh and then his mouth was upon hers, hard and demanding. His tongue thrust beneath her teeth and demanded a response.

Madeleine melted from within. Her mouth cleaved to his. Her body molded to the harder shape of his. Her innards turned to liquid, and all she could do was cling to him and return his kiss.

Every time they touched, the heat between them grew wilder. Her world narrowed to this moment, this man. His scent surrounded her, his strength pressed against her, his taste filled her.

Thomas slid his hands to her hips and pulled her against him. His hard length pressed into her belly, telling of his desire for her.

An answering desire lit in her and bloomed through her senses. She couldn't get enough of him, couldn't be close enough, couldn't stop.

The wall at her back was shockingly cold through her bliaut.

He nudged her feet apart and stepped between them. Then he was lifting her, his hands beneath her bare thighs, wrapping her legs around his hips.

The contact of his erection at the apex of her thighs sparked through her, and she moaned her need into his hot, hungry mouth. She knew what happened next, what fit where, but nothing had prepared her for the primal ache to complete the act.

Inside her was a hot, wet place begging for Thomas.

He moved his hands to her buttocks and squeezed her pliant flesh. His long fingers slid along the slit between her thighs.

Madeleine bucked against him, needing more.

"Ahem."

They froze.

Breathing heavily, Thomas lowered her legs to the ground.

With shaking hands, Madeleine smoothed down her skirts and then, together, she and Thomas faced the intruder.

Relief flooded through her when Peter stepped into the room and closed the door behind him. "Children," he chided, "that's how an entire storm of trouble begins."

Madeleine bowed her head, shame weighing it down. She knew better than to court the sort of trouble of which Peter spoke. This fire between her and Thomas raged unchecked and burned them both in its path.

Had she come into his chamber, dressed as she was, to fling herself into the fire?

"Maddy," Thomas said, his voice soft and compelling. "The shame is mine and not yours. I should have stopped myself."

Shaking her head, she met his gaze. The blame, they carried together. "No, Thomas, I was with you in all ways.

"Your honesty humbles me." A soft smile tilted his mouth. "In many ways, you're so like your father."

A tendril of mischief wriggled out from beneath her mortification, and she grinned at him. "But not in all ways?"

"No." He barked a laugh, the handsome lines of his smile gentling his face. "Most assuredly not in all ways."

"Lady Madeleine." Peter bowed, his tone firm. "I believe you're missed in the hall."

Faced with his clear dismissal, she could only creep from the chamber, thanking the Lord for her deliverance as she went. Deliverance from what, however, she wasn't clear about.

* * *

Thomas watched Madeleine go with the sinking certainty that he was about to have his ballocks handed to him. And he fully deserved it.

"Right." Peter bowed Madeleine out and shut the door behind her. "First, let us care for that wound of yours."

Thomas waved him off. "It's fine."

"And this is where we began." Peter growled and closed the distance between them. He nudged Thomas's arm. "Lift."

Already deep in the mire, Thomas obeyed and lifted his arm for Peter to access the wound.

Unlike Madeleine's gentle touch, Peter slapped salve on his injury and bound it again. He tidied the chamber in sharp, jerky movements.

Thomas bided his time. He knew Peter far too well to consider he might have nothing to say on what he'd interrupted.

Blood heating at the memory of her skin and her scent, the eager reciprocation of her mouth to his kiss, the soft, wet flesh between her thighs. Jesu help him! The predictable result to his body threatened and he breathed deep.

Peter finally spoke from where he stood staring out of the casement. His words were not the ones Thomas had expected. "You like her."

"I desire her." Thomas rolled the idea of liking Madeleine as well as desiring her around his mind. A fiery, opinionated, willful, stubborn pain in his arse, but one with a knight's honor and a woman's wiles. He was in trouble deep enough that only his eyeballs peered above it. "And, yes, I like her plenty."

"I wasn't surprised to see what I interrupted." Peter tapped the casement. "I also suspect it's not the first of those scenes to have taken place."

"No." The need to unburden himself swelled in Thomas, and he sank on his bed. "I can't be trusted alone in the same room as her."

Peter chuckled. "I don't believe the problem is yours alone. The woman I observed not ten minutes ago lusted for you as much as you for her."

Triumph swelled in him. "Really?"

"Heed me, Thomas." Peter shook his head at him. "I know you well enough to know how much abusing Sir Richard's trust would cost you."

The gravity and truth of his obligation to Madeleine's father slammed into him. "I despise myself for it."

"Well, I wouldn't take it that far." Peter nudged him and laughed. "You're a handsome cur with a healthy appetite, and she's lovely and lively and appears to have the same appetite. The need isn't the sin, Thomas. The acting on the need without the blessing of her father and God is the sin."

His path lay clear before him, and Thomas set his feet on that path without hesitation. "I'll speak to Sir Richard."

"Good. I strongly suggest you do so soon." Peter rolled his eyes. "You might also tell him we strongly suspect Wilfred is the one trying to kill you."

Chapter Twenty-Two

As she fled Thomas's chamber, Madeleine tried to pull herself together. Heat still ran through her blood and made it pound. She must be the most fickle and inconstant woman alive. From the day her mother had met her father, neither of them had looked elsewhere. What ailed her that she had only to near Thomas to forget Robert?

Heather hurried toward her. "There you are." She stopped when she reached Madeleine and fussed with her bliaut and her hair. "No guessing what you've been doing, but we need to put you to rights."

"Why?" Objecting took a degree of hypocrisy she hadn't the spirit for. She stood still. "I'm not sure I'll go to dinner."

"You must." Heather heaved her bodice up an inch. "There's something big happening in the hall."

"What?" She helped Heather smooth her skirts.

Heather frowned and shook her head. "I don't know, but Robert is in the thick of it."

"Robert?" Alarm spiked and got her moving toward the hall. If Robert were in trouble, she might be able to help him.

Silence, thick and heavy cloaked the hall. Heather nudged her and they crept forward.

Father stood on the front of the dais, Robert by his side.

Beside them, Edward looked grim, Andrew wore his normal lack of expression, Simon looked bored and Oliver thunderous.

Mother had her mouth pinched together in a way that meant she was so angry it would be best to start riding the fastest horse out of Elford. Mother didn't often lose her temper, but when she did, it was spectacular.

All eyes in the hall were on Father and Robert. Except for Posy, who was looking right at her and smirking.

From behind her, Heather sucked in a soft breath and grabbed her hand. "Breathe," she whispered. "Breathe and give them nothing."

"What?" Her belly tightened into a knot of trepidation. She wasn't going to like the next five minutes; her every instinct, plus Heather's reaction, screamed it.

Movement at the hall entrance drew her gaze that way.

Thomas and Peter slipped into the hall and eased into the tense throng.

Briefly, Thomas glanced at her. He gave her a questioning looking, and she understood he was checking on her.

She nodded that she was fine. The brief contact bolstered her. Putting her shoulders back, Madeleine returned her attention to Father.

He was looking at her. Rapid emotion flickered across his face. Fury, distaste and sympathy. For her?

She tightened her grip around Heather's hand. This was all making a horrid sort of sense and she lacked the courage to look fully into the face of her burgeoning conclusions. Conclusions were only real if she acknowledged them.

Looking grim, father said, "I have glad tidings." Over the heads of the gathered Elford folk, his gaze held hers. "This night, I announce the betrothal of Robert of Rutherford to our own Posy."

Throughout the hall, scattered applause broke out.

Robert paled.

Madeleine's grip tightened around Heather's hand until Heather hissed and forced her to release her stranglehold.

Robert was engaged to Posy.

It couldn't be true.

Just yesterday, he'd been whispering sweetly in her ear. Was it because she'd danced with Thomas and not him? Had her petulance led to this? She must have done something to drive Robert away.

Against her will, her gaze crept to Posy.

Cheeks pink and eyes sparkling, Posy accepted kisses and hugs from those around her. She looked so pretty and happy.

It speared Madeleine and robbed her of breath. She stood and waited for emotion, any emotion, to reach her, but inside she'd become hollow. Words and people echoed around her but found no response within her.

Father didn't announce a feast. Why, of all details, this one stuck out, she couldn't say. No feast meant he wasn't pleased. Perhaps Father, like her, had held dear hopes for Robert to be hers. No, Father had never favored Robert, so it made little sense that he looked thunderous. He'd organized this entire tournament to try to persuade her to look elsewhere. In the end, Robert had looked elsewhere.

Reality snuck past her unnatural calm. She had lost Robert to Posy.

Why? How? When?

Mere moments ago, was it not she who had succumbed to passion with another man? Robert must have known.

It all became startlingly clear to her. Robert had known about her and Thomas and acted out of spurned pride. It was all that made sense. That was why Posy looked so smug. She must have seen Thomas with Madeleine and carried stories.

Madeleine could picture her pretty mouth twisted into scornful, angry lines as she spewed her vitriol into Robert's ear.

Father's gaze met hers again. From across the hall he was trying to convey a message she couldn't grasp.

"Madeleine," Heather whispered. "You're so pale. Shall we leave?"

"No," she croaked. To run and hide with everyone watching her would be worse. "I just need—"

What? She couldn't finish that thought.

Then she could. Answers flooded her mind. She needed it not to be true. She needed to wake in her bed and find it had all been a nightmare. She needed to roll time back like a stone and have the last minutes not happen.

When the night was over, she would burn her red velvet bliaut and never see it again. She'd set out with such hopes tonight, only to have them destroyed.

A group of girls surrounded Posy, giggling and hugging her. Posy whispered to her friends, and as one, they turned and stared at Madeleine.

Their scorn burned through her. They saw her as spurned, ruined, rejected.

Gripping Heather's hand, she raised her chin and met their stares. She was the daughter of Richard of Elford and Margaret de Guilles. No man, or woman for that matter, would see her bleed.

From her bloodline, she drew the strength to walk the fourteen steps it took to reach Posy. Margaret de Guilles had walked across a bloody battlefield, her head held high, her future in the balance, and parleyed for her life and the lives of her people. Her daughter could do this.

Her face stretched into a smile. "I have yet to wish you the best on your engagement."

Posy gaped at her. "Oh."

"May you have many years of happiness." She glanced toward her mother, and the pride on her mother's face gave her the strength she needed to finish. "I wish you and Robert all the best."

"Indeed." Posy preened and looked to her dwindling audience. "You shouldn't feel too bad." Leaning closer she stroked her belly. "I'm afraid Robert and I have been rather wicked."

She met Father's gaze, and the truth rang like a bell. Father would never allow a man to get a child on a woman and walk away from his responsibilities. He would also make sure he had the right man. The man who had put the child in Posy was the one marrying her.

Madeleine's belly lurched. While Robert had been whispering in her ear, he'd been tupping Posy. He'd talked marriage with her and rolled in the sheets with Posy. Her mind ground to the inevitable conclusion that every word out of Robert's mouth must have been a lie.

And Posy knew it. Her victory shone in her big eyes as she smirked at Madeleine. The humiliation rose and stuck to her, thick and gummy.

God's balls, but Madeleine of Elford wouldn't slink from the field of battle, beaten, cowed and whipped. "Feel bad?" Her hard laughter cut across the hall. "Why would I feel bad?"

"You know why." Posy didn't look so sure of herself now. She glanced to her coven, but they shrunk back, no longer so certain of their victory. Licking her lips, Posy squared her shoulders. "You were in love with Robert. Everyone knew it."

"Madeleine," Heather whispered. "Let's leave now."

Out of the corner of her eye, Madeleine caught movement on the dais, her mother or her father rushing to her rescue. Perhaps even one of her brothers, hastening to save her from the consequences of her folly.

She would save them the effort. "In love with Robert?" Her laughter sounded more natural. "Is that what you thought?"

"What else?" Posy tossed her head. "Everybody knows you've been in love with Robert for months."

Faces turned her way. They knew. They all thought the same. They saw her shame, her humiliation. They saw the pathetic castoff of a man who had gotten his lover with child. "Well, of course they did." A wildness overtook her. Damn the consequences. Nothing could be worse than humiliation. "It's what I wanted them to think. I couldn't tell them the truth."

"Madeleine." Heather yanked her hand. "Let us leave here. Now."

Posy's look of scorn seared her to the bone. "You're making up stories now. You loved Robert, and he's to marry me, and you hate that."

"I don't care who Robert marries."

"Yes, you do." Posy jabbed her finger at her.

"No, I don't. I'm already promised. To another."

"Bugger." Heather's whisper resounded in the suddenly silent hall.

Posy threw her head back and cackled, so sure of herself. "You lie."

"I tell the truth." Heat flooded her cheeks. The ground wavered beneath her feet as the waters of her deceit lapped at her ankles. The entire hall now saw her as a liar.

"If you're betrothed"—Posy stepped closer—"then name him."

His warmth and strength hit her moments before his arm wrapped around her waist. He tugged her back against the hard, solid bulk of him, a safe place in a storm of her making. "To me," Thomas said. "She's betrothed to me."

* * *

Thomas sat beside Madeleine on the dais all through the interminable meal that followed. He smiled. He laughed. He drank and even, he imagined, did a passable imitation of a besotted sot.

Moments after his announcement in the hall, Lady Margaret had called for a celebration.

And all the while, he read his approaching demise in the eyes of the Elford men. Wilfred, because Peter was convinced that was the man who had hired the archer, may have to wait his turn to end Thomas's life. Madeleine's brothers already regarded his head as an unnecessary addition to his body. Sir Richard gave him one long, hard look that reeked of accusation, and after that, hadn't looked his way again.

All of that meant nothing compared to the tangled roil of emotions tearing through Madeleine. She sat beside him so tense he feared she would crack. With the entire hall glancing, and speculating, he couldn't speak to her and give her the reassurance she needed.

Instead, he did the only thing he could think of, and kept her wine goblet filled and answered well-wishers on her behalf. At last, the wine did its work, and she eased into him, laying her head on his shoulder.

"Thank you," she whispered. "But I'm very much afraid Edward means to kill you."

As Edward chose that moment to glance up at him, death in his gaze, Thomas agreed with her. "He will try."

"Thomas." Sliding her delicate hand to his thigh, she dug her nails in. "Thomas. You can't kill my brother."

Peter must be laughing his sanctified arse off. Madeleine had stood before that smug bitch and dug herself deeper and deeper into a hole. He'd moved before he'd even thought through his intent. All he'd known was that he couldn't leave her to face the enemy alone.

He'd opened his mouth and said the one thing that would save her.

In response, her taut spine had relaxed, and her body had cleaved to his, as if she surrendered to his rescue. Warrior to her core, Madeleine had given herself into his hands.

"I won't kill anyone." Unable to resist a moment longer, he slid his arm about her waist and pulled her against him. "I'm sure the same can't be said of your brothers."

"You saved me." She sighed and collapsed into him, tucking her face into his neck. Her skin burned hot against his. "Why?"

He'd no answer for that. Or he did have an answer, but he chose not to confront it.

Lady Margaret shifted toward him from the other side. "Is she all right?"

"A trifle drunk," he whispered.

She nodded and smiled as if they were sharing a happy chat. "Take care of her."

"Always."

"I know that." Lady Margaret turned to face him. "Which is why I'll stop my husband and sons from ripping you apart long enough for you to explain why this is the first we are hearing of this."

Her sense of betrayal burned, and he said, "I appreciate that, my lady. Matters proceeded faster than we would have hoped or expected."

"There is no secret arrangement between you?" Lady Margaret sipped her wine. "I didn't think there was, and neither does Sir Richard, which begs the question why you acted as you did. What is there between you and Madeleine?"

Not really knowing what his answer should be, he didn't know how to answer her. "Madeleine and I have grown closer."

"Closer?" Lady Margaret's eyes went colder than a winter morning. "How close?"

"It's not what you think. I haven't—she and I haven't..." Heat flamed his cheeks and he couldn't finish.

"You're telling me you've not lain with her." Margaret looked at him, her gaze searching and demanding the truth.

He'd come close, and if Peter hadn't interrupted them tonight, he might not have been able to answer as he did. "I haven't lain with Madeleine."

"Thank you, Thomas. I knew my faith in you couldn't be misplaced." Margaret sighed, and some of the tension drained from her.

The hours dragged past as people continued to celebrate the two engagements. It was past midnight when Sir Richard turned his cold, blue gaze on him. "Come with me."

Thomas rose immediately.

As expected, all four of Madeleine's brothers crowded in behind him.

Edward barely waited until Thomas had entered the armory before he swung. His fist landed on Thomas's jaw and sent him reeling back.

"Stop it." Madeleine stood between him and her circle of angry brothers. "He doesn't deserve your anger. He saved me."

"I see." Sir Richard raised an eyebrow at his daughter. "I might have guessed you were in the middle of this."

Madeleine reddened. "I'm not. Well, I am but I—"

"There was no agreement between us," Thomas said. "We were not engaged, but now that I have announced it, I stand by my declaration."

"Not yet, you don't." Edward scowled at him. "You don't deserve her, and saying you do won't win our approval."

"I can speak for myself." Richard shoved Edward to the side and stood before them. "I regard you as one of my sons," he said. "Which is the reason I won't let this pack at you before I hear your explanation."

"It wasn't his fault." Madeleine raised her chin and met her father's scowl. "The fault is all mine."

Richard glared at her. "I wasn't speaking to you."

"But you should have been," she said, proving she'd very little fear in her. "Thomas didn't want to marry me. He only said we were engaged to save my pride."

Richard looked at him. "Is that true?" He cut Madeleine off with a raised hand. "I'm speaking to Thomas. Kindly hold your tongue."

As much as lying would have been the easier route, Thomas couldn't. He owed this man his honesty, and to be worthy of his trust. What had been happening with him and Madeleine endangered both those things. "No, sir."

Madeleine started and stared at him. "Of course you meant only to save my pride."

Keeping his gaze on Richard, Thomas said, "The truth is that before I entered the hall, I had made my mind up to speak with you."

"What are you talking about?" Madeleine gaped at him.

"Be quiet, Madeleine." Lady Margaret glided into the room. She kept her tone even, but Madeleine snapped her mouth shut. "Why were you coming to speak with Richard?"

"I meant to ask permission to court Madeleine."

Edward hissed in a breath. "God's bones, but if my mother were not here, I would take you apart for that audacity."

Lady Margaret sent her oldest son a look that would silence a hall. "Are you in love with her?"

Again, Thomas took a position of truth. "I really can't say for sure that I am, but I desire her as I have never desired another."

"When Edward is finished with you, I'll destroy what's left." Oliver cracked his knuckles. Even Andrew looked murderous. Simon poured a mug of mead and sipped it. He understood their anger. The sudden announcement of a betrothal appeared mightily suspicious and underhanded.

Lady Margaret turned to Sir Richard. "Thomas has assured me things haven't progressed past the irreparable, and I believe him."

"You can't mean what you say." Madeleine shook her head at him, a dazed look on her face. "You intend to court me?"

"Yes." With Lady Margaret in the room, he could afford to take his eye off the brothers for a moment. "I was going to request permission to court you."

"Why?"

That stung his pride, and he spoke without thought. "You know why. You also know what will happen if things keep going the way they are."

"Thomas. Did you lie to me at table?" Lady Margaret's silky tone made his hackles stand on end. "I'll kill you myself if you've dishonored my daughter and broken my trust."

"Mother." Madeleine's blush bled down her neck. "It's nothing of the kind. It's not like that between us."

"Then how is it between you?" Sir Richard's eyes had gone colder than the grave. "Explain yourself, Thomas."

Thomas valued his neck too much to risk the details, so he shrugged. "I would make her mine. I didn't come here for a bride, but I would very much desire to leave here with one."

"I have a better idea." Edward shifted Madeleine out the way and went toe to toe with him. "How about you never leave here? We could make you part of the soil."

"That's not helping, Edward." Sir Richard clasped Edward's shoulder and tugged him back. "There are entirely too many people seeking his demise already."

"I should have asked you first." Thomas spoke quickly while he had the chance. "I intended to do this the right way, but when —I should have spoken to you days ago." He refused to put blame on Madeleine.

"You can't allow this." Madeleine stepped in front of her father. "He doesn't really want to marry me. He only spoke up to save me."

"Perhaps, perhaps not." Richard kept his gaze locked on Thomas. "Is your desire one sided?"

Thomas shook his head. "I don't believe so."

"Madeleine." Sir Richard turned to his daughter with a stern expression. "And hear that I'll tolerate no lies. Is Thomas correct? Do you desire him as he does you?"

At this rate, Madeleine exchanged one blush for another. No sooner had the first blush ebbed than another replaced it. "I—we —he's correct."

"Then you're betrothed," Sir Richard said. "But I'm not convinced about the suddenness of this. It wasn't long ago you disliked each other."

Perhaps their strong feelings for each other had merely disguised feelings of a different kind.

"Thomas will remain here for the next thirty days. If, at the end of the time, you're still sure you wish to marry, we will proceed." He offered his arm to his wife. "Come, Maggie. We have much to talk about." As he walked, he said over this shoulder, "Andrew, Edward, Oliver and Simon. You will join us."

And they were alone.

Madeleine looked up at him and the tears in her eyes startled him to silence.

"I'm so sorry," she whispered. "Thomas, I'm so sorry. Once again." She squeezed his hands. "I'm stupid and I'm impetuous and because of this you've suffered."

"I would only have suffered if your brothers had taken it into their heads to beat me," he said. The guilt in her pretty eyes ate at him. He didn't deserve her remorse. True, he'd hated seeing her brought low by that vicious little hen, but he'd also acted in his own best interest. She'd merely given him a perfect opportunity to take what he wanted.

"We will wait the thirty days, and then you can go your own way," she said.

Not if he'd anything to do with it, but it required careful handling on his part. If he pushed too hard, Madeleine would dig her heels in. "I was going to request permission to woo you."

"You were?" She frowned, and then it cleared. "I see now. Because you respect my father and you felt as if you were betraying him by...well...the things that happened between us."

"I was betraying his trust." The need to kiss her was a constant in her company. "Madeleine, you were in my chamber earlier this night. You know what happened, and you know what would have happened if Peter hadn't interrupted us."

"Perhaps not." But she looked no more convinced than he. "But still, you can't wish to marry me."

"Why not?" Did she find him so repulsive? Clearly, not physically repulsive.

"We fight all the time." She took his hands.

"Not all the time."

She blushed and giggled. "All right, I'll grant you not when we're doing that." Her voice grew breathier and stroked the always-hot embers of his desire for her. "But marriage can't be only that."

"We know each other well," he said. "And your father likes me."

"But my brothers don't."

"Edward doesn't." He drew her closer to him, needing to hold her. "But Andrew and Oliver are coming to see my good qualities, and Simon is too indolent to suffer an emotion as strong as hate."

She let him fold her against his chest and slid her arms around his waist. They fit together, and he wanted to stay there all night. At least until other urges gave them something better to do. But for now, it was enough. It felt good, connected and intimate.

"I believe I would make you a good husband, Maddy." He buried his nose in her fragrant hair. "But I can also see you need time to be convinced."

"You're so sure you could?" She peered up at him, challenge and mischief dancing in her eyes.

"I stand as good a chance as any other man." He gave in to the lure of her smile and smiled back. "Let us take these thirty days for us, Maddy. If at the end we are ready to kill each other, we shall have our answer." He kissed the tip of her nose. "Let me woo you, Maddy."

She wrinkled her nose at him. "I can't picture you wooing anyone."

He forced himself to step away and settle for kissing both her hands. "Then I have thirty days to accustom you to the sight."

Chapter Twenty-Three

Madeleine spent a restless night, and when she did sleep, her dreams were full of Robert and Posy and Thomas. They blurred together in a confusing jumble of weddings and mockery.

Her last dream of Posy marrying Thomas and both of them turning and laughing as she stood naked in the church behind them as they spoke their vows, was enough to wrench her out of bed.

She sat in her window embrasure and watched the sun rise over the land. Her heart felt tender about Robert marrying Posy. Her brothers had tried to tell her, even Thomas had tried to tell her, but she'd refused to listen.

Stubbornly she'd stayed on the path she'd decided, despite what others and logic told her. Heather had never liked Robert, and she was an excellent judge of character.

Her pride hurt too. All the time Robert had been making eyes at her, he must have secretly been bedding Posy. She played back events, and in light of yesterday, so much became clear.

That day when Thomas had first arrived at Elford, she'd gone out to the old chapel to see Robert. Posy had been running through the wood, and Madeleine had never considered for a moment that she'd come from Robert.

She went through more scenes and found Posy there as well. They had been having their love affair right beneath her nose, and she'd been too stupid to see it. No, she was worse than stupid, because her loved ones had been trying to tell her the truth, and she'd deliberately ignored it.

Her chamber door opened, and Mother came in. She was already dressed for the day. Lady Margaret woke early and went about her duties as chatelaine while the castle guests still slept. "Good morning." She carried a small tray with her. "I thought we might break our fast together."

Madeleine stood and took the tray from Mother and placed it on a small table.

"How are you this morning?" Her mother cupped Madeleine's face between her palms and studied it. "You had an eventful day yesterday."

"I didn't sleep much." Lying to her mother had never come easily. "I was just now thinking how the signs of Posy and Robert were there all along, and I never saw them."

"Ah, well." Mother poured honey into both bowls of porridge then added butter and cream and a handful of nuts. "These things are always so much easier to see in hindsight."

Not really hungry, Madeleine accepted her bowl, because Mother would insist she ate. "Did you know about them? Before the announcement."

Mother stirred her porridge. "I suspected, my darling. That Posy is a sly one, but she's not always that clever at hiding what she has been up to. The desire to gloat was always her downfall."

"I think my heart is broken." A huge sigh worked its way out of her chest in a huff.

Mother patted her hand and gave her a gentle smile. "If you merely think your heart is broken, then it augers well for it being mended soon enough."

"I thought you might say something like that." She poked at

her porridge with her spoon. If she poked at her feelings, she felt like a fool for not knowing about Robert and Posy, and she had only a slight twinge in her heart. A larger part of her got stuck on the fact she was now betrothed to Thomas and had no idea what that meant. How would they go forward?

Mother put her bowl aside and dabbed her mouth with a napkin. "Now. Let me get to what brought me here this morning.'

She'd rather thought Mother had done so already. Madeleine put aside her barely touched bowl and waited.

"When your father and I met..." Mother took her hands. "As I have told you, our first meeting took place in a tent on a battle-field, in the midst of one of the battles our marriage was intended to prevent."

Madeleine had heard the story many times, and she nodded.

"Your father asked everyone to leave but him and me, and then he asked me what I wanted from this marriage." Mother's face softened in memory. "Not what I wanted for my people or to attain power, what I as a woman wanted."

Her father had always been a man who thought more than most. Pride warmed Madeleine. Sir Richard had never blindly followed but always thought for himself, and he'd taught them to do the same.

"I asked for a few things." A slight flush crept over Mother's face. "And one of those things was that if we had daughters, those daughters would have the choice over who they married."

Madeleine had heard this all before. "I know that. And he has always given us that choice."

"You're not listening, dearling." Mother patted her hands. "You've the choice regardless of what else happens."

And then Madeleine understood. Mother was saying that despite what had happened in the hall, they would stand by her if she chose not to marry Thomas. Her family would stand behind her whatever her decision. "I don't know what I'll do," she said, searching her thoughts as she spoke. "But for now, if

Thomas doesn't mind, and he appears not to, the engagement stands."

"Very well." Mother stood and gathered the bowls. "But a warning, my dear girl. If you make the decision to lie with him, you marry him. Our tolerance doesn't extend to that."

* * *

Any hope that yesterday might have dispelled some of their visitors died the moment Madeleine entered the hall later that morning.

If anything, the hall seemed more crowded than ever. Most of those gazes snapped her way as she entered.

Tristan raised his cup to her across the hall. By announcing her betrothal to Thomas, she'd lost all her suitors in one telling blow.

Madeleine raised her chin and greeted a few people by name.

She joined a group of women sewing by the casement and took her place among them. They were mending the bed linens, not her favorite task, but if she left now it would look too much like a retreat. So, she threaded a needle and bent her head to her work.

Whispers made her look up. Two girls had their heads together, whispering and giggling. One of them caught her looking, nudged her friend and they stopped.

Sir William entered the hall, and Madeleine gave him a smile of welcome, but he dipped his head in acknowledgement and kept moving. Now that she was betrothed, apparently all flirting and teasing was at an end. Which was as it should have been, but William's reaction upset her. She sensed it was something more than her being betrothed.

Then she caught Posy's smug expression across the hall, and it all made sense. Posy had been speaking about her behind her back. As she watched, Posy whispered to her friends, and inclined her head toward Madeleine. They all laughed.

Catriona took the seat beside her. She bent to her sewing as she whispered, "Keep your chin up. Don't let them see they wound you."

Spoken as a woman accustomed to doing just that. As much as Madeleine wanted to ask Catriona more, she was grateful for the support.

The word "desperate" drifted her way, and then more laughter, shriller and louder this time.

Heat crept up Madeleine's cheeks. She jabbed her finger with a needle and cursed.

Someone sat next to her and jostled her. It was Adelaide, and Madeleine sagged in relief at seeing her.

After a few moments, Adelaide whispered, "What's happening? The mood in here is thick enough to stab."

"They're talking about Madeleine." Catriona kept her voice low. "The spiteful plump one is saying her betrothal to Thomas is false."

Adelaide went silent, looking about her, and then stood. "Well, enough of that." She hurried from the hall.

Madeleine sat there alone but for Catriona sewing steadily at her side. Nothing of what Catriona thought or felt appeared on her face. It was an expression she wore often, and there could be all manner of thoughts and feelings hid behind her bland mask.

Cackles erupted from Posy's corner.

Madeleine kept her head over her sewing.

"They only know they wound you if you show them," Catriona said. "Give them nothing."

Madeleine straightened her spine. She wanted to run and hide, but she refused to give them the satisfaction.

Giving the gigglers a dirty look, Heather bustled into the hall and took the seat Adelaide had left. "Posy has been busy."

"Catriona told me." Madeleine glanced at Heather and forced herself to smile. "I can't think why. She already won Robert."

"Yes." Heather grimaced. "But you robbed her of her moment

with your announcement. Talk in the hall last night was all of you and Thomas. They were barely mentioned."

Her stab of satisfaction over that wasn't nice, but then, neither was Posy. "And now she wants her time in the sun. Other than that my betrothal is false, what is she saying?"

Heather glanced at Catriona and they both grimaced. "You're not going to like it."

"Really?" Madeleine feigned shock. "And here I thought they were all wishing me well."

Rolling her eyes, Heather sat up straight. "She's saying that you're trying to make Robert jealous and using Thomas to do so. As well as telling everyone who will listen that your betrothal isn't real."

That was close enough to the truth to send scalding heat through Madeleine's cheeks. She addressed the only part she could without lying. "I'm not maintaining this betrothal to make Robert jealous."

"I know that." Heather nudged her. "But it did happen suddenly, and people have heard you speak badly of Thomas enough for her words to find receptive ears."

Damn! She needed to guard her tongue. Her family had been warning her of consequences forever. "Why does she hate me so?"

"Are you really asking that?' Heather gave her a hard look.

Madeleine couldn't understand it. "Yes."

Heather looked at Catriona.

Catriona shrugged and said, "Because they have always had it, they don't understand how beautiful what they have is."

"Right." Heather's smile held secrets, and those were sad secrets, as she took Madeleine's hand. "Maddy, of course she resents you. You have everything she wants. You come from a wealthy, powerful family who adore you. Your father grants you more freedom than any other girl I know. Other than the power a marriage to you represents, your dowry is also obscene."

"I wouldn't call it obscene." Vulgar, perhaps, but obscene

seemed a little strong. She'd never thought of her and Posy in these terms.

"Obscene." Catriona shook her head. "And I thought mine was large."

"And when your father merely floats about the offer of a possible chance at your hand?" Heather's arm swept the hall. "Elford is overrun by every available man who stands a chance at winning you. Of course other women resent you."

"You don't." Madeleine glanced around the hall at the other girls.

"There are times when I do." Heather smiled to soften her words. "But more for the way your father and brothers adore you and would never force you into anything you didn't want."

"And they certainly do adore you." Catriona watched Edward as he entered the hall. She got up and gathered her things. She smiled at Madeleine and her eyes were kind. "You are loved, Madeleine, and valued. Don't let anyone make you feel otherwise. Their envy is not your failing but theirs."

Catriona slipped out of the hall without Edward noticing.

Or had he?

Once she was gone his gaze slid to where Catriona had sat, so quickly, that had Madeleine not been watching him she would have missed it.

"What we're saying is that Posy envies you," Heather said. "It makes her unkind."

Guilt nipped at Madeleine. Posy was the oldest of eight children, five of them girls. Her family expected her to marry well. By securing her match with Robert, she'd done that.

At the same time, it would be easier to be sympathetic if Posy's spiteful little face wasn't gloating at her from across the hall.

Adelaide returned to the hall, and she had Thomas with her.

Looking handsome and virile in a leather working tunic, he headed directly for her.

The hall went silent as he did so.

Leaning down he pressed a soft kiss on her mouth. "Good morrow, sweeting."

"Good morrow." Even knowing he did it to prove a point, her heart still skipped a beat and her body responded to his nearness. Of all the reasons she could think for them not marrying—and she couldn't recall one at this exact moment—their mutual attraction wasn't one of those reasons.

He tugged her to her feet. "Come. Ride with me."

And he always knew exactly the right thing to say when she needed him to say it most. Madeleine retuned his smile with a dazzling one of her own. "Anywhere you lead."

Chapter Twenty-Four

Her hand safely tucked into his, Thomas and Madeleine left the hall. Watching them go with a hard stare, Posy had nothing to say for the first time that morning.

Remembering Catriona's counsel, Madeleine slammed a lid on triumphant thoughts.

Posy had won Robert, but that may be more reason to pity her than anything else. A man who had played one woman false, could do so with another. As much as it galled her that Posy and Robert had carried on their affair behind her back, she tried to view it as Posy would. How hard must it have been to watch the man you loved, your lover, court another for her hand?

Feeling pity for Posy was new to her, and it would take some getting accustomed to.

"You're troubled." Thomas's deep voice rumbled through his chest.

He read her emotions well. "Adelaide didn't tell you?"

"She mentioned you were having some trouble in the hall." He tightened his fingers around hers. "I rode to your rescue immediately, my lady."

"I'm most obliged." She returned his smile.

Their mounts stood ready for them outside the stables.

Madeleine's smile widened. "You also prepared ahead."

"Always." He grinned and threw her into her saddle. "There are very few things you like more than to tear through the day on this beast of yours."

Brute tossed his head, impatient to be off.

"I see Brute is well."

"Come, Maddy." He checked her stirrup. "Let's ride with the wind and leave our troubles behind."

She couldn't resist that opening and grinned down at him. "Or I could leave you behind."

Spurring Queen, she cantered out of the bailey before he could reply. But he was right. The sun on her back, the wind in her face, the powerful surge of muscle beneath her did clear the rattle in her head.

Hooves pounded up behind her, and Madeleine urged Queen faster. The wind whipped her laughter away. She and Queen knew this land so well.

Thomas rode as if Brute were part of him, but with his greater weight and heavier horse, they were no match.

Madeleine threw a glance over her shoulder, a blatant challenge.

Up went one of his eyebrows.

The ground thundered beneath them, striking an answering resonance through her bones and pounding the rhythm in her blood.

Neck and neck, they dove into the forest.

Madeleine tucked her head beside Queen's neck, and trusted Queen to find the path she knew well. Not so sure of the path and not as agile, Brute fell behind.

Queen's ears pricked. Some horses were born to run and win, and Queen loved the challenge of a race.

With Madeleine in the lead, they broke from the forest and took the flat path beside the river. Soon they would draw rein and rest the horses, but if she could reach the bridge to the village, she would declare herself the winner.

A weight hit her from the side, carrying her off Queen's back and straight into the murky green river.

Madeleine screamed, hit the water and nearly swallowed half of it. She went down, water closing over her head. Kicking her legs, she popped back out again.

Breaking the surface, a hand's length from her, Thomas came up grinning. "I win."

"That was cheating." She slapped water at him. "And you could have killed me."

"I know you can swim." He rolled his eyes, snagging her around the waist. "It was a perfectly timed maneuver. Executed with consummate skill."

"It was a fool's chance to take." She braced her arms on his shoulders. Her legs tangled with his beneath the water, her skirts wrapping around her legs. "What would my father say if I told him about it?"

"Who do you think taught it to me?" Thomas's eyes warmed, his expression growing sensual. His gaze dipped to her mouth and he drew her closer to him. "Now for my prize."

"Cheaters get no prizes." But it was hard to speak with her breath lodged in her chest.

He touched his lips to the corner of her mouth. "Even if they beg sweetly to be forgiven?"

"Even then." The thrill of the race and the shock of being toppled from her horse drifted away to be replaced by a different thrumming through her blood. As much as she wanted to stay angry, already she responded to the light brush of his mouth across hers.

"Madeleine," he murmured. He slid his lips to her ear and sucked her lobe into his hot mouth. "This betrothal isn't a trial for me."

She tried to keep track of the conversation, but it was hard with her blood thrumming and her nerves alight. "You can't mean that."

"But I do." He kissed his way down her neck, wet, heated

kisses that made her tingle everywhere. "I don't need thirty days to know if I want you or not."

"You can't know that."

He stopped his distracting kissing and looked at her, their noses almost touching. "But I do know, and I won't be walking away without you thirty days hence."

"Thomas." Her thoughts dashed here and there and back again and wouldn't settle. A bare handful of days ago, she'd been deeply in love with Robert, convinced she had her future all planned out. Now, a different vista spread before her, and she didn't know how to feel about it. She craved simple and clear.

Pushing aside all thoughts, she sunk deep into the moment. The sun shone warm on her head, but the water chilled her skin. She floated, weightless, in the river, her form pressed to Thomas. As if her body knew what it wanted, it cleaved to his hard lines. "Thomas," she whispered and let the full sensual thud of him hit her.

Water darkened and spiked his thick lashes together. A drop clung to his cheek, and little rivulets meandered down the side of his face.

His arms about her were strong and sure, and they made her feel delicate and womanly. Upon his large shoulders, she could lay her worries and rest there for a while.

Her hips floated closer to his and they nudged beneath the water.

"Madeleine." His hot gaze stuck on her mouth. "What are you about?"

She was done with words and she elected to show him instead. Wrapping her legs about his waist, she brought herself closer to him, anchoring her body with his. In all the confusion of the last two days, this she knew. She desired Thomas of Draycott, and he desired her. In their mutual passion she didn't need to think, just surrender to feeling.

He groaned, his hands flexing on her back as he drew her closer.

Gripping his head tightly she pulled his mouth to hers.

For a long moment, he didn't respond, merely let her explore his lips with hers, let her touch her tongue to the seam of his mouth.

And then he opened to her exploration and took over the kiss. His hands slid down her back to cup her bottom. His kiss grew hungrier, more ardent, as if he couldn't taste enough of her.

His lust called to a wildness within her that was all base need and craving. She returned his kiss with equal fervor, her senses heating and her limbs growing warm and pliant. Her breasts grew sensitive where they pressed into his hard chest, and between her thighs she ached for him.

Finding his footing beneath them, he walked them out of the water.

A distant warning sounded in her mind. There was nobody there to stop them now, and they were rapidly approaching the point where neither of them would make the effort.

Reaching the bank, Thomas slid her down his body, their wet clothes sticking to them and providing no barrier to their heated flesh.

Thomas tore his mouth from hers and stepped back. His chest heaved as his gaze scalded her. He tugged off his jerkin and tossed it. His chemise followed, which he laid on the ground.

Chest bare to the sun, he was even more magnificent than she remembered. Strong and hewn like he'd been carved from wood solely to delight her sight.

He closed the small distance between them and opened his mouth over hers. Their kiss became voracious, uncontrollable, and Madeleine gloried in it.

His firm grip on her hips kept her flush against him. She'd never seen a man's aroused rod, but she felt it now, pressed against her and it thrilled her. She knew what it meant and what could happen next. And she wanted that like she wanted her next breath.

He cupped her breast, his thumb strumming her erect nipple.

Lust coursed through her, and she pressed into his touch. She wanted to feel his bare skin on hers and she struggled with her laces.

Thomas released her breast for long enough to help her. Together they tugged her wet bliaut over her head and Thomas dropped it beside his chemise.

Her white linen shift clung to her, see-through now that it was wet. The pink circles of her nipples, the dark hair between her legs, all on display for him.

And Thomas looked, as if he could never look away. He reached out with one hand and stroked a line from her shoulder, over her breast, and down her belly. He caught her hip and brought her closer to him. "You're lovely."

She felt lovely. With only her wet shift between them, the heat from his chest seeped into her and melted any lingering resistance.

"Madeleine." His breathing sawed through him. "I have little resistance left, but I'll stop if you tell me to. If you want to wait, I will honor that."

"I don't want you to stop."

His expression gentled, and he slid one hand about her nape and drew her closer to him. "You slay me, Maddy."

Being called Maddy by Thomas felt more intimate, like a slim bond between them.

He touched her reverently, his big hands surprisingly gentle as he explored her body, the fullness of her breasts, the dip of her waist, the roundness of her bottom. His expression intent, he watched his hands shape the wet cloth to her.

Madeleine explored him in turn, traced the firm rise of his chest muscle and lingered on his flat brown nipple.

He hissed in a breath.

She ran her fingers over the dips and swells of his belly, so different from her and so intriguing.

Thomas undid her lacings and gripped her shift. He raised it slowly up her legs.

Cool air caressed her calves and then her knees. The shift came higher, fabric bunching in his fists and Madeleine shivered. Excitement pounded with every heartbeat. Thomas would introduce her to a side of herself she'd yet to explore.

Dipping his head, he fastened his mouth on hers. This kiss was slower and deeper, a thorough exploration of her mouth. He broke the contact to pull her shift over her head.

Her nakedness left her feeling vulnerable, but Thomas kissed her, his big hands roaming down her back to cup her bottom and lift her against him.

He lowered her to her back and stood a moment over her, looking at her, his gaze hungry and slumberous. Making short work of his boots and braies, he stood there and bared himself to her gaze.

His rod jutted from between thick, muscular thighs, and for the first time, she felt apprehension.

Lying down beside her, he propped his head on one hand. His other hand spread over her ribcage, his skin dark against her fairer tone.

"My lovely Madeleine." He plumped her breast and lowered his mouth to her.

The sensation of his hot, wet mouth on her nipple made her cry out. She forgot her shyness as he suckled her. He moved to her other breast, sliding his hand over the jut of her hipbone to the apex of her thighs.

Madeleine was momentarily jolted by the new touch on her most private place.

He slid his fingers between her thighs and nudged them apart.

She was wet where he touched, and his fingers slid through her sensitive flesh. He found a place where she was so tender, she jerked into his touch.

Raising his head, he whispered sweet words, comforting words, words that told her how much he wanted her.

She opened her thighs, wanting more of what he offered, sensing a greater conclusion to come and needing that.

He stroked her, easing a finger inside her and then out again.

All the while, he caressed the sensitive part with his thumb, driving her need higher and higher.

Sensation built within her. Like an unstoppable flood, it pressed against her.

"Let it come," Thomas whispered. "Hold nothing back."

Her climax coursed through her in a wash of unbearable pleasure. Her back bowed off the ground as sensation carried her with it.

Thomas guided her hand to him and wrapped her fingers around his shaft.

"Like this," he wrapped his hand around hers and showed her how to touch him.

Madeleine watched her hand pleasuring him, fascinated by the sight. What she did to him reflected clearly on his face. An expression part pain, part pleasure, all earnest intent creased his features.

"Enough." He took her hand from him and kissed it. "I'm too close as it is."

He slid between her thighs, his weight resting on his forearms. His rod nudged at the apex of her thighs, but he merely pressed against her, letting her feel him.

Madeleine braced for what would happen next. But Thomas didn't thrust inside her. Instead he moved against that bundle of nerves until need rose in her again.

Thomas bent his head and kissed her, slowly, as if he'd all the time in the world. He gripped her thigh and coaxed her to bend her knee, wrapping her leg about his back, opening her even more to him.

Madeleine raised her other leg, and he growled as he slid against her wet, willing flesh.

"This might be uncomfortable." He fit the head of his rod against her and pressed.

The intrusion felt strange, and she tensed.

"Easy." He kissed her softly, working his rod deeper inside her. "Let me in, Maddy. Let me love you."

She breathed deep and relaxed, and the strangeness gave way to the pull of stretched flesh and a new fullness inside her.

He took his time, seating himself fully within her. Sweat beaded on his forehead, and he held himself rigid above her. "Are you well?"

"Yes, Thomas." She tilted her hips up to receive him deeper. "I'm more than well."

Any lingering discomfort melted as he stroked slowly in and out of her. He let her dictate the pace, watching her intently for what she wanted, sensing when she needed him to go faster, thrust deeper.

Their skin slid and slapped gently as he owned her with his body. Another precipice loomed for her, and Thomas slid his hand between them and stroked the sensitive place again. This time, when she shattered, it came from deeper within her and took her higher and kept her there for a longer, breathless moment.

Thomas thrust harder and faster into her, his face grim in his urgency, before he emptied inside her with a shout. Gathering her closer, he rolled until he lay beneath her. His chest heaved and he folded her tight against him.

Madeleine lay there, content to stay in the warmth of his arms.

As the world once more intruded on them, she was grateful for his warmth against the slight nip in the breeze.

"Madeleine." He kissed the top of her head. "How do you render me so helpless?"

"In much the same way you do the same to me." She propped her chin on her hands and stared up at him. She felt looser in her limbs, with a lingering sense of contentment.

He cupped her bottom and then gave it a light slap. "We should dress and return." He planted a lingering kiss on her mouth. "I must speak with your father immediately."

Chapter Twenty-Five

Madeline's contentment popped like a soap bubble. "I beg your pardon."

"I must speak with your father." Thomas frowned up at her as if his statement was obvious.

Scrambling to her feet, Madeleine searched for her clothes. She couldn't have this conversation unclothed. The fool lay on her shift, and she grabbed it and tugged. "Move."

"Madeleine." He took his time moving and handed her the shift. "What are you doing?"

"Getting dressed." He had gone and ruined everything. The effort of wriggling into damp clothing had her panting. In frustration she was forced to accept his help.

"I can see you're getting dressed, but you're angry, and I don't understand why."

"You want to tell my father what we did." She nearly hit him, he was so dense. "And I forbid it."

Up went one of his dark brows. "Forbid? That's a strong word."

"I have strong feelings about this." She shoved him off her bliaut and tugged it over her head. Once more she was forced to accept his help with the laces. She waved her hand at his clothing pile. "I don't want my father and mother knowing we did this."

He stood there naked as the day he was born and frowned at her.

"Get dressed." She threw his chemise at him. "I can't speak to you when you're like that."

Making no move to clothe himself, Thomas jammed his hands on his hips. "Madeleine." And she hated that tone of voice. It made her feel like a chastised child, and he knew she was no child. "What other outcome did you expect after you had lain with me?"

She shoved his braies into his belly. "I wasn't thinking then."

"I was." Jaw set in a stubborn line, he finally took the hint and jerked on his clothing. "I told you our betrothal was real for me."

Well, for the love of God. She threw her hands up in exasperation. "How was I to know that's what you meant when you said this betrothal was no trial for you?"

"What else could I mean?" He glowered at her as he yanked his boots on. "Especially when you and I consummated our relationship right on the heels of those words."

"I didn't put the two together." She hunted her boots and hauled them on. He really was the most annoying man. "At no point did I see a connection between what you said and what we did."

He shrugged. "It matters not. Your father still needs to know matters are now irrevocable."

"Irrevocable?" That sounded particularly final. With all the insouciance a girl who had just lost her virginity could muster— not that much—she said, "I think you're making too much of this."

"Do you now?" Abruptly his face and tone gentled and he stepped closer to her. He tucked a strand of wayward hair behind her ear, setting off a trail of sweet warmth in the wake of his fingers. "Do you really think so little of the loss of your innocence?" He cupped her chin. "If so, it's a good thing I consider it a rather weighty event."

"Thomas," she managed to whisper. He disarmed her with his gentleness. His bombast and posturing, she could manage. She'd grown up around big, domineering, arrogant men and felt no fear. But when Thomas used tenderness against her, she had no defense. "I don't want my father to know what happened here today." Cursed tears filled her eyes, and she wanted to smash them away. "He will be so disappointed in me."

"Maddy." He gathered her into his arms, smelling of sunshine and warm skin. "Two people were involved in the deeds of this day." He kissed the top of her head. "I feel sure he and your brothers will be too much occupied beating me to within an inch of myself to think much of your part."

She managed a wet chuckle. "Why are you so sure they need to know?"

"Two reasons, sweeting." He rested his head against her, and despite their current argument, Madeleine drew comfort from the contact. "Firstly, you could be carrying my child even as we stand here. You know what we did leads to children?"

She nodded. Mother, and later Adelaide, had explained all of this in mortifying detail.

"And secondly." Thomas's deep voice rumbled against her ear. "My honor demands I tell a man whom I respect like a father."

Men and their infernal, bedamned honor. Madeleine snorted. "But your honor comes at the price of my father's respect for me."

He sighed and held her for a long while. "All right, Madeleine. What do you suggest?"

"Can we not wait first to see if I'm carrying your child?" She peered up at his grave, stern face. "If I am, then our course is already set."

Thomas looked at her, waiting for more.

"But if I'm not, then we still have twenty-nine days in which to decide if we are suited."

His face darkened, and she would almost swear that hurt flickered in his eyes. "When I gave in to the desire to make love to you, I had already made my decision. I told you so."

"Now you're being stubborn." She almost stamped her foot, but she was trying to get him to listen to her as a mature woman. "You hardly know me. As a woman, I mean. You couldn't possibly know you want to marry me."

"Can I not?" One of his dark eyebrows rose, but his features were now carefully inscrutable.

She tried to read him. "Can you?"

"I have a counteroffer for you," he said. "I don't tell your father about what happened here today, and in twenty-nine days, you stand before him and your mother and make them believe you want nothing more than to marry me."

"I don't see how that's a counteroffer." She wished she could discern his thoughts. "It's more in the nature of an ultimatum."

Thomas shrugged. "Call it what you will." Anger hardened his features and turned his gaze chilly. "I made you mine today, Madeleine. In every sense of the word." He cupped her face in his palms, firm but not painful. "No other will lie with you. No other will take your hand and declare before God you're his to protect and nurture. You're mine." He pressed a hot kiss on her mouth. "But you can have your twenty-nine days to become accustomed to the idea if you need them."

* * *

"What are you sulking about?" Peter asked him over dinner.

Thomas shrugged because Peter was wrong. He wasn't sulking; he was seething. A man had tried to kill him, and he should be giving that the attention it demanded. Instead he was transfixed by a tawny-haired vixen who tied him in knots without even trying.

How could he be so sure he wanted to marry her? She'd stood there with her blue eyes all sincerity and asked him how he could be so sure he wanted to marry her. The answer to which was engraved on his soul. How could he not?

He'd wanted to bellow at her. Instead, he'd mounted his horse and ridden back to the keep. Yes, he should have assisted her to mount but in that moment, he'd been so angry he'd doubted he could put his hands on her without shaking her.

Did she think he went around deflowering the daughters of men he held in awe? She must, and Thomas knew exactly who he blamed for her poor opinion of men.

Locking gazes on his prey, he stared at Robert.

Robert must have sensed his intent because he looked up from his dinner, paled, and ducked back to his trencher.

Yes, that worthless maggot should hide his head. He'd trifled with Madeleine, and that in itself was bad enough. But a worse crime in Thomas's estimation was Robert had somehow persuaded a fiery, beautiful, clever, and fearless young woman that she deserved less than a man's entire heart, body and soul.

Madeleine, uncharacteristically subdued for once, sat beside her mother on the dais wearing a gown the shade of the emeralds he would like to shower her with. And damned if, angry as he was with her, he craved nothing more than to take her in his arms and comfort her.

Christ on the cross. Give him something he could swing his sword at rather than this slow seeping poison. He could still recall the silk of her skin beneath his hands, the taste of her kiss, the way she moved beneath him—innocent and wanton in her passion.

She looked up and caught his gaze. A light flush spread over her cheeks.

Without looking behind him, he raised his cup to be refilled. He'd it in mind to get blighted drunk tonight.

"Thomas?" Peter frowned at him. He glanced from Thomas to Madeleine and back again. "Have you done something you ought not have?"

"No." He'd no hesitation in his reply. He was born to love Madeleine of Elford, and she'd been his for as long. Making love with her was the natural extension of their connection. As he was raising his cup to his mouth, a faint bitter tang of unripe tomatoes stopped him.

Twice now, an attempt had been made to end him, and his guard was up. Where normally he would have thought the smell peculiar and dismissed it, now he took his goblet from his mouth and sniffed.

Peter still watched him. "What is it?"

"I'm not sure." Thomas sniffed his goblet. The smell definitely came from there. Bad wine at Draycott was expected, but not at Elford. He handed it to Peter. "Smell this."

While Peter did, Thomas searched the hall for who had poured his wine. A balding, thickset serving man with a pitcher in his hands scuttled for the entrance.

"Stop him!" Thomas leaped to his feet.

Without looking behind him, the man dropped the pitcher and ran.

"What is it?" Sir Richard pushed to his feet.

Thomas vaulted the table and went after the man. Peter would stay behind and give any needed explanations.

He reached the corridor outside the hall.

Empty.

Running, he took the stairs into the bailey. Nothing. Nobody moved in the near moonless night.

"Blast his soul." Thomas walked across the bailey. At the well, a young girl was drawing water, and he rushed her, startling her. "Did you see someone run through here?"

The girl paled. "N-no, my lord."

Retracing his steps, Thomas ran into Edward and Sir Richard at the top of the stairs.

Sir Richard looked carved from stone, and angrier than Thomas had ever seen. "Anything?"

"No. Nobody went that way."

Edward cursed. "Andrew is searching the chapel, and Oliver took above. If he's still in the keep, we'll find him."

"This is becoming a habit." A new anger burned away his frustration with Madeleine. "We cannot be certain it is Wilfred until we catch the bastard, and catch him, we will."

Sir Richard slammed a fist into his palm. "Somebody makes free of my keep and abuses my hospitality."

"Why you?" Edward cocked his head. "The cut girth, I could see as a way to disable you. Perhaps even the arrow we could put down to a similar reason, but poison?" He shook his head. "Poison is a weakling's weapon."

"Or a coward's," Thomas said. The sort of coward who knew he could never best Thomas in combat, someone nursing a deep resentment for Thomas. Regardless, it ended now.

Edward frowned. "Who is this Wilfred?"

"Someone I should have rid myself of years ago." With Madeleine now in his life, he had even more reason to live. More than that, he was now responsible for her safety, and this coward threatened that. "He grows bold, and that will make him careless."

"Thomas." Sir Richard clapped a hand on Thomas's shoulder. "I want you to know that you owe me nothing. If you need to go and deal with this cur, you must do so. I don't know how matters lie with you and Madeleine, but you're free to leave before the thirty days are over."

Guilt almost choked him, and he forced himself to meet Richard's gaze. "I'm afraid that's now impossible."

"What can you mean?" Richard looked baffled. "I tell you now, you can leave. If you want it, I release you from your betrothal.'

Edward lacked his father's faith in Thomas and stepped into him. They were of a height and Edward's fury blazed from his eyes. "Tell me I misunderstood you."

"Edward!" Richard gripped Edward's shoulder. "Let us not compound the ill suffered by Thomas under our roof."

Thomas didn't flinch. He was no liar.

"You whoreson." Edward's punch connected in a sickening

crunch against his nose. Blood spurted from his nose and down his cheek.

Richard got between them. "Edward." He bellowed. "I demand to know why you insult our guest."

"Ask him." Edward grit between clenched teeth. "Ask him why it's too late to withdraw from his betrothal. I want to see if he can look you in face and lie to you."

"Why would..." Richard stilled, and a chilling fury took over his face. "Thomas?"

"She's mine." Thomas made himself hold Richard's gaze. "Mine to marry and mine to keep."

Thomas would have carved into his living flesh to avoid seeing the profound look of disappointment and betrayal on Sir Richard's face. Stepping aside, Sir Richard nodded to Edward and walked back into the hall.

Edward planted his fist in Thomas's gut, followed by a second to his ribs. Jesu! The man had fists like hammers.

He jacked at the waist and heaved to catch his breath.

But Edward followed with a swift upper cut that caught his bent head and sent it snapping back on his neck.

His lip split, and Edward might have loosened a tooth.

"Edward!" Madeleine shrieked, her slippers pattering on the stone floor.

Edward paid her no heed and caught Thomas a blow to the cheek and another solid shot to the belly.

Thomas's dinner threatened to escape the pounding.

Madeleine pushed between them.

With a curse, Edward managed to pull his next punch before it landed on Madeleine standing between them.

"Edward." She pushed Edward's chest with both hands. "Have you lost your mind? Somebody tried to poison Thomas, and you do this to him?"

"He has cause, sweeting." Thomas tried to move her aside. He deserved everything Edward thirsted to hand him and more. He'd broken faith with Sir Richard. He'd taken what wasn't his yet to take, and he deserved to be beaten to a bloody pulp.

Wide gaze searching his face for answers, Madeleine winced and touched his lip. "Why would you say that?"

"Get out of the way, Madeleine." Edward hadn't cooled one whit. Instead, his anger hardened by the second into something cold, calculating and infinitely more dangerous.

"No, Edward." She turned on her brother. "You've no reason to…" Like her father, Madeleine didn't always need everything spelled out for her, and she turned back to him. "You didn't."

"Yes. He did." Edward answered for him. "Father heard it."

Nothing Edward could hand out could hurt more than the look of betrayal Madeleine bent on him. Hurt gleamed in her beautiful eyes, her lip quivered, and she shook her head. She turned and ran from him.

Thomas went after her. He needed to explain.

Edward stepped in front of him. "Not so fast, you whoreson."

Chapter Twenty-Six

Madeleine sat beside Adelaide in the chapel. Catriona sat beside Adelaide and gave her a smile. Both offered their silent support and Madeleine took it. The congregation's gazes lay heavy on her shoulders.

Standing tall and proud, light streaming through the window behind the altar and gilding his hair, Robert stood and awaited his bride.

For so long, she'd dreamed she would be his bride. That he would stand thus and wait for her. Now she felt numb, detached, as if Robert had happened in another lifetime. Like hawks, the congregation watched to see her cry or break down. The very absence of any such emotion confused her, and that confusion was by far the most dominant emotion she experienced.

Adelaide stirred, and Thomas slid past her and into place beside Madeleine. He looked down at her. "Are you bearing up?"

The marks and bruises on him drove all other thoughts from her mind.

"Me?" Her voice came out too loud, and she quickly lowered it. "I'm not the one who looks like he was trodden on by a destrier."

Thomas grimaced, and then winced and touched his finger to the corner of his split lip. "That bad, eh?"

"Yes." Along with his split lip, he sported a puffy and bruised eye, a bruise on his cheekbone and one side of his jaw was swollen. A savage need to punish whoever had injured Thomas coursed through her. "Did Edward do this to you?"

"He had good reason." Thomas took her hand and threaded his fingers with hers.

Madeleine studied the rough, unbroken skin of his knuckles. Unbroken because Thomas hadn't fought back. He'd stood and taken a beating from Edward. Dismemberment might be too tender a punishment for Edward. Thomas might not be able to fight back, but she could.

"So fierce." Thomas winked at her. "Sweeting, if you had been my sister, I would have done worse."

She met Edward's gaze and sent him a look loaded with all she would do with him when they were out of the presence of the priest and their parents. He had taken matters too far.

Unperturbed, Edward raised an eyebrow at her.

Thomas had not fought back, and she had left him with Edward to take a beating.

Posy appeared in the chapel doors. Flowers were woven through her long raven hair. Her gown of pink silk clung to her full figure and complimented her coloring. But it was the look on her face that made her truly lovely.

Posy glowed, and enemies they might be, but every bride should look as lovely on her wedding day. The smile Posy fastened on Robert beamed her joy. She really did love him. Posy's hope for a glorious future shone from her eyes.

Thomas's fingers tightened around Madeleine's.

His touch reminded her that they now stood together. They were a couple. She rested her head against his shoulder. Thomas had this way of making the shifting world go still around her with his presence. She didn't know if she felt better or worse for Posy's love being real. Had Posy watched Robert with her and experienced doubts and wounded feelings?

As happy as Posy looked walking toward him, Robert looked miserable. It took Madeleine a moment to understand the grim look on his face. The petty part of her got a quick flash of satisfaction. Posy floated on a cloud of joy toward a groom who looked like he was being disemboweled.

Robert had played them both false. By the look of misery on his face, he felt no more love for Posy than he had for her. By the end of today, Posy would be tied to Robert forever, whereas she had a strong man beside her who held her hand through the ceremony, in case she needed him.

Madeleine wanted to jump up and shake Robert and tell him to get that look off his face. He was not the one enduring the worst of today. His actions had brought this wedding about. He had stayed constant to nobody, and he did not even deserve Posy.

Yes, Posy had cast her lures his way, but nobody had forced Robert to snatch them up. He'd lain with Posy and made the child she carried.

As Madeleine had lain with Thomas.

Unlike Robert, Thomas hadn't waited to see if she was with child before he confessed his seduction. He'd taken the beating for being honorable. Even though she still could not face her father and had endured an agonizing conversation with Mother.

Warmth crept into her chest, and she snuggled closer to Thomas. Precious gems couldn't be more valuable than this. Every bruise and mark Edward had given Thomas proclaimed Thomas's honest intention to stand by her and any child they might have created.

Thomas looked down at her and raised his eyebrow in question.

Not ready to explain, she shook her head and smiled at him.

His answering smile stoked the warmth in her chest.

The priest took Posy and Robert through their vows.

Posy's voice lilted as she spoke hers.

Bloody, bloody Robert sounded as if he were being tortured.

Father Mark blessed the congregation, and it was done. Robert and Posy were tied together for the rest of their lives.

As they passed her, Posy looked up and smirked. It was hard to maintain her empathy in the face of Posy's gloating, and Madeleine smirked right back. Say what you would about Robert, he wasn't Thomas. Her thoughts tumbled ass over tip to an abrupt halt.

Father led the congregation out of the chapel in Father Mark's wake. As he passed, he glanced at Thomas. He stopped and took a longer look at Thomas's bruises. Then he nodded. "It is done." He winked at Thomas. "I would have done worse."

"I'm aware." Thomas snorted. "But I do beg your forgiveness."

Father glanced at Mother, who glared back. "You have it." Father clapped him on the shoulder. "I'll be proud to call you son."

Snap! The jaws of her irrevocable future shut around Madeleine. Her future was decided, the course set, and it suddenly felt as if her opinion hadn't been required.

"Breathe." Thomas tugged her hand through his arm and joined them to the procession.

Distracted, she almost forgot to hiss a threat at Edward.

Almost, but not quite. "Even if he won't fight back, you can bet your black soul I will."

"Maddy." Edward gave her a look loaded with older brother condescension. "He took what wasn't his to take. Thomas accepts it. Make your peace."

As if a wall were going over in a rumble of tumbling rocks, flattening her beneath it, Madeleine could make peace with nothing more. Her life seemed to have been snatched out of her hands and was being tossed amongst Robert and Posy and Thomas and her family. Her chest constricted and labored her breathing.

"I'm going for a ride," she said in Thomas's general direction and separated from him.

She rushed through the hall and out into the bailey. Still, she couldn't draw a deep enough breath to satisfy her demand for air.

She saddled Queen herself. Nobody would miss her for hours. A feast was taking place in honor of the marriage, and all eyes would be on the happy couple. The half happy couple, at least.

The bailey was all but deserted, and she let Queen have her head. They flew out of the bailey, through the gatehouse and over the drawbridge.

The sentry shouted for her to slow down, but she needed the speed. She needed to outrun her thoughts and escape the jaws of her life.

Queen's smooth gait did what no amount of chatter or wine would, soothed the roiling emotions inside her and stopped her thoughts. She pushed Queen faster, delighting in the speed and concentrating on keeping them both safe.

When the ruined church appeared, Madeleine drew rein and slowed Queen to a walk.

Her life fell like an apple pared into two parts, the time before Thomas had come and the time after. Here, she'd stood and nearly begged Robert to kiss her. On that day, nothing could have persuaded her she would be at this point, Robert married to Posy and her betrothal to Thomas a certainty.

But that memory wasn't pure, corrupted by what had probably been going on between Robert and Posy before she reached him. Had they lain there and rutted? Had he not wanted to kiss her because he had so recently tupped Posy?

A heedless sun climbed a clear, endless sky, and she slid off Queen and tethered the horse to a gorse bush.

On this fallen section of wall, she'd stood and watched Robert ride away. Then Thomas had come from behind the tallest remaining section of the ruin. Even as she had despised him, the woman in her had thrilled in response to him.

Their attraction had been immediate and powerful.

Madeleine sat in the shade of a gnarled old elm and propped her back against the trunk. She hadn't slept well last night. Long hours had passed as she waited for Father and Mother to summon her about Thomas's declaration that they had been lovers.

Instead, Mother had only come this morning as she was dressing for the wedding.

"Well, darling." Mother had cupped her chin and looked at her with infinitely patient and understanding eyes. "What is done is done, and I'm not enough of a hypocrite to lecture you about acting out of wedlock." Mother's misty, nostalgic smile hinted at something she held dear. "All I need to know are these two things."

Not sure what Mother would say, Madeleine had nodded.

"Did he please you?"

Her face had nearly burst into flame at that question, but she'd managed to nod and mutter. "Very much."

"Good." Mother winked. "Does he make you laugh?"

"When I'm not fighting with him," Madeleine answered as honestly as she could.

Mother had warned her to come to her if her monthly courses were late and left her to get ready.

Of course, Heather could never leave it there and had besieged her with questions. What was it like? Did she enjoy it? What did a naked man really look like?

None of which she'd answered.

Queen looked up from cropping grass when Madeleine chuckled.

The day was warm, and insects buzzed and chirped in the long grass. A meadowlark fluted and called to his mate. It was too lovely a day for dark thoughts to win.

Peace came with each breath of sweet, fresh air, and Madeleine closed her eyes. She let her mind drift and it meandered to her and Thomas and their lovemaking. Before he'd ruined everything with his talk of telling her father, it had been wonderful.

Now that Father knew, and they were heading straight down the aisle anyway, she could see no impediment to more of the same.

She must have fallen asleep because the sound of hoofbeats woke her.

Queen blew a soft greeting to their visitor as Madeleine opened her eyes.

Still dressed in his wedding finery, Robert threw himself off his horse and stalked toward her. "I thought I might find you here."

"What are you doing here?" Madeleine yawned and stretched before getting to her feet. Her heart ached a little at the sight of him dressed for his wedding. "You should be at your wedding feast."

"Feast?" Robert's face twisted into a sneer. "I couldn't stand it a moment more. Sitting there pretending to be happy."

Anger curled like slow rising smoke through her. "She's with child, Robert. Your child. You liked her well enough to get her that way."

"I knew it." He grabbed a handful of hair. "You're angry with me."

Madeleine gaped at him. She couldn't find the words to express what boiled inside of her. All she could manage was, "Of course I'm angry with you."

"Madeleine." He raised his hand to her. When she didn't react, he dropped it again and sighed. "You can't understand what I have been suffering."

Had he suffered a thing? She couldn't imagine what that might be.

"You were always there. It was my intention to marry you all along." He tugged his hair. "But marriage is for life, and your father would never tolerate me taking a leman."

Neither would she, but his admission was so eye-opening she didn't want to stop him now.

"I wanted to...try something different. Someone different."

He stared at his feet. "But then, she fell pregnant and went to your father. Now I'm wed to her, and you will marry another. I wanted an adventure before I was married." He grabbed her and pulled her to him. "I can't tolerate the idea of you with him. You're mine. You've always been mine."

He bent his head to kiss her and froze.

"I don't share," Thomas said from behind Robert. "And she's very much not your woman."

The knife at Robert's throat was held in Thomas's large, calloused hand.

Robert swallowed hard and sweat beaded his forehead. "I was merely saying goodbye."

"Say it." Thomas pressed the dagger point to Robert's skin. "Say it and go away before I change my mind and gut you."

Robert dropped his hands from her. "I should get back to my bride."

"Yes, you should." Thomas stepped back, but only so far as to allow Robert to move away from her. "Join your woman. This one is mine."

Chapter Twenty-Seven

Madeleine watched Robert ride away, his last look burned into her mind. Robert had given her such a haunted look of betrayal, it scored her to the bone. Yes, she understood his hypocrisy, but some part of her still felt his reproach.

"Did you arrange to meet him here?" Thomas looked angrier than she'd ever seen him. His eyes went like onyx, and he clenched his jaw.

His anger distracted her from the question, but only for a moment. "Of course I didn't arrange a meeting. It's his wedding day."

"More to the point, Madeleine, you are a betrothed woman." Staring after Robert's retreating form, he caressed his blade's edge with his thumb.

"You agreed to thirty days."

His eyes glinted dangerously. "I rescind that offer."

"Just like that?"

He nodded. "Just like that."

Madeleine was so bloody bedamned tired of the men in her life pushing and shoving her about like a bale of hay, taking it upon themselves to decide what she thought and even what she felt, talking amongst each other and settling her future for her.

Well, blight, blast and bugger to that. It ended now.

She rounded on Thomas. "How dare you?"

Up went one supercilious eyebrow, and he crossed his arms. "I dare because of that child you carry."

"What child?" She tossed her arms up. "Thus far, this child is nothing more than a phantom."

He shrugged.

Shrugged!

He hadn't even the decency to produce a verbal argument.

Madeleine went toe to toe with him and let her frustration, confusion, fear and even heartbreak come roaring out. "You don't own me. You've no right to stomp around in your huge boots all over my life. You had no right to say what you said to Robert. You've no rights where I'm concerned at all. No rights. Not one."

Thomas stared at her, his jaw set. "Are you finished?"

Was she? Not quite. "You also had no right to go to my father carrying tales. Now look where we are. You trapped me into this betrothal." She poked his chest. "And that means I'm not bound by it."

Her back hit the stone wall behind her. Breathing hard, Thomas pressed into her front. His eyes glittered down at her. "You've a hearing problem, Madeleine."

"Get off me." But her tone lacked her fire of two minutes ago.

He was infuriating packed in an intimidating wallop. And dangerously delicious.

"You oaf."

"Any more names for me?" His breath was warm on her face.

"Brute."

Gaze hotter than the sun, he stared her down.

"Lout."

He pushed his hips into hers and she gasped at the hard ridge of his rod.

"Thug," she whispered, not giving the insult nearly the heat it deserved.

"Uh-huh." He breathed in her ear. "What else?"

"Boor."

He nuzzled her neck on a soft groan and bit her. He blew on the spot and soothed it with his tongue.

Heat scalded her skin and shot to the junction of her thighs. Anger melted into molten desire, and she dug her hands into his hair and tugged.

"Do I have your attention?" He scooped her legs and wrapped them around his waist. Pressing forward, he kept her in place with his hips and grabbed her skirts and tugged them up to her hips. He gripped her bottom with both hands and ground her against him. "Open your stubborn ears and listen."

Sensation shot through her and made her crave more. Thomas robbed her of thought and speech. He'd only to touch her or come near her and she became wax for him to warm and mold. God, it was almost galling. If it had been one mite less addictive, she would have resented his mastery of her senses. She refused to roll over without a fight. Madeleine nipped at his lip.

He hissed in a breath.

She sucked his lip.

Thomas pulled back and stared at her. "I should slap your arse."

"Try it and see what I do." She raised her chin and met his gaze.

He tightened his grip on her bottom. His fingers slid into the slit between her thighs. "This tells me what you refuse to admit."

She found it hard to speak with his fingers stroking her private place, playing lightly over the pleasure spot. Writhing against him, she tried to increase the pressure. "And what's that?"

"This tells me you're mine." He slid two fingers inside her.

Madeleine arched at the thrilling invasion. She wanted to fight his claim and tell him it wasn't true, but with him pumping his fingers within her, all of her being concentrated on the pleasure he brought her. "Thomas."

"What, Maddy?" He thumbed that sweet place. "You're mine. If you were as honest as your body, you would admit that you've been mine since we first encountered each other right here."

"No." She panted, unable to draw a full breath. As pleasurable as his fingers were, she wanted his rod, yearned for him to complete her with his flesh. "It's merely rutting."

"No." He brought her closer to the peak and slowed. "It's so much more than that, Maddy. You're mine."

"No." Frustrated to the point of screaming, she moved against his still hand. When he didn't obey her prompting, she almost shrieked his name. "Thomas."

"What?"

"You know what."

His gaze remained implacable on her face. "Tell me you're mine. Admit it, you stubborn wench."

She uttered a sound half sob, half laugh. "I want you."

At last, he moved his fingers slowly inside her. "More."

"I need you."

He stroked her aching bud. "Closer."

She was close to screaming, and she dug her nails into his shoulders. "I lust for you. I desire you. I crave you."

"Say it, Maddy." His eyes glittered down at her. A flush rode his cheekbones. "Say what we both know to be true."

"God's balls. You win." She would do near anything to get him to continue. "I'm yours."

"Yes, you are." The intensity of his gaze was as flame to her skin. "There will be no broken betrothal. This ends with you wed to me, sharing my bed, sharing my life, bearing my children."

"How can you be so sure?" Tears prickled behind her eyes.

He rested his forehead against hers. "I'm sure, my fiery Maddy, because as much as you're mine, I'm yours. Wholly, completely and immutably."

His declaration burrowed into her chest and created a warm place to nestle.

Thomas drew his hand from her and dropped her legs.

Madeleine cried out her frustration.

He dropped to his knees in front of her and pushed up her skirts. "Hold these."

She grabbed her skirts as his dark head lowered to her thighs. So close to her that it made her breath catch in her throat. She'd no idea what he was doing down there.

Lifting her leg, he draped it over his shoulder, opening her to him.

Nobody had seen her thus and she tensed and gripped his hair. "What are you doing?"

"Feasting on what is mine." And he put his mouth on her.

Madeleine shrieked, shocked rigid, but also thrilled by the hot wet slide of his tongue along her intimate flesh. She should object. This was probably a sin. But dear God in Heaven, if he stopped now, she'd beg.

He licked, sucked and drove her closer to a dizzying precipice that left her panting and moaning and uttering strange sounds that couldn't possibly be escaping her mouth. She soared over the edge in a tightening of every part of her, and a streak of ecstasy that buckled her knees and left her breathless.

Thomas rose and cupped her cheeks. "Say it."

"I'm yours. All yours." Her bones melted into the stones behind her.

Clasping her to him, he lowered them both to the floor.

He knelt on the ground and opened her legs over him. "Maddy, there is no going back."

Beneath her, he pressed harder than ever and she needed all of him. To take him within her and join them in the most elemental way possible, to find that place together where they were no longer two separate beings. "Finish this." She wrapped her arms about him and kissed him. "Finish us. Take us both there."

"Maddy." He groaned and shifted beneath her. "You will be the death of me."

She helped him free himself and find her. "Till death do us part, Thomas?"

He chuckled and stopped, his face caught in a rictus part torment, part bliss as she lowered herself onto him.

Like this he filled her completely, and Madeleine clung to him, clasping his head to her breast.

Thomas moved his head, fastening his hot mouth on her nipple through her bliaut. He gripped her hips and showed her how to move on him, rising and falling.

The sensation was unimaginable. She was in command. She drove them forward and she reveled in her power.

Too soon, she felt her completion tightening through her belly. "Thomas." She tightened her channel around him.

"Yes, Maddy." His fingers dug into her hips as he took control, driving her down onto him, relentless and consuming.

She exploded on him.

He joined her and both of their cries rang out in unison.

In the aftermath, she clung to him with her arms and her thighs, loath to let him go and release the moment. Like this, they didn't argue. Like this, they were in perfect accord. Like this, she could fall into her future with him without any qualms or doubts.

Thomas shifted beneath her and moved her to the side. He righted himself.

Still basking, it took Madeleine precious moments to see that his reaction wasn't the same as hers.

Face close and expressionless, he looked frigid and separate from her.

Madeleine struggled to her feet on legs that still shook. "Thomas?"

He looked up at her. "I shall see you back at the hall."

"Thomas?" His coldness lanced through her. "What's the matter?"

"Madeleine." He shook his head and caught the saddle on

Brute, preparing to mount. "I'm not proud of who I become around you."

"What?" That hurt more than anything. "I don't understand what you mean by that."

"No, I suppose you don't." He turned to her, and his gaze held a blight in their depths. "For want of you, I broke faith with a man who has been more than a father to me. Mad with jealousy, I used your desire for me to wring a confession out of you." He mounted his horse in a fluid motion. The sadness on his face was the worst of all. "But a confession extracted from a woman in the throes of desire means nothing at all. I'm so desperate for you, Maddy, that I sought to drive Robert from your mind with my body." He gathered his reins and clucked to his horse. "And once the aftermath has cleared of making love to you, I find myself ashamed of the man I am."

Chapter Twenty-Eight

T homas's shame kept him company on the ride back to Elford. He'd no command of himself when she was about, making a mockery of how he strove for mastery of himself in all that he did. With Madeleine about, he dove from despair to elation and back again, bouncing against lust, fury, frustration, hope and delight along the way.

She slayed him. He was dirt beneath her pretty feet, and the warrior within him, fierce and wild, fought her hold.

His rage when he'd come upon her and Robert had driven him close to lunacy. Through shimmering vision he'd hungered for Robert's blood, hot and fresh, on his hands. He'd seen his dagger driven deep into the cur's gullet. Some wisp of reason buried within him had risen in time to stop him.

Her standing there brimming with challenge and defiance had driven his warrior into a frenzied need to master her, and he had, to an extent. However, her capitulation as soon as he'd wrung it from her had turned to ash. He'd used her desire as a weapon against her, and for the first time in his life, he had taken from a woman what she had not willingly given. He loathed himself for that. Her desire for him was a gift she bestowed, and he'd used it as a weapon and sullied them both.

Arriving back at the stables, he leaped from his mount and tossed the reins to Saul.

"You well, my lord?" Saul held Brute's reins and squinted at Thomas.

Not in the slightest but the explanation would take too long. "Aye."

He took the keep stairs thrice a stride to the hall, praying nobody would hail him. Unfit for company and still raging at himself, he sought the solitude of his room.

He caught a kitchen boy halfway through the quiet hall. "I wish to bathe."

"Yes, my lord." The boy ran for the kitchens.

To scrub from his skin the taint of his dishonor and his shame. Madeleine deserved so much better than him, but she was stuck with him. That was his blame to shoulder as well. Had he kept his hands and his lust to himself, she wouldn't have given her virtue to him and would not be possibly carrying his child.

In his chamber, he stripped his doublet and chemise. He paced, his mind churning. If she wasn't with child, would the honorable thing be to release Madeleine from their betrothal? Everything within him rose in rejection of such an idea. Unworthy as he was, she was still his, woven into the weft of his being. Meager offering as it was, she owned his entirety.

A knock at the door stopped him, and he opened it.

Drudges entered with a bathing tub and water buckets. Clearly, the boy hadn't hesitated to convey his wishes.

Thomas stripped the remainder of his garments and climbed into the scalding water. It stung his skin, but he forced himself to endure the discomfort. The need to punish himself kept him from reaching for cooler water.

Eventually he grew accustomed to the heat, and it took some of the tension from his muscles. He lay back with his head on the edge of the tub and closed his eyes.

Since he'd first run into her at that abandoned chapel, Madeleine had been playing merry hell with him. He couldn't think, function, as himself with her about. She was like an illness to him. But an illness he craved like his next breath. What in God's name was he to make of all this, do with all this?

His door opened, blowing a cool draft of air over his shoulders. "Go away, Peter. I can do without one of your sermons now."

"I can promise I'm not here to sermonize," Catriona said.

Thomas sat up and stared at her. "Catriona?"

"Yes." She leaned against his doorframe and held up a pot. "I came to wash your back."

"What?" Aware he was taking too long to put the pieces together, he stared at her. "You shouldn't be here."

"Really?" She sauntered into the room, her hips swaying. "Because it wasn't that long ago that the chatelaine would make herself available to an honored guest." She trailed her fingers over his bed curtains. "To assist with his bath, of course."

If Edward saw her in his chamber, there would be death. Edward wouldn't wait around long enough to hear how Thomas would never consort with a married woman. "You need to leave."

"Do I?" Catriona pouted. "Are you sure you would like me to leave?"

"Yes." He didn't even give it a moment's thought. He wanted her out, and now. "Not only are your Edward's wife, but I'm promised to Madeleine. Nothing good can come of you being here."

She flinched, and her shoulders slumped. The temptress dissolved into a young woman who didn't look nearly so certain of herself.

"Catriona?" He gentled his tone. "You should leave."

"I know." She plopped onto his bed. "I can't carry on like this."

Arranging his knees for modesty, Thomas gave her the chance to speak. From what he'd seen at Elford, it was an opportunity rarely afforded her.

231

"You should hate me for being here." She sighed. "It will only cause trouble for you."

"Because Edward and I are at each other's throats?"

"Yes." A lone tear slid down her cheek, all the more heart-breaking for its isolation. "He doesn't love me, you know. He doesn't want me here. Seeing you with Madeleine, the way you look at her." Another lone tear joined the first. "I wanted that—want that. Not this cold, slow death day by day. I thought if he caught me here, with you, he would send me away. Madeleine loves you. She would never believe you had betrayed her."

It was one of the worst plans he'd ever heard. But it didn't matter anymore. All he needed to do was see her on her way and get some clothes on.

Catriona blinked her big green eyes at him. "Might I sit here for a moment and catch my breath?"

She'd left the door ajar. Anybody could wander in. While she sat on his bed and caught her breath. Damn his soft heart, but her tears disarmed him, and his head went ahead and nodded.

Stilling, Catriona glanced through the slight door opening.

A shadow darkened his door.

Thomas tensed.

"Oh, Thomas." Catriona lunged toward him and threw her arms around his neck. "Take me, Thomas."

Thomas surged to his feet and away from her. "What? No."

Water splashed over Catriona and doused the floor.

Edward stood in the doorway. He stilled and looked about. His gaze lingered on Catriona glaring at him defiantly, sitting in a pool of water, her gown soaked above the waist. He stared at Thomas. "Would you care to explain?"

"What explanation could you need?" Catriona stumbled to her feet. "You caught us. Everything is as it appears."

"No!" Thomas couldn't believe what he was hearing. He didn't know whether to clap his hand over Catriona's mouth and stop her or clap his hands over Edward's eyes so he couldn't see what he had seen.

"Everything is as it appears?" Edward's derision scored the air as he looked at Catriona. "What I see is you arranging matters to suit your story. Once again." His voice was so cold Thomas flinched. "I'd wager Thomas is even more surprised than I." The scorn on his face could cut steel. "Was I meant to demand justice? Kill Madeleine's betrothed?"

"I..." Her eyes beseeched him, but Thomas couldn't help her. Nor did he feel inclined to. In that bare breath between knowing Edward approached and Edward opening the door, Catriona had made a decision. The wrong decision for all of them.

She slumped. "I did not think you would kill anyone. I hardly thought I mattered enough to you to warrant such a reaction."

"Catriona?" Madeleine stood in the doorway. "What is all this?"

Thomas tried to cover himself with his hands.

Madeleine looked at Catriona, and then Edward. Finally her outraged gaze found him.

As he watched, Madeleine reached the wrong conclusion. With a look of outright scorn, she whirled about and stalked away.

Edward grabbed Catriona's hand and tugged her from the room. "You have caused enough mischief."

Suddenly alone, he contemplated chasing Madeleine but erred on the side of getting dressed first.

* * *

Madeleine couldn't be certain what drove her anger higher. She'd come in search of Thomas to let him know how she'd felt about him running away from her, and found him in his chamber naked, with Edward and Catriona.

Robert had made a fool of her, and she wouldn't allow another to do the same. Something about the scene didn't suggest seduction, but her hurt drove away reason. Thomas had treated her ill, and then she'd found him with Catriona. The man had insisted on marrying her, gone behind her back so that she'd no choice, and this was how he behaved.

"Madeleine," Thomas called.

She quickened her step. The words that had brought her to his chamber, searing her throat in their urgency to escape, now disappeared.

Thomas's footsteps pounded behind her. "Madeleine."

"I have nothing to say to you." She broke into a run.

"God's balls, wench!" Thomas gripped her by the waist and yanked her to a stop. "If you make me, I'll chase you across this entire demesne."

He wore only his braies, and his mussed hair stood up at the crown. She drew her shoulders back and glowered at him. "I don't want to speak to you."

"Good, then I shall speak."

The effrontery of the man left her speechless.

"Catriona came to my room. I didn't invite her, and I was in the bath when she came," he said.

Madeleine snorted and stared past him at the wall. However, his story did make sense. "Why would she do that?"

"She was there to seduce me," he said. "At least that's what she thought she was doing."

"What?" Her gaze whipped back to him. "You're not making any sense."

"I know that." He pushed a hand through his hair, disturbing it further. "None of this makes any sense. She was using me to anger Edward, in the hopes he would send her away."

"Have you lost your wits, Thomas? Why would Catriona want to leave Elford?" But even as she said it, the truth tinkled like a silver bell in her brain. Catriona had been unhappy for a long time.

Thomas gave her a steady look. "You know why."

And she did

Edward entered the hallway. "He speaks true. My wife desires that I send her from me."

Thomas whirled to face Edward. "She told you what she was about? I didn't invite her to my chamber."

"I'm aware of that." Edward sighed. "If it helps, I'm not sure she'd any intention of seducing you."

It didn't help one whit. "That did not prevent it from creating mischief."

"She begged that you and Madeleine speak with her." Edward motioned Thomas to precede him. "If you would?"

Madeleine's relief at discovering Thomas spoke true was swiftly replaced by her shock at Catriona. Edward and Catriona had been married for around two years, and the keep knew well how they didn't get on. True, she had never spent much time with Catriona, and the last few days they had spoken more than usual. Catriona had even offered her support as she sat sewing. What she had done now would not only hurt Edward, but her and Thomas as well.

For that alone, Madeleine wanted answers.

Thomas moved off with Edward and Madeleine joined them. If they were going to get to the bottom of it, then so was she.

In Edward's chamber, Catriona sat on the bed, in a sodden disheveled mess. Tears streaked her cheeks, and a red mark swelled her cheek.

"You hit her?" Madeleine rounded on Edward.

Edward reared back with a look of distaste. "Of course I didn't. She got that in her struggles against me."

"How?" Madeleine approached the bed. She stopped short of Catriona. "Are you all right?"

"Yes." Catriona pushed a hank of hair back. "He didn't hit me. I got this from the bedpost."

Madeleine glared at Edward, but she didn't believe her brother would hurt a woman, particularly not his wife. "Is what Edward says true?"

"Yes." The look Catriona threw Edward seared the air between them. "I can't—" She straightened. "No matter. I caused both you and Thomas pain, and now you must hate me."

Edward crossed his arms, his face an inscrutable mask, but Madeleine caught the flicker of hurt he hid as fast as it came. His silence shrieked with what he refused to say.

"Edward?" Surely this had hurt him too.

Catriona dropped her head and picked at the bedding.

"She made her choice," Edward said. "My lovely wife finds her time with me insuperable. So much so that she would risk your betrothal to get away from me."

Catriona glared at Edward. "You don't want me here."

"What I do or do not want hardly matters now." Edward's tone was as cold and implacable as his eyes. "You lied your way into this marriage, I should not be surprised that you sought to lie your way out."

The way Edward and Catriona flayed each other with words saddened her. She knew Catriona had done wrong, but there had to be more to the story. Madeleine perched on the edge of the bed.

Thomas tensed and moved closer.

With a sad look, Catriona shrugged. "I am sorry, but I thought the damage would soon be undone."

"Could you not have spoken to one of us instead? Adelaide? Mother?" Madeleine asked. The sad lines around Catriona's face tugged at her heart. "We love Edward, but we're not blind to his faults.

"I'm not one of you." Catriona threw Edward a look so weary, it made Madeleine ache for her. "You are all so close, and Edward is adored here. I am merely his troublesome Scottish wife."

Thomas cleared his throat. "You do appear as a united front."

"What does that mean?" Madeleine glanced at Edward, but he was staring at Thomas.

"It means that without meaning to, you create a barrier between your family and the rest of the world." Thomas gave Catriona a gentle smile. "It is easy to feel as if you are not a part of the family."

That couldn't be right. They had welcomed Catriona amongst them. Or had they? Before that day in the hall with Posy and her snickering friends, Madeleine could count on one hand the amount of times she had spoken with Catriona beyond every day matters. Had Catriona's loneliness amongst them driven her actions? Did Thomas feel the same way as Catriona?

Edward made an impatient noise and looked at Thomas. "As the injured party, it's your right to decide the punishment."

Catriona tensed.

"Madeleine?" Thomas looked at her. "What would you do?"

Raising her head, Catriona met her gaze.

Madeleine asked the question it seemed to her that nobody asked of Catriona, "What do you want?"

Blinking, Catriona drew a shuddering breath. "I would like to leave here."

Edward scoffed. "After all the lies you told to get here?"

"Edward." Madeleine motioned him to be silent. "Would you like to go home?"

"I can't go home." Catriona flinched. "My father would never accept me back. He would make it...unpleasant for me to be there."

Madeleine's father was leagues different from Catriona's, but it didn't make her blind to how other men treated their daughters. A woman returned to her home by her husband would be branded a failure, regarded as little more than used goods and treated as such. "There is always Rutherford?"

Catriona gave a tiny nod.

Edward cursed beneath his breath.

"Send her to Rutherford. She is a member of this family." Madeleine stood and looked at Edward. "Perhaps this can be the start of letting her know that her wishes matter to us."

Chapter Twenty-Nine

With all the evening's excitement, Madeleine ate dinner in her chamber. Poor Catriona. Even knowing what she'd done, Madeleine felt for her. And poor Edward. She had no idea what either of them would do now.

Not that her own betrothal situation was simple. Building storm clouds outside her casement echoed her growing confusion over Thomas, and she sat and watched them churn and grow.

That she would marry him didn't seem strange, and a growing part of her accepted that reality, even welcomed it. Her mother and sister had both married for love, but Madeleine had seen what passed for marriages for other girls her age. Some had husbands who ignored them, others prayed for a husband who would ignore them, and still others lived in an amicable arrangement that left them free to find love elsewhere. Witnessing Catriona's desperation firsthand today only made the situations other women suffered poignantly clear.

Madeleine had grown up with parents who loved and adored each other. The passionate connection between her parents was undeniable and had even embarrassed her when she was younger. Now that she was looking to marry, it made her want nothing less.

She'd thought she was in love with Robert, but had she really been in love with him? Given the revelations about Posy, she might not even have known him as well as she had supposed. She prodded at the sore place left by Robert's desertion and betrayal. If anything, her pride hurt more than her heart.

Should something happen to Father—God forbid—Mother would be inconsolable. When Stephen had died, part of Addy had died with him, and she would always carry him in her heart.

Madeleine had come too far down the honesty path to ignore the truth, that what she felt for Robert paled by comparison.

Abandoning her dinner barely touched, she sipped her wine and looked into the spectacular storm brewing over the mountains.

What she'd felt for Robert hadn't been love, but knowing that didn't make it any clearer how she felt about Thomas. She'd been so sure she loved Robert, she'd gone against what her family and friends said, ignored all advice trying to steer her away from him. Her certainty had been so unassailable she'd gambled her entire future on it.

The keep was quieter tonight. A few of their guests had already left, and others were getting ready to leave. She looked forward to having her home back. Of course, Thomas would stay. They had another twenty-seven days to their agreement.

As the storm raged outside her chamber, she climbed into bed and blew out her candle. Lightning lit up the sky, followed by low rumbling thunder.

"Madeleine." Thomas startled her as he slid into bed beside her. "I didn't see you at dinner."

She shrugged, glad he was there. "I wasn't much for company this night."

"Did I cause that?" He lay on his side beside her, his voice deep and quiet in the dark.

His question shook her into turning to face him. "How could you have?"

"Today. At the ruined chapel." He studied her face intently. "I wasn't in control of myself, and I might have hurt you."

"But you didn't." She could set his mind at rest about that. "I enjoyed it."

A smile creased his serious face. "Did you now?"

"Uh-huh." Darkness hid her hot face. "Is that why you're here?"

"Yes." He shifted to his back and tucked his hands beneath his head. "We don't speak much, you and I."

She couldn't deny the truth of that. "No, mostly we—"

"Yes." He cleared his throat. "It struck me that you might not know me well enough to know that today was not typical of me."

"Well, that's disappointing."

He gave a short laugh and turned to look at her. "I meant my loss of control."

"I know." She snuggled into his warmth and put her head on his chest. "And I do know you, Thomas. Even if we spent those years fighting."

"You did the fighting, mostly. I defended myself."

He needn't think he could get away with that, and she pinched him. "You did your fair share of provoking."

"True." He caught her hand and kissed it before laying it back on his chest. "But that was me as a boy. As a man, I'm as much a stranger as the rest of your slathering pack of suitors."

One of the things she was learning about Thomas, the man, was that he had a possessive streak. "Do you think you've changed that much?

"Not really." He chuckled. "Perhaps my bad habits have grown worse."

"The same could be said for both of us."

Lightning illuminated his strong profile. The crack of following thunder sounded like it came from right beside the casement. "Tell me something," she said. She traced the strong line of his jaw with a fingertip. His skin was warm and smooth and tempting. "Tell me something that I should know about you that I don't."

After a pause, he said, "I'm quite possibly the most ineligible suitor you have here."

"Why?" She rolled to her tummy and propped herself on her elbows.

"I'm not wealthy. I cannot offer you the life you have grown up with." Thomas spoke it as a simple truth, without false modesty or self-deprecation. "My manor is sorely in need of improvement. I have spent most of the coin I earned from my sword making the land profitable, ensuring my people will have a warm winter, comfortably fed. The manor has had to wait. It will take a lot of coin and time to make it decent."

Her dowry would certainly help with that. He said she didn't know him, but she had no concerns he wanted to marry her merely for her dowry. "In that regard, at least, you are betrothed to the right girl."

"Do you consider yourself betrothed?" He turned, his eyes glinting in the near dark.

"I do." It was her feelings on the matter that required clarification. Despite his poor demesne, marrying Thomas would be no burden. He had a strong back and had worked hard to restore his land, and he treated her as if they were partners in their betrothal. "Do you?"

"For certain." He put his arm about her and tugged her to his chest. "You are already mine."

His certainty was reassuring, and his heartbeat sure beneath her ear. Having him there, in the intimate dark, gave her more ideas like at the chapel. She pressed her mouth to his throat.

"Madeleine." His voice held a grumbled warning. "I came here to speak with you, beg your pardon."

"You're completely forgiven, and we have spoken." She trailed her finger into the open lacings at his throat. "Now we need to discuss reparations."

"Reparations, hmm?" He caught her finger and sucked it into his hot mouth.

The sensation made her breath catch. "It will have to be a punishment that matches your transgression."

He hummed and dipped his head. His mouth on her throat sent thrills dancing over her skin. "What do you suggest?"

"A lot more of that," she said.

Laughing, Thomas rolled her to her back and came down atop her. "Maddy?" His voice grew serious. "I'm serious about today. I shouldn't have lost control with you."

Madeleine studied the play of shadow on his beautiful, grave face and something within her melted. Thomas was such a strong man, and so contained and capable, it was easy to forget that a warm heart beat behind all the steely control. "Thomas, I feel no fear of you." And that she knew to her soul. "And you would never hurt me."

"Madeleine." He kissed her softly. "I didn't come here to make love to you."

"Thomas." The other thing Madeleine knew to her soul was that he needed to rid himself of his pesky honor in her bed. Here, it was only her and him, and not her father or Thomas's sense of right and wrong. "You spend a lot of time telling me you don't want me."

He reared back and raised an eyebrow. "You're a vixen."

"But I'm your vixen." She nipped at his chin. "And as of this afternoon, I have promised myself to be your vixen."

"Mad—"

Done with talking, she fastened her mouth on his.

* * *

Thomas woke with dawn still a couple of hours away.

A warm, fragrant, silky bundle, Madeleine slept against his back. In twenty-seven days, he would be entitled to wake with her thus every morning. For now, however, she wasn't his in the eye of

God and man, and he needed to leave before someone caught him there.

He loved her. As simple and astounding as that, the realization had hit him in the night. From the day he'd seen her at the chapel, she'd wormed her stubborn, willful way beneath his skin. God help him, because he would never again know a moment's peace.

He shifted beneath her and rolled to his back.

Murmuring sleepily, Madeleine made a new nest for herself beneath his chin.

When he was with her, she would bedevil and torment him, and when he wasn't, he would bedevil and torment himself wondering how she was and what she was up to. With Madeleine, there would always be something she was up to.

Fool that he was, he even loved that about her. Life with Madeleine could never be boring. She would be a partner, a strong woman to stand beside him. Together they would make strong sons and determined daughters. Together they would make Draycott prosper again, but her dowry was her own. He wouldn't touch it.

Cupping the smooth curve of her ass, he summoned his resolve. He really did need to leave.

Already, their child could rest within her. If they kept this up, it wouldn't be much longer before that happened.

"Sweeting." He kissed the top of her head. "I must go."

"No." She burrowed closer to him.

It felt like lopping a limb. "It's getting late, and I don't want to run into anyone."

"You're so proper." She giggled and kissed his jaw. "People would never guess what you do to me when they're not about."

Heat flooded his neck and cheeks, and he wanted to squirm. "I must go."

She rolled away, taking her warmth and silk with her. "I'll see you when we break our fast."

"Until then." He couldn't resist one last kiss before he left.

He pulled on his chausses and chemise and carried his boots as he let himself out of her room.

The flags chilled his feet.

"Thomas." Edward appeared out of the darkened corridor. "I need to speak with you."

Blight on it! Edward was the very worst person to catch him sneaking out of Madeleine's chamber. His jaw hadn't yet forgotten the potency of Edward's right fist. He tried for composure. "Edward."

"It's about Catriona." Edward shoved his hands behind his back. "I owe you recompense."

It must have cost Edward much to wrestle his pride into submission. What a pity that Thomas felt too mellow and pleased to want to take advantage of the rarity. "You owe me nothing."

"She tried to seduce you." Emotion blazed from Edward's gray eyes. "She could have caused untold mischief between you and Madeleine."

"I gave the decision to Madeleine, and she made a wise choice."

Edward's eyes narrowed. "Given the circumstances, I shall consider your presence in my sister's chamber to be about discussing her decision."

"My jaw would be grateful." Thomas couldn't stop his reflective wince.

Edward chuckled. "As will my ribs."

The sound drew a smile from Thomas, and also reminded him of the times they had played together, and when the competition had still been amicable. "When did we start disliking each other?"

Edward stilled and cocked his head as he thought. "I'm not sure I ever disliked you so much as envied you."

"Envied me?" If Edward hadn't been standing in front of him, Thomas might not have believed his ears. "This from the boy who had it all: the perfect family, the wealthy and illustrious father, the riches, the power. And you had the effrontery to be good at everything you turned your hand to."

"But not the best." Edward raised a brow and dared Thomas to argue. "I always wanted to be the best, and I would have been had it not been for my father's pestilent ward."

"I owe your father much." The penniless son of a dead fourth son, Thomas would never have fostered as well if not for Sir Richard. "He has been more than kind to me."

"He blames himself for your father's death." Edward shrugged. "I wasn't there, so I can't say, but my father counted yours as a friend."

"I always tried to make sure he didn't regret his generosity."

"He still doesn't." Edward cleared his throat. "I find this jawing thirsty work. Would you care to join me in a cup of ale?"

"It's early."

Edward laughed. "Or late, depending on how you look at it."

Despite the hour, a drink sounded right, and Thomas motioned Edward to precede him. "I'd like that."

They were both sitting before a blazing hearth with a mug before Thomas spoke again. "When does Catriona leave?"

"In the morning." Edward stared into his tankard. "I gave her the day to pack all her belongings."

"She won't be back?" Thomas was sure Madeleine hadn't intended Catriona's banishment to be permanent.

Edward swirled his tankard. "No. It's best for both of us if she should stay at Rutherford."

Thomas hadn't attended Edward's wedding, but Richard had given all his children their choice of mate. "You don't go well together?"

"Well together?" Edward barked a bitter laugh. "We can barely be in a room together without drawing each other's blood."

Nobody had ever accused Thomas of tact, so he asked, "Why did you marry her then?"

"I loved her." Edward sipped his ale and stared into the fire.

"Or perhaps it was merely lust, but whatever it was, from the moment I saw her, I was sunk."

"When did you first see her?" Edward's story was familiar.

Edward got a wistful look on his face. "In a forest glade. I thought she was fae for a moment." He chuckled. "And then she caught me spying on her." He shook his head and stared into the fire. "That seems like a lifetime ago."

Thomas wouldn't have guessed Edward's response. "You chose her?"

"Yes." Edward nodded and stretched his legs to the warmth. "I saw her, quite by chance, or so I believed, when I was out hunting."

After replenishing both their mugs, Thomas sat back in his chair.

"It was only later that I found out it was all a carefully calculated plot to bag a rich prize."

"Are you considered a prize?" Old habits died hard.

Edward laughed and shook his head. "Hard to credit, is it not?" Then his face settled into unhappy lines. "I was the prize, and I fell into the trap completely. I loved her, and she...tolerated me."

That had to hurt, and it struck close to Thomas's heart. He knew he loved Madeleine. Like Edward had been, he was ensnared, ensorcelled, enchanted. But God help him, he'd no reason to believe Madeleine felt the same.

Chapter Thirty

Most of her family was gathered already when Madeleine reached the hall the next morning. She greeted them before taking her seat.

"Our company grows thinner." She indicated the hall to Adelaide.

Adelaide gave her an arch stare. "They're leaving now that you're taken."

"Am I taken?" Madeleine attempted an innocent look.

Adelaide snorted and turned back to her meal. "Thoroughly taken if rumor is to be believed."

Madeleine's face glowed with heat.

"I heard what happened with Catriona," Adelaide said.

"Yes." Madeleine's good mood wavered. "She must have felt completely alone."

Adelaide sighed. "I think we should change that. I have decided to visit her at Rutherford and get to know her better."

"Edward won't be pleased."

Adelaide rolled her eyes. "Edward likes to forget how in love with her he was. He must have wanted her for a reason, and I want to find out if I can discover it."

All thoughts of Edward and Catriona disappeared as Thomas

strolled into the hall. She even forgot about Adelaide sitting right beside her.

"Our Thomas seems to have an extra swagger in his step." Adelaide nudged her. "Would you happen to know anything about that?"

Her face heated, but Madeleine kept her eyes on Thomas.

A smile on his face, he approached the dais. It was like it was only the two of them in the hall. Leaning down, he kissed her cheek. "Good morning, my lady."

"Good morning." Was it so terrible she wanted to drag him off to where they could be alone?

Adelaide made space for him on the bench. "You had best sit here."

"My thanks." Thomas wedged himself between them. "It's a fine morning."

"It is for some of us." Adelaide sighed. "It's hard not to be envious of you two."

Thomas sipped from Madeleine's tankard. "Have you thought of remarrying?"

"Thomas." Madeleine nudged him. None of them spoke to Adelaide about remarrying. Her heart had been so broken before.

"No." Adelaide propped her chin on her palm. "I wouldn't want to remarry, but that doesn't mean I would spurn company."

Now that Madeleine had experienced what it was to lie with a man, to be adored by him and have him show you the joy of being with each other, she could better understand how much Adelaide must miss that intimacy. "You could take a lover," she said.

"I could." Adelaide shook her head and laughed. "But that's perhaps a conversation we should have without Thomas."

Thomas was blushing and looking anywhere but Adelaide. It was adorable, and Madeleine kissed him.

His expression grew slumberous. "I believe we should go riding after we have broken our fast."

"Riding?" Heat suffused her limbs.

"Horses." He dipped closer and kissed her. "At first."

Adelaide made a strangled noise and shoved her fingers in her ears. "I beg you. I don't want to lose my meal."

They finished their meal and Adelaide excused herself to her sewing.

Her hand in Thomas's, Madeleine went with him to the stable.

He must have sent a message ahead because Queen and Brute stood ready to go.

It was a fine morning. The sun rose high in a cloudless sky. A playful breeze kept the worst heat at bay.

Both horses were ready for exercise and responded gleefully when given their heads.

Madeleine took the lead, moving in the opposite direction from the old church. Part of her felt like this morning was a new beginning, washed clean by last night's storm. She led them to where the land rose gently but steadily into a range of craggy hills. They had to slow when the ground grew stonier. The stiff breeze carried the hint of chill as the rise grew steeper and grass grew sparse amongst the rocks.

Madeleine stopped at a lookout point and dismounted. From there, the demesne of Elford spread out below them. The castle rose against the horizon like a honey-stoned sentinel. Clustered at her foot were the cottages of Elford. Velvety green swathes were broken by tilled land here and there. Patches of forest wove through the open land.

Madeleine breathed it all in with the wind. This was her home, and it struck her for the first time that she would leave here once she was married.

Coming up behind her, Thomas put his arms about her. "What?"

"Hmm?" She appreciated the warmth of his big body.

"Why did you look sad?"

He must watch her constantly to know her expressions so well. "I was thinking."

"What?"

"If we get married—"

"Madeleine," he growled.

"All right." Must he be so pedantic? "When we get married, I'll leave my home."

He shifted behind her and wrapped her tighter to him. "I can't promise you anything so grand as Elford." He cleared his throat. "Quite the opposite, in fact."

"It doesn't matter to me."

His chuckle carried a hard edge. "You say that now, but you won't be nearly so sanguine when you see my home."

"Our home." She covered his hands with hers. "It will be our home."

"Indeed." He kissed her temple. "I still must earn my keep, Madeleine."

"I know that." His mood had turned somber, and she wanted to lighten it again. "That's why you're marrying a rich wife."

"Madeleine." He titled his head and looked down at her. "I'm not marrying you for your dowry."

"I know that." He didn't seem inclined to let her change the tone of their talk. "But I have a large dowry, and we can make our home as we would want it to be with it."

Eyes dark and unreadable, Thomas watched her. "That's your money. You should keep it for our daughters."

"But Thomas." She shifted away from him to turn in his arms. He wasn't making any sense. "Why would we not use my dowry to improve our demesne?"

"I'll do that for us." His jaw took on a stubborn line.

"How?" She wanted to stamp her foot, but she must have been learning because she managed to keep a civil tone. "Your way is to wage war, and as good as you are at doing so, every time you step onto a battlefield, you take your life into your hands." She gentled her tone and took his hands. "I'm growing fond of you. I would like to keep you with me."

Thomas frowned and stepped away from her. "Maddy?" An

odd expression crossed his face. "You know I'm not marrying you for your dowry."

"I do." She wanted to touch him, but the distance between them seemed much larger than the scant arm's length.

"But do you know why I'm marrying you?" Thomas folded his arms. His face was inscrutable and yet she sensed a lot depended on her answer. It was like stumbling through a strange room blindfolded.

"You like me." Heat flooded her cheeks. "You desire me."

He laughed, a harsh sound, and turned from her. "You're fond of me. I like you and desire you."

"Yes." She closed the gap and touched his arm. "I don't understand, Thomas. We are arguing, and I don't know why."

"No, you don't." He stepped away from her and faced the view.

"What is it now, Thomas?" His back remained to her. Tension eked from him, and she really didn't understand what she'd done. "I have clearly angered you. The least you could do is tell me in what way I have transgressed this time."

"You really don't understand." He spun to face her. "And that's my own stupidity, but I had thought—it doesn't matter." Turning about, he strode for Brute.

That really was the outside of enough. "Don't ride away from me again." She did stamp her foot this time. "If you ride away again, you can stay away."

"Don't threaten me, Madeleine." He closed the distance between them and loomed over her. "I'm not going to patiently wait for you to call me to heel."

"And I'm not your whipping post." She wanted to shove him, but she resisted the urge. It probably wouldn't move him a breath anyway. "You're constantly getting into a temper with me. I can't think why you want to marry me if I anger you constantly."

"That's the problem." He grabbed her by the arms and drew her closer to him. "Let me make it clear for you then, Madeleine. I'm marrying you because I love you."

His declaration crashed through her and left her speechless. She could only stare and blink at him.

"Yes, Madeleine." He almost pressed his nose to hers. "I love you. God help me, but I do, and it maddens me that you don't love me back."

His gaze raked her as if searching for something. He wanted her to say it back. She could feel it in him. Part of her desperately wanted to give him what he wanted, but doubt whispered louder and louder to her and she couldn't.

"Right." He let her go. "Just so."

With her feet stuck to the ground and her thoughts in disarray, Madeleine watched him mount and ride away.

Even after the scene between them, Thomas would never take his perturbation out on his mount. That tiny piece of knowledge penetrated the icy fog surrounding her, and she wanted to call him back and speak to him. "Thomas!"

But he was already too far. He kicked his mount into a canter.

Madeleine ran to Queen and flung herself into the saddle. About to kick Queen into a gallop, Madeleine stopped.

Thomas's hurt lingered in the place he'd stood and told her he loved her. She believed him too, for the simple reason that Thomas would never say such a thing if he didn't mean it.

Her heedlessness rose to haunt her.

In myriad tiny ways, he'd been telling her he loved her before the words came out of his mouth. It had all been there for her to see, if she hadn't been stubbornly fixed on Robert.

She rode back slowly, thinking.

Thomas was also not a man to trifle with. His honor and nobility demand she behave in kind. He loved her, and before she said it back, she needed to be sure she felt the same.

She liked him. A lot. She desired him, more than she'd ever thought possible. He made her laugh, he frustrated and angered her as well, but she would put her life in his hands. By marrying him, she was doing exactly that.

None of her feelings for Thomas were tepid. It was as if he

was painted across her in bold, brash shades, shades that matched her own emotions. With Thomas she never had to censor or dim herself lest she overwhelm him. Solid, powerful and constant, like the rock to her tide, Thomas stood sure as she broke over him.

But was that love?

"Dear God," she whispered to the wind. "I'm not sure what love is. I only know what it's not."

Peter stood by the stables as she rode up. Face grim, he helped her dismount and handed her reins to a stablehand. "Thomas rode in a short time ago."

"We argued." There was no point lying to Peter.

Peter nodded. He'd known that already. "He rode out again."

"What?" Her own demand rose to haunt her. She'd told him if he rode away from her again, he could stay gone. "When is he coming back?"

"I can't be certain. He had matters to tend to." Peter looked at her. "What did you say to him?"

The possibility that Thomas might not ride back through Elford's gates strangled the breath from her. Her chest ached, and her thoughts whirled. "It's more a case of what I didn't say to him."

Chapter Thirty-One

Madeleine went for dinner that evening, but Thomas didn't. His place beside Peter remained empty.

With a shrug to her enquiring glance, Peter returned to his meal.

She couldn't leave it there, so she took a seat beside Peter. "Where is he?"

"Gone." Peter wouldn't even look at her.

"Peter?" She demanded he look at her.

With obvious reluctance, he turned his gaze her way.

"I hurt him," she said, and the words seared her as she did. "He told me he loved me, and I didn't say the same."

"Why?" Peter's eyes flashed ire at her. "Why can you not see what is obvious to the rest of us?"

"What do you see?" She must be blind. "Because all I see is that I wouldn't have wished to hurt him for anything, but saying I love him when I'm not yet sure can't be the answer."

Peter opened and shut his mouth. He studied her as if trying to read her thoughts. "What makes you think you don't love him?"

"I didn't say I don't love him. I said I needed to be sure, and that has nothing to do with him." She knew her trouble lay solidly at her door. "Thomas is all I would want in a man." She took a breath and admitted her true fear. "But not so long ago, I thought the same of another man. I wouldn't trifle with Thomas and tell him something only to make him happy."

"He would see through that anyway." Peter sighed and handed her a goblet of wine. "I hate that you do, but you make a valid point. Your pairing has all come about suddenly."

"For both of us." She relaxed. "All I know, at this precise moment, is that I'll marry Thomas and I'll be glad to do so."

Peter studied the depths of his goblet. "He went hunting," he said. "We have discovered where Wilfred is hiding." He squeezed her hand. "He'll be back."

* * *

But not the next morning, he wasn't. Heart sinking to her boots, Madeleine took her place beside Adelaide. Thomas had ridden away from her angry and hurt, and he hadn't even turned about to make sure she got back to Elford safely.

UnThomaslike behavior, for certain, and she didn't like it.

Over the long, stuffy night hours, she'd stoked her ire with every slight and transgression she could lay at Thomas's feet, trying to avoid her fear that Peter was wrong and Thomas would never come back.

Some time between the watch calling two and the first crowing of dawn, Thomas's faults had become a stream of things she did like about him. She liked how he made her laugh, how he always hovered close enough if she should need him but trusted her capable enough to give her room. She liked his strength and his prowess, and how other men seemed less in his presence. Her father thought much of him too, and that weighed heavily with her. Father gave his approval grudgingly, and it had to be earned.

The memory of Thomas dancing with her made her laugh until tears leaked down her cheeks, and then she'd stopped laughing, but the tears had kept coming. She'd injured him, and he'd done nothing to deserve being hurt.

Even Heather had left off teasing her as she had gotten dressed for her day.

If Thomas were here, she could speak to him, explain it wasn't that she didn't feel the same, she merely wanted a short time to be sure. Make him understand that she really did want to marry him.

Now that the specter of him not coming back had entered her mind, it made her achingly aware of how it would feel not to marry him.

She left table with her meal barely touched. Looking for air and space clear of people, she climbed the stairs to the battlements. From there she could see clear past the village. Out there, somewhere, Thomas roamed, and she really wished he would stop it and come back.

"Madeleine." Robert joined her at the wall and put a hand on the crenellation near her shoulder. "What are you doing up here?"

Nothing she would share with Robert. "Getting some air. It looks to be hot today."

"Hmm." He studied her face. Then he touched his finger to beneath her eyes. "We have known each other for too long to lie, Maddy. You've barely closed your eyes all night."

"It was warm." She shifted her face from his light grasp.

"I have barely slept either." Robert moved closer. "Not since my wedding day, have I closed my eyes."

"Robert." Madeleine grabbed for her patience. She didn't want another of those discussions with Robert. "This isn't right. These conversations have to stop."

"Don't ask that of me." He grabbed her by the arms. "Ask me anything, but don't ask that I forget you."

Dear God, the man had the skin of an ox. "Whatever we had, Robert, is done. You're married to Posy now, and I'm betrothed to Thomas."

"Blight upon them." Robert gave her a small shake. "You

know as well as I do that it should be us together." He yanked her to his chest and covered her mouth with his.

His lips were wet and sloppy, and his tongue thick in her mouth.

Madeleine ripped out of his arms. "Stop it!"

"I can't." He lunged for her and caught her about the waist. "You're mine, and I'm yours. It will always be you for me."

"No!" Posy stood by the battlement door with her hand over her mouth and her eyes filled with tears. "What are you saying, Robert?"

"He speaks without thought." It must have been awful for Posy to witness. "He doesn't mean it."

"Yes, he does." Posy's voice rose to a shriek. "He has always meant it. He doesn't want me. He wants you. This child I carry" —she cradled her belly—"he looks at it and wishes to his soul it was yours."

"Posy." Madeleine backed away from her. All that she said was horribly wrong. "That's not...it's your child with Robert, and that's as it should be."

"Don't." Posy dashed away tears, and her voice grew even louder. Curious heads turned up from the bailey and appeared along the battlements. "Don't pretend that you care. You've always wanted him. And he has never loved me." She thrust an accusing finger at Madeleine. "It didn't matter what I did. It's you he loved, and you he still loves."

"Hush." Robert grabbed Posy's arm and turned her about. "You're making a fool of yourself."

"Really?" Posy threw back her head and gave a grating laugh. "I rather thought you had done that for me."

Face pale, eyes blazing, Robert hauled her down the stairs and away from the battlements.

"Good Lord." Andrew came to stand beside Madeleine. "That was a nasty little scene."

"Yes." Madeleine was glad Thomas hadn't been there to witness it. "But Robert is mistaken."

Andrew cocked his head. "Is he?"

Her feelings for Robert had been those of a child. "Yes."

* * *

Another morning, another fast broken, and another empty place where Thomas should have been.

"He will be back." Mother patted her arm. Without Madeleine saying a word, somehow everyone in the keep knew she and Thomas had quarreled and he'd ridden off.

Because it was to her mother, she let her fear show. "Are you certain?"

"Darling." Mother wrapped her in a lavender-scented hug. "That man would do anything for you. But Thomas is a proud man, and he needs time to realize there is no place for pride in love."

It gave her hope and lightened her burden. "I thought I might go for a ride after breaking my fast."

"That's a wonderful idea." Mother patted her cheek. "I have some herbs I want to send to the old mother near the ford. Would you mind taking them for me?"

Anything to get her out of the keep waiting for Thomas to stroll in. "Gladly."

After her meal, she went to the stables and saddled Queen. The stall where Brute had been mocked her with its emptiness. However, his men still milled about the barracks. A couple of them nodded to her as she rode past. Perhaps it was her imagination, but they seemed glad to see her. If Thomas was done with her, would he not have made them all leave?

Fresh wind flattened the grasses in the meadow beyond the keep. Gray clouds hung over the treetops and promised rain later, but she would be well home before then. Perhaps Thomas was looking at those same clouds and rushing for Elford before they broke.

It was a silly, whimsical thought, but it cheered her.

"Madeleine," Robert called.

For a moment, she had the unholy desire to dig her heels into Queen and ride away before he caught up to her. Shoving that deep, she turned and waited for him.

"Madeleine." He drew his mount closer to her. "Thanks for waiting."

"What is it, Robert?" Another encounter like yesterday would fray her temper. There was nothing more to discuss, and Robert's insistence that there was only made her like him less and less. "I'm on an errand for Mother."

"I know." He twinkled at her. "I overheard her asking you. I snuck down to the stable and left before you."

"Why?"

"It wouldn't do to have people see us together." He grew serious. "Not after yesterday."

She nudged Queen into walking on. "About yesterday, Robert, it must not happen again. It's not fair to Posy or Thomas."

Robert sighed and rubbed a hand over his eyes. "I know that, Maddy. I really do, and I'm more sorry than I can say for yesterday. I just..." He shrugged. "I'm a man who made one grievous mistake, and now it seems I'll live my life having it thrust in my face." He stared at the meadow. "Be patient with me, Maddy. I'm slow to realize the things I should."

She and Robert had been friends for years. They had grown up together, and for a long time, she'd been sure it would be the two of them binding their lives together. "I'm going to marry Thomas," she said, and then added, "I want to marry Thomas."

"I understand." Anger flashed across Robert's face and then disappeared. "I'm not going to make another distasteful display of us, but I did this to us, and my anger is at myself."

Madeleine had nothing to say to that. If Robert had realized his feelings for her earlier, she would have married him. It didn't seem kind to let him see her relief. Posy had not had such a lucky escape.

They left the meadow and entered green wood. Thick oaks cut the wind and drew heavy shade about them.

Robert cleared his throat. "May I ride with you? We left the keep separately and nobody need know."

"My ride is rather boring." She didn't know how to tell him no. She didn't want to wound him.

"It's not the ride I care about." His sad smile rebuked her impatience with him. "Give me this one ride, Maddy, and let me pretend we are still as we were."

Discomfort nipped at her. Thomas would thunder and rage if he found out. She even missed him looming over her and telling her what she ought to do.

"Maddy?" Robert awaited her answer with an anxious look on his face.

If Thomas wanted to tell her what to do, he'd best be around to do so. "Fine."

"Thank you." Gone was the sad face, and Robert was more like himself. "Enough of that. We shall enjoy this day and hope not to get rained on."

They chatted easily as they followed the road through green wood and through a long sweep of fields. Between the rows of wheat and rye, rose the humped backs of those who tended the grain.

"Morning, Lady Madeleine." Jack the Strong waved from beside the road. "Be sure to turn back before that hits us."

Madeleine followed his pointing finger to the darkening clouds. "I haven't long to go from here."

Robert nodded to Jack. "Morning, Jack. How is that pretty little hunting bitch of yours?"

"Good, Sir Robert." Jack looked at his feet. "She's as canny as ever."

"That's the way it ought to be." Robert leaned down and clapped Jack on the shoulders. "You be sure to send me one of those puppies when she next whelps."

"Yes, Sir Robert." Jack sidled away from Robert's horse. "Please convey my best to your parents, Lady Madeleine."

"I certainly will." Madeleine moved on.

They passed through the village, with a couple of stops for a chat here and there. Mother always stopped to speak with the villagers. For once, Robert didn't seem to mind how many times she stopped. He even made it a point to greet every single person she did.

He caught her studying him as they rode beyond the village and into the sparser farmland beyond. "What?"

"I thought you hated chatting to the villagers."

He gave her a long stare. "A man can learn the error of his ways, can he not?"

"It seems he can." She spurred Queen forward. Robert had the look he got when he started in on his regrets and how they should be together.

"Maddy?" Robert had stopped at a small path to their right. "Do we have a minute to look in on an old friend?"

She really didn't want to be caught in the rain. "I don't—"

"Please, Maddy, it would mean so much to Nurse if you did."

"Nurse?" She hadn't heard from nurse in a long while.

Robert gave her an arch smile. "I had a dark purpose in joining your ride. Nurse has instructed me to abduct you if necessary, but I must bring you to her today."

"Why today?" If Nurse wanted to see her, she had only to request it, and Madeleine would gladly go. "I really must deliver these herbs."

"Maddy." Robert gave her a reproachful stare. "Have you forgotten what today is? You couldn't have forgotten."

Her mind worked rapidly and came up with nothing, but Robert didn't know that. "Of course I haven't forgotten." She forced a carefree smile on her face. "Lead the way to Nurse."

"See if you can keep up with me." Robert's horse lunged into a gallop.

Madeleine almost didn't follow, but if Nurse was expecting

her, she would hate to disappoint her. She dug her heels into Queen.

Laughing over his shoulder, Robert raced across the pasture.

Maddy raced right after him.

They had left the village far behind when Robert finally drew rein. They were almost at the old church, and they were definitely going to get wet. She couldn't be sure she absolutely remembered where Nurse lived, but it didn't seem reasonable it was out near the chapel.

"We should turn back." Madeleine drew even with him.

"Shut up, Madeleine." Robert raised his hand. "I'm so sodding tired of the sound of your carping."

Robert's arm fell, and pain exploded behind her eyes.

Chapter Thirty-Two

Madeleine woke to a pounding head and churning belly. She barely rolled over in time before she vomited. Pain spiked through her head, and she had to lie down again.

When she next woke, her head had calmed to a dull throb and her stomach had settled. The smell of vomit threatened to change that, and she eased herself into a sitting position. Her eyesight dipped and swayed and slowly formed shapes. The shapes took on meaning in her sluggish thoughts.

She was in a cottage she didn't recognize. Aside from the cot on which she lay, there was a rough wooden table, a bench near the hearth, and a bucket in the far corner. The fire smoldered and provided meager heat.

Shivering, she stumbled to her feet and threw another log on the fire. Her limbs didn't work as well as they should, and she had to sit on the bench while her head stopped swimming.

The bucket was filled with water, and after swilling out her mouth, she used as much as she dared to clean the floor.

As she worked, her mind collected the disparate pieces of memory and put them in order. Robert must have rendered her senseless and brought her here. None too gently, if her sore head and body were any indication. Why remained a mystery.

She tried the door. Unsurprisingly, it was locked, as was the small shuttered casement. She rattled the shutters and then the door, but they were sturdy and not moving.

Pressing her eye to a small gap in the shutters, she tried to make out what surrounded the hut. Tree trunks and undergrowth crowded a bare earth clearing. She was in a wood or forest, and it must be beyond the old chapel. That didn't help. Long shadows and the hut's chill persuaded her it was late evening.

Gently she eased the cricks in her joints and limbs and sat on the bench. Before she'd lost awareness, that flash of Robert's face had been no Robert she'd ever seen. In that moment, he'd looked like a cruel, angry stranger.

Her situation was like a strange dream from which she wished she could awaken. Only if it was a dream, she wouldn't be growing colder, and she wouldn't need to relieve herself.

Robert could be thoughtless, and impatient when he grew bored—which he did rather easily. He had never liked to be thwarted and didn't like losing.

Still, it made no bedamned sense.

Perhaps it was an elaborate jest, and he would reappear with a laugh. Hitting her on the head wasn't her idea of a joke.

Robert's short temper and churlishness over losing took on a new, more sinister meaning. As a child, he'd bided his time to get even with a childhood slight, which could be seen as cunning.

Since Thomas had appeared, Robert had changed. Or more accurately, since Thomas had appeared and bested him at everything. When it had been merely the other men her father had invited, Robert had continued to tease her and keep her at arm's length. But Thomas had been so much more of a threat than all the others combined. For the first time, Robert couldn't be so sure of her.

Was that what this was all about? Marriage?

That didn't make any sense either. Robert was married to Posy. Abducting her wouldn't change that.

She pulled the blanket from the cot and huddled before the fire. She'd only one log left, and she didn't know how long she would be there.

Her imagination flew on that thought. Perhaps Robert planned to leave her there until winter. She would starve long before that. Either way, it would solve his problem. Except if he planned to kill her, why go to the bother of bringing her there and locking her in?

Queen! What had happened to her horse? If Robert had hurt Queen, or worse, she'd rend him limb from limb.

She heard hoofbeats coming through the wood. They stopped outside the cottage.

Madeleine grabbed the last log and hid to the side of the door. It wasn't much of a plan, but she had the advantage of surprise.

The door opened and Robert walked in.

Madeleine swung for his head.

Robert ducked and whirled, taking the impact on his bracer. He tossed the log and cuffed her.

Madeleine hit the wall and slid to the floor.

"Maddy." Shaking his head, Robert tossed the log in the fire. "You're not in your father's hall anymore. Here, you will learn to behave like a proper woman."

Cold rage burned through her. Robert had hit her, and hard. Her shoulder ached from where it had hit the wall and her cheek throbbed. "What do you want, Robert?"

"The same thing I have always wanted." He crouched in front of her. "You."

"I would rot in hell first."

"Cheer up, sweeting. It's not you I want in the carnal sense. Posy is much more to my taste there. It's the other delicious morsels that come with you, that dowry for a start."

Wanting to keep her distance, Madeleine drew her knees up to her chest, and tucked her skirts around her ankles. "I don't understand, Robert."

"Of course you don't." He stood and picked up a sack he'd dropped when she'd tried to hit him over the head. "You're too much of a spoiled bitch to understand what need is."

His anger shocked her and she turned the conversation to another pressing concern. "Where is Queen? Where is my horse?"

His expression darkened. "She got away after I clubbed you. You fell off and I couldn't catch her." He sneered at her. "Stupid and willful, just like you. I cannot fathom why your father would allow you to ride such a beast." A chilling smile replaced his sneer. "But all that changes. Now that I am in command you will know your place."

She'd come within a hairsbreadth of marrying this lout. "What is your plan in bringing me here?"

"You've yourself to blame there." He pulled bread, cheese and a cooked chicken from his sack and placed them on the table. "You were supposed to marry me. God knows you were eager enough for it."

The truth of his statement seared her. She'd all but begged him to marry her. She'd thrown herself at him. "I would have married you, too."

"I knew that. Everybody knew that, even your family. Although they were none too happy about it."

She almost laughed aloud. "They didn't think you were worthy of me."

"Worthy?" He spun on his heel. "They should have bent the knee and thanked me for having you."

Madeleine chose not to remind him of how he'd bent the knee for her.

"No, but they would rather have Thomas." He pulled a jug of mead from his sack. "Your father always had some maudlin attachment because Hugh died unnecessarily."

"It wasn't that." Madeleine didn't know why she bothered to correct him, but speaking somehow pressed back the nightmare.

"Hugh was loyal to my father from the days when he'd nothing but his sword. He died the night my father married my mother. All that Hugh had wanted was peace between Elford and Rutherford, and he died moments before he got to see it realized."

Robert sneered. "How tragic. He left poor little Thomas behind. And now that poor little Thomas is all grown up, of course he must marry you."

Thomas hadn't yet been born. Hugh hadn't even known he had a son on the way. "My father still gave me the choice of whom to marry," she said. "If you must know, nothing had been agreed between Thomas and me before you announced your betrothal. I only said it had as a salve to my pride."

"Really? I felt sure it had." Robert raised a brow and sipped from the mead jug. "You were like a bitch in heat the moment he came near you."

"I—"

"Please, spare me your maidenly protests." He took another slug of mead. "You're a lusty one, all right. It made the idea of marrying you bearable."

That hurt. Even coming from that cur, it took a piece off her. "None of this changes your marriage to Posy."

"A marriage I shall easily have annulled. I haven't touched her since the marriage."

He must be cracked. "She's having your child. Whether you've bedded her after the vows or not hardly matters now."

"Yes, but it's only my child because she says it is."

Posy wasn't above lying to get her way. "She's not pregnant?"

"Oh, she's breeding all right." He broke off a piece of bread and ate it. "And it's mine. I took her maidenhead. But only she and I know that."

"And now me." Poor Posy, and that sentiment grew every time Robert revealed some new treasure about himself.

"You're not a problem." Robert took a bite of cheese. "By the time you leave this hut, you will have learned to behave." He took another piece of bread. "You will know what to do with that mouth of yours and when."

He would die and become worm food before that happened. She saw no need in popping his daydream. He would find out he was wrong soon enough. "That leaves Posy."

"Who has hardly made herself any friends." Robert chuckled. "She's known for a liar, and I have several men ready to claim she came to their beds many times. It will be the word of a vindictive harpy against theirs and mine." He shrugged. "She played so nicely into my hands with her hysterics on the battlements."

It wasn't much of a plan and relied heavily on chance, but far be it from her to assist him in plotting her downfall.

"Lesson one." Robert held up the bread. "I brought food enough for us to share. Then you tried to escape, so now you will be punished." He slapped cheese on the bread. "If you behave, I'll save a crust for you to break your fast in the morning."

"I need the privy." She wouldn't beg him for a damn thing.

"After I have eaten, I'll take you outside." He sat on the bench and leaned against the wall. "And I'm not inclined to hurry." He sipped mead. "You can help me settle my horse for the night."

The very real possibility of rape rippled through her. She took deep breaths to calm herself. If she gave in to fear, she would be useless.

Father had always told them fear and anger were your enemy. They crowded your mind and slowed your thoughts. Calm brought the ability to think your way out of a situation.

"I'm with child," she said. She could very well be.

Robert frowned and looked at her. "I'll say it's mine."

"Thomas won't believe that."

"That might be a problem." Robert smiled. "But he won't want you once I'm done with you. I'll claim the child as mine, and it will save me the effort of having to keep it up long enough to do the job myself."

It was as if he wanted to flay her with words and then deeds.

Did he think she minded one whit that he found her repulsive? No. She was thanking God with every breath.

"We needn't go through with this." She gestured the hut. "We can say that this is your child today."

"Maddy." He wagged a chiding finger at her. "I know you too well for that. Besides—"

His grin made her go cold.

"I'm going to enjoy setting you right."

Not wanting to see his smug face anymore, Madeleine closed her eyes and leaned her head against the wall. His plan was madness. But it didn't matter how she saw his plan. It only mattered that Robert had embraced it, and that meant he was going to execute his plan.

"I'm not sure how this will all play out," Robert said. "I made sure it's known we are both not at the keep tonight, and we were seen together by many in the village this morning." He stretched and yawned. "If it comes to it, I have a priest who isn't too fussy about the truth."

Chapter Thirty-Three

Madeleine tried to watch for Robert's vigilance to lessen, but eventually she fell asleep. She woke to a gray morning, and Robert already up and about.

As much as the vulnerability rankled, she said, "Robert, I need to relieve myself."

"Good morning." He gave her a sunny smile. "I thought you might." He motioned the cottage door. "After you."

Outside, forest surrounded the cottage. None of it looked familiar. Peering through the tree cover, she located the sun and tried to work out her position. They had to be within a day's ride of Elford. Scotland was north, the sea to the east. From there, she could make a plan.

Robert motioned her to precede him into the trees. "It's not what you're used to." He chuckled. "But it won't be forever. See it as an adventure."

Adventure her arse, but arguing with him was pointless. Her energy was best conserved with finding her way out of the bind. Robert had more chance of whistling for the wind than getting her to marry him.

He stayed about ten feet back as Madeleine hunted for a good bush. Finding one, she slipped behind it.

Thick branches concealed her from Robert, and she held her breath. She took one step back and then another.

"Madeleine?" Robert looked toward the bush.

"Yes." She stilled. "I shan't be long."

Robert grunted and leaned a shoulder against a tree. "See that you're not."

She slipped further back into the trees. She couldn't outrun him, but perhaps she could get deep enough to evade him.

The forest floor was strewn with debris, and she watched every step she took. Stealth must win over speed. She put enough distance between her and Robert that she couldn't see him anymore.

Soon he would realize and come for her. Every instinct screamed at her to run, but he would find her too soon if she did. Father had spoken about how, when in battle, instinct needed to be weighed against reason.

She slid further into the forest.

A twig cracked and her head was yanked back by her braid. "I thought you would try something." Robert tightened his grip on her hair. "But against my better judgment, I gave you a chance."

Madeleine screamed her frustration and tried to free her hair.

He yanked her head back and made her neck ache. "Shut up, you stupid sow." His face twisted in a cruel mask. "You did this to yourself."

"I'm sorry." He dragged her behind him, and Madeleine had to concentrate on not falling over her feet. "I won't do it again."

"No, you won't." Robert gave her hair a twist. "Because you can soil yourself before I trust you outside the hut."

Kicking open the hut door, he shoved her inside.

Madeleine lost her balance and slammed knees first into the hard-packed earthen floor. "I'm sorry, Robert, but you would have tried as well. I really do need—"

"Here's what you're not understanding, Madeleine." Robert dragged her over to the central support pole. He shoved her against it hard enough to jar her back against the wood. "I don't care what you want or what you need. You're nothing to me." He yanked her hands behind her back and bound them with rope. "All those months I've spent kissing your toes and begging for scraps are over."

Finished binding her, he stood over her. His face was flushed and his gaze burned. "I'm in charge here, and you will pay for every slight you dealt me and every time I had to humiliate myself in front of you."

"It wasn't like that." Madeleine hardly knew the man looming over her with murder in his eyes. "I loved you."

"More fool you." Scoffing, he brought his face close to hers and yelled, "Because I never loved you. Not once. Not even for a second."

All this time he'd been pretending? "Why?"

"Why do most men want your hand, Madeleine?" He tapped the side of his head. "Think about it."

"Money?"

"There we are." He jabbed his finger at her. "You're a smart one. I grew up begging for crumbs from your father's table. I won't spend the rest of my life doing the same."

The way Robert saw their lives bore no resemblance to her picture. "My father respected you. He trusted you as one of his own. He certainly never saw you as a beggar."

"Please." Robert scoffed. "At best, he only ever tolerated me." He scowled. "Not like that whoreson, Thomas. Thomas could do no wrong. The sun shone right out of Thomas's arse."

Father might not have merely tolerated Robert, but he'd also not favored him. "This can't work." Her arms hurt and the rope chafed at her wrists. "You can't keep me here until I agree to marry you."

"You say that as if your agreement matters to me." He chuckled. "And you had better hope it does work." His grin made her blood freeze. "You won't like the alternative."

* * *

Four days, and Robert hadn't given her so much as a chink to slip away through. He watched her constantly, and when he couldn't, he tied her to the pillar. He left her tied up for all of that first day and night and had then released her the next morning.

Madeleine had been grateful enough to promise him anything to get some movement about the cabin.

One day, he'd left her tied to the pillar for most of the day. Madeleine had barely kept from soiling herself. Fortunately, he hadn't held good on that threat and took her out twice a day.

She was forced to accustom herself to him watching her relieve herself.

"Fire needs tending." Robert lounged with his feet on the table. "And don't get any ideas with that wood."

She could feel his eyes on her every move. If she kept doing as he said, he might start to relax with her, and then she could take her chance. "Shall I make dinner?"

"Yes." He smiled. "Heat the water."

Madeleine put water in the pot and moved it over the fire. He delighted in giving her menial tasks to do. Well, his petty revenge had failed because doing something kept her from losing her mind.

Surely her family had realized she was missing and were already looking for her. If Queen had returned without her, they would know something was amiss. Except, Robert had made sure he was seen with her in the village on the day he took her.

"Look at you." Robert chuckled. "You might even make a worthy wife at some point." He yawned and stretched. "Not that I care. I have given it some thought, and I'm pleased you're with child. It will save me having to do the job."

One day, she would get free, and then he would pay for every insult, every cruelty and every indignity. She would relish carving them out of his flesh with a dull knife. Her thoughts kept her going.

Madeleine kneaded the bread dough and set it aside. "What should I make for dinner?"

"I haven't yet decided." Robert sniffed. "Is that you I can smell?"

Her hair was stuck to her head and her dress was stiff with dirt. She wouldn't be surprised if it was her. For her part, she hoped her smell made him sick to his stomach.

"I can't make dinner if you don't tell me what you want."

Robert stared at her. "I would have thought you couldn't make anything." He gestured her bread. "I would never have guessed you were more than a useless bauble."

His insults fell right off her. To think, she'd spent so much of her life caring what this sod thought of her.

When his insult failed to penetrate, he grew petulant. "I can't think past the stench of you." He stood and kicked the table. "I won't be able to eat with that reek."

What a pity. Inside she cried a million tears for his hardship.

"Come." He grabbed her nape and shoved her toward the door.

That was new, and Madeleine grew fearful. Thus far, all her new discoveries about Robert had been awful. "Where?"

"You stink."

"I can't help that." She wished she could say the same, but Robert had provided himself with fresh raiment and washed each night.

He tied a rope around her wrists and dragged her into the forest.

"Where are we going?" She concentrated on keeping up with him. If she fell, he would only drag her behind him until she managed to regain her footing. She still had the scrapes on her knees and shins from the last time that had happened.

Robert strode through the forest, going further from the cabin than they had before. The trees thinned as they ended beside a small pool fed by a sprightly stream.

With her first clear view of the sun, Madeleine estimated she was north of Elford.

After untying her hands, Robert shoved her at the stream. "Bathe."

The water was so welcome, she wanted to fall right into it. "Could I have some privacy?"

Robert smirked and sat on a nearby log. "Bathe yourself or I'll do it for you."

It was no idle threat, and turning her back, Madeleine shimmied out of her clothing. She rushed for the concealment of the pool and had to sink to her knees for the water to cover her.

Sitting straight, Robert stared as if he could see through the water. "I like my women with more meat on them, but you're not repulsive."

Dear God, the last thing she needed was him taking that sort of interest in her.

"Did Thomas see you?" He laughed, his eyes glittering. "I like knowing that I have seen what he has."

Madeleine sunk deeper into the water.

"I shall like it even better knowing I have had what he has." Robert waded into the pool, lust suffusing his expression. "I've certainly tupped worse."

Staying low, Madeleine scooted away from him. She'd grown complacent around the fear of rape. She tripped over a rock beneath the water and tumbled back.

"It's time for you to make this worth my effort." Robert lunged for her, grabbing her by the nape and dragged her toward him.

Her toes found the rock, and then she managed to grab it.

Robert's eyes widened and he tried to duck.

Desperation drove her and Madeleine crashed the rock down on his head.

He cried out and tried to grab her hand, but Madeleine hit him again. And again. And again, until he slumped into the water, his head sinking beneath it. Blood streamers colored the water pink.

More rocks scraped her feet as she scrambled for the bank. Snatching up her dress, she ran with it.

Robert hadn't allowed her any shoes, and the ground hurt her feet, but she ran until she was out of breath. Then she stopped and struggled into her dress.

Forcing herself to calm, she took her bearings.

By the sun's position, it was late evening. She set off south.

Chapter Thirty-Four

Madeleine kept moving. She couldn't take the chance Robert hadn't drowned, and she wasn't going back to check.

A brisk night breeze chilled her sweat on her skin, and her feet felt like she was walking on the bare bleeding bones. Still, she didn't stop.

Around sundown, she came upon some berry bushes, filled her pockets with what she could grab, and stuffed her mouth as she walked. Fear kept her pace to a fast hobble. God alone knew how far she'd yet to go, and she wanted to conserve her strength if she needed to run suddenly.

As the sun rose, exhaustion dragged at her legs and made them feel like lead weights. Soon, she would need to find a hiding place and rest.

A dog appeared in front of her so suddenly that she shrieked and leaped away from it. It pushed through the hedgerow and stood in front of her, hackles raised.

Responding as was its nature, growling and snarling, the dog pursued her.

"Oy!" A man pushed through the hedgerow after the dog. "What's all that noise?"

Madeleine shrank back.

"Lady Madeleine." He pressed closer to her. "Is that you?"

The dog continued barking, and Madeleine struggled to find her words. The man knew her, he knew her. Did that mean she was safe?

"Shut up." The man lunged at the dog. "Don't you be showing your teeth to our Lady Madeleine."

She found her voice. "Am I on Elford land?"

"Yes, my lady." He hauled his cap off his head. "It's me, Alfred, the carpenter from the village."

"Alfred?" She blinked until his face became clear. "Alfred Carpenter?"

"Yes, my lady." He shoved his cap back on his head. "Where've you been, my lady? There's been that big a fuss and bother over you being gone. Since that horse of yours returned without you, the men have been out day and night looking for you."

"I..." Queen was safe. She was safe. Tears rose so suddenly she couldn't stop them. They clogged her throat and poured down her face. Her body shook under the strength of her sobs.

"See now, Lady Madeleine." Alfred patted her shoulder awkwardly. "You don't take on so. Alfred will see you home."

* * *

Madeleine woke the next morning in her own bed, in her own chamber. She'd vague memories of arriving home to lots more tears and even more hugs. Even Edward had looked glad to see her. She had yet to see Thomas, and he was the one she wanted to see most.

Her family had taken the news of Robert's perfidy as she would have expected. Mother had gone very silent and then looked at Father. Father had nodded at her brothers and they'd all left Elford within the hour.

Not a scrap of pity for Robert bothered her. He would get what he deserved, reaped what he'd sowed.

A knock sounded on her door, and Mother peered around. "Good you're awake."

Madeleine struggled into a sitting position, her limbs still sore from her escape.

"I have ordered a bath for you." Mother sat on the edge of her bed. Her face was grave. "Your father sent me to ask you...if..." She cleared her throat. "If Robert..."

And then Madeleine got it. "No, he didn't touch me. Until the last day, and I clobbered him."

"Good." Mother's eyes took on a bloodthirsty gleam.

"He told me several times how unattractive he found me. He was glad when he discovered I might be carrying Thomas's child."

Mother raised a brow. "Are you?"

"Um...not as far as I know." Her face flamed. Madeleine stared at her bedding and prayed for a hole in the earth to drop through. "I only pretended to be with child to keep Robert away from me."

"That was clever." Mother smoothed her skirts. "I have news for you."

"News about Thomas?" Madeleine hadn't seen him when she'd stumbled into the hall last night. She hadn't been in any state to ask either. "He must have returned by now."

"Yes, he did." Mother frowned out the casement, and then turned to her and took her hand. "He came back hours after you rode off the morning you disappeared."

Thomas was back. That made her dizzy with joy. "He found Wilfred?"

"Alas, no." Mother grimaced. "Wilfred was gone by the time Thomas arrived. He spent a few days trying to track him but to no avail."

There was something about Mother's manner that made Madeleine nervous. Mother was parsing out the truth like she feared how Madeleine would take it. "Where is Thomas?"

"Not here." Mother took a deep breath. "He came back to the news that you had gone, my darling, and Robert was missing too.

Your argument with him and Posy on the battlements was brought up and used as evidence that you and Robert had run away together."

"What!" Madeleine bolted upright. "How could anyone believe that was true?" A nasty suspicion wormed into her mind. "Did you believe it was true?"

"Me?" Mother looked affronted. "I knew better, but Thomas..."

Her stomach sunk. "Thomas couldn't have believed them."

"Posy was convinced of it, and her outrage was most persuasive. Even Simon and Edward believed it possible." Mother looked apologetic. "Once Queen returned without you, your father sent men out immediately. He didn't believe it either."

At least her parents knew her better. But Thomas couldn't believe she'd run away with Robert.

Why not? Whispered a poisonous voice in her mind.

Thomas had come across Robert trying to kiss her at the old church. Thomas's guilt and concern that he'd hurt her might also be added to the witch's brew. Then there was the scene her mind ducked away from repeating. Thomas had told her he loved her, and she'd stood there like her lips had been sewn shut.

As much as she wished for the distracting heat of outrage, she couldn't find it within. Thomas had believed her in love with Robert, and that she didn't love him.

How stupid she'd been not to recognize she was in love with Thomas earlier.

"Madeleine?" Mother took her hand. "I'm sorry to tell you this, but Thomas left. He believed you had..."

"Run off with Robert." Madeleine swallowed the lump of disappointment in her throat. Through her ordeal with Robert, there had been so many times she'd wished for Thomas, dreamed that he would burst through the door at any moment.

Peter had been wrong. Thomas had given up on her.

It hurt so much, like a vise around her chest, squeezing the air out of her. "I did this."

"Sweeting." Mother gathered her into a hug. "Matters are rarely so defined. Whatever you did, Thomas must have done his part too."

"No." She clung to Mother's comfort like a small girl. "All he ever did was try to love me, and I was too stupid to let him."

* * *

That night, she was called to the hall. Her father and brothers were back. She doubted they would be back so soon without Robert, but she didn't know if he was dead or alive.

Lingering fear tightened her belly. She wanted to yank it out of her, exorcise it. After all Robert had done to her, this felt like the worst. He'd made her fearful. Because the fear inside her wasn't that she'd killed him, but that he could find her again and make her suffer those days again.

Clasping her hands together, she forced herself to walk into the hall.

Robert was alive, although he looked battered, bruised and bloodied. His gaze flickered to her. "Madeleine. It seems you've bested me."

"Yes." And it had cost her anyway. Robert had cost her Thomas. "I didn't think to see you here alive."

"It was a close thing." He glanced at Edward and grimaced. "But here I am."

Even bound and on his knees before the hall, Robert remained arrogant. No trace of him begging her forgiveness could be detected. Perhaps he couldn't see what he'd done as wrong, or perhaps he didn't care.

She looked to her father. "What will you do with him?"

"His father is a good man." Father looked pained. "It grieves me to take his son from him."

Robert paled. "But she's well." He jerked his head at her. "I didn't kill her. I didn't even defile her. Tell them, Maddy. If you ever had a sprinkling of the love you swore for me, tell them that much."

His conceit staggered her. After what he'd done, he still looked to her as if sparing his life was his due.

"Then don't," she said to her father. "Don't kill him."

"Maddy." Robert beamed at her. "I knew I hadn't been wrong in you."

"Strip him of everything but the clothes on his back. Have him marked a betrayer and banished from our demesne. Then send word that whoever shelters him shelters the enemy of Elford."

Robert's look of shock left her feeling hollow. Not even the evening of the score between them could make up for what she'd lost.

"What about Posy?" At last Robert's voice contained fear. "She carries my child. She will speak for me."

"Posy has left for Rutherford," Father said. "She has said she doesn't want to come back to Elford and has washed her hands of you."

Robert looked aghast. "She wouldn't have."

"Ah, but she did. Are you certain you want to banish him?" Andrew surveyed Robert. "I think he would look much better without his head."

Robert looked appalled. "We grew up as brothers."

"We were not brothers." Andrew's face was colder than a winter's eve. "These are my brothers." He pointed to Simon, Edward and Oliver." Then Andrew gestured her. "And that's my sister. You forfeited your life the moment you put your hands on her."

This was her more rational brother.

"I suggest you start emptying your pockets," her father said, stepping closer to Robert. "You owe my daughter your life because I'll honor her request. My sons on the other hand—" Father shrugged. "I have no control over them. I could do nothing if they took it upon themselves to sneak away and indulge in some hunting."

Madeleine didn't care if her brothers did or didn't. She turned and went back to her chamber.

She opened her door to Heather ready to put her to bed and Adelaide sitting on her bed. Tired and wanting nothing more than to sink into her bed, Madeleine suppressed a groan. She wanted to skip the girl chat.

"We've been waiting for you." Adelaide's cunning smile got Madeleine's hackles rising. "We wanted to speak to you."

"I'm tired." She turned so Heather could unlace her bliaut. "Can we not speak in the morning?"

"We could." Adelaide tilted her head. "Or you could be spending the morning differently."

Heather helped her out of her bliaut and threw a robe over her chemise. "Hear what we have to say and then decide tonight."

"You're in league with my sister?"

"Yes." Heather hopped on the bed beside Adelaide. "We are in perfect agreement."

Feeling annoyed and somehow betrayed, she washed and dried her face. Heather sat beside her sister and looked smug.

"Have your say then, and let me sleep." She joined them on the bed and started combing her hair.

"Thomas left," Adelaide said.

"I'm aware of that."

Heather poked her shoulder. "And he's still gone."

"Really?" She made her tone as scathing as she could. "I hadn't noticed."

"That's certainly the way it appears." Adelaide gave her a meaningful stare. "It appears as if your betrothed left and you care nothing."

Sharp hurt lanced through her. "That's not true."

"I told you so." Heather smirked at Adelaide.

"Then why doesn't she go after him?" Adelaide smirked right back.

Madeleine stared at the two of them as if they'd gone daft. "I can't go after him."

"Because she's scared." Heather jerked her head to indicate Madeleine. "She's scared and hiding here."

"For all the good that will do." Adelaide snorted. "Thomas had his heart and his pride wounded. He won't come back without inducement."

"I have destroyed his love for me." Tears choked her voice.

Adelaide and Heather stared at her, then at each other, and burst into laughter.

It shocked Madeleine's tears away.

"I'm sorry." Heather attempted to stop. "But if you think that, then you're more of an idiot than Thomas is."

She was insulted for both her and Thomas. "I beg your pardon."

"Uh-oh." Heather giggled. "It's her frosty tone. Beware."

"What do you two want from me?" She gave up on them. They were behaving far, far beneath her notice. "If he'd wanted to see me, he would have waited for me."

"But he didn't." Adelaide gave her an admonishing stare. "So, what are you going to do about it?"

Heather nudged her. "Yes, what are you going to do? Somebody has to march right up to him and let him know how wrong he is."

"Someone whom he's besotted with. Someone he can't think straight around," Adelaide said.

Heather smirked. "Someone who holds his delicate little heart in her hand. That someone should get over there and kick his arse before he does more thinking with it."

They had both taken leave of their senses. There was no other explanation. "You think I should go to Thomas?"

"Exactly." Heather beamed at her with pride as she said to Adelaide, "I told you she wouldn't need much persuading."

"I can't do that." Madeleine's thoughts sped. She said she couldn't do that, but was that really the case?

She could get Queen and ride after him. Father knew where his manor was. Indeed, they might as well do it right. Father, Mother and a full escort could take her to Thomas. Let him look at her family and her and tell them all that he'd surrendered his fight for her.

"He left without even speaking to me." Hurt slithered away under the harsh light of anger. "He's always making these assumptions where I'm concerned, and I'm well tired of it."

"Isn't that just like a man?" Heather pursed her lips. "They can never see further than the tip of their noses."

"I'm going after him." Maddy's purpose firmed as she spoke, and she marched for the door. "I'm going to ask Father for a full escort and for him to accompany me." Her idea bloomed by the heartbeat. "And those brothers of ours can leave off Robert and join us."

"You do that." Adelaide waved her fist.

Heather whooped. "Go and get that man."

Madeleine stopped with the door ajar. "Come on, you two. This was all your bloody idea in the first place, and you can jolly well come with me."

Chapter Thirty-Five

As dawn broke, Madeleine led her column of Elford folk out of the castle. Her brothers, both parents, Heather, Adelaide, a few castle folk, and a substantial escort all joined her expedition.

God help her if he didn't want her anymore, because she was going to have to hear it in front of all these people. But news had spread through the keep the previous evening and anyone who felt they had any investment in her and Thomas had decided to come.

Despite the size of the party, Father kept them to a brisk pace, and they camped that night just inside Elford land. They rose early the next morning—Adelaide whining—and got underway again.

Mother rode beside Father, looking far too young for her years.

As they rode, her parents kept their heads close together. They still had that magic togetherness bubble about them. In the bustle of castle life, it often got lost, but out here, it was in clear evidence.

That's what she wanted. That's what she'd been looking for.

Adelaide poked her arm and indicated their parents with her

head. "We grew up with the expectation of having that." She sighed. "It makes it hard to accept anything less."

"But you loved your husband." Madeleine watched her father lean over and whisper something to Mother that made her laugh. "You had that."

"I'm not sure I had that." Adelaide wrinkled her nose. "I loved Stephen, and what we had was good, but I'm not sure it was that."

Yes, her parents were husband and wife, but the friendship underpinning their marriage went soul deep. "They're partners. Equal partners in everything they do."

"Exactly." Adelaide tapped her pommel. "With Stephen, we shared everything, but he was young. Looking back, I can see how he was more of a boy at times than a man."

"What's the difference?" Madeleine looked over to where Simon was trying to pull Oliver from his horse.

"Shouldering your responsibilities." Edward nudged his horse between hers and Adelaide's. "Protecting those who look to you. Carrying your weight."

Edward never spoke about his marriage, and somebody needed to ask the question Catriona couldn't. "Is that what you wanted?"

"Yes." Edward glanced at her, and then stared at the horizon. "Once we are done sorting you, Madeleine, I think it's past due that I deal with my own family situation."

Adelaide clapped a hand on her thigh and grinned. "We'll get Thomas and Maddy sorted and then it's your turn."

Shaking his head, Edward gave a wry laugh. "I have a feeling I'm going to need all the help I can get."

* * *

Dusk on the third day of traveling put them near enough to see Thomas's manor. Built of pale stone, it rambled along the brow of a small hill, commanded a view of the land on three sides, and overlooked the sea on the fourth.

Father sighed and looked about him. "Hugh chose the prettiest spot for his manor."

"Yes." Mother looked about her. "The holdings look prosperous enough."

Father shook his head. "Thomas's uncle beggared the land and the people. Thomas has done much to improve things. He took care of his people first."

"I have a large dowry," Madeleine said.

Mother touched her cheek. "That you do, my darling. And a family who will do what they can to help."

Clustered together on the seashore, whitewashed cottages showed signs of having been repaired. The village looked to be busy with fishing lines strung out to dry, smoke swirling from chimneys and children playing between them.

"That will be all Thomas's doing," Father said. "His uncle near stripped the land and people before Thomas grew old enough to take charge."

Mother turned to her. "Before we enter that manor, be sure, Madeleine, that you want to be his helpmate in all of this. You and Thomas deserve nothing less."

Madeleine nodded. "I have a strong back and a pair of willing hands." This was where she wanted to be. She was sure, more than sure. The only thing she wasn't sure about was if Thomas would welcome her.

People trickled out of the manor as their party approached. The guards were alert but relaxed.

Thomas's tall form filled the doorway, and then he emerged into the dying light. His gaze picked her out and stuck.

Madeleine's mouth dried, and her mind emptied. Her entire party looked to her, waiting for her to act.

Why had she thought this was a good idea?

Thomas frowned and looked their party over. "Sir Richard." He bowed to her father. Then her mother. "Lady Margaret."

"Come along." Andrew stood beside Queen. "Down you get. This is your dragon to slay."

Despite Andrew's help, she more stumbled than dismounted.

Adelaide winked at her.

Heather jerked her head at Thomas and made faces at her to get on with it.

Thomas looked at Father. "I don't understand. I thought she would come when—"

"As soon as she got back." Mother beamed at him. "We brought her as soon as she got back. She has something to say to you."

Right! They had all come here for this, best she got to it.

"Thomas." Madeleine stopped three feet from him. He looked so good to her Thomas-starved gaze. The lines of his beautiful, strong face as uncompromising but dear to her as ever. Those dark eyes that could freeze like frost or burn like flame.

He gave her a stiff bow. "Lady Madeleine."

They were back to Lady Madeleine, were they? She rather thought not. "I returned to Elford to find you gone."

"Yes, I could not find Wilfred. I am still searching." He shifted and glanced at her hovering party. "We thought it best—"

Adelaide cleared her throat. "I really think you should not speak and listen instead."

"Why are you all here now?" He growled his frustration. "What is this all about?"

Madeleine had the answer to that. "You made me a promise. To marry me." She gestured her party. "We are all here to ask why you broke that promise."

He gaped at her, and then anger suffused his face. "I did not break—"

"You left Elford." Edward stared hard at Thomas. "You left before Madeleine came back."

Thomas gaped at Edward and then anger suffused his face. "You know damn well why I did that."

"Yes." Edward smiled beatifically. "But Madeleine is unaware of why you left. She thinks—"

"I can speak for myself, Edward." Her family really took too much upon themselves. "You believe I left with another man. Robert. You think I left you for Robert."

Thomas blinked at her.

"I see how you would think that." She grasped for her courage. "But let me fill in the gaps in your knowledge. I didn't run away with Robert; he abducted me. He kept me in a hovel for five days before I managed to escape and find my way home."

Thomas stilled. Violence simmered beneath his unnatural lack of motion. His gaze went to Father. "He abducted her?"

"He did." Father looked relaxed as he sat his horse. "Robert has been dealt with."

"Not by me he hasn't." Thomas's jaw hardened. "You have him?"

"We can speak of that later." Father waved a hand. "The matter is in hand."

"Not until it's in my hands." Thomas took a step closer to Father's horse.

Edward snorted. "Stand in line. Whoever gets him first gets first blood." Then he pointed to her. "I suspect you've other matters to attend to. Urgent matters."

"I returned home, not to find my loving betrothed waiting for me"—Madeleine risked poking him—"but to find he'd decamped and left me."

"I didn't—" Thomas shut his mouth and shook his head. His eyes were harder than ever as he looked at her. "Did Robert hurt you? Are you well? You look well." He clasped her chin and stared into her eyes. "Are you well, Maddy?"

"I was frightened and humiliated, but not hurt." She covered his hand on her chin with her hand. "I was hurt to find you not at Elford. I understand why you left, what you thought, but you were wrong about other things too. Not just Robert."

"What else was I wrong about?" His expression softened, and his gaze warmed.

"You were wrong if you thought I didn't love you." Surely his worry for her well-being augured well for him still loving her.

He jerked and looked doubtful. "Don't lie to me about this. I don't need or want your lies. This is too important."

"I love you, Thomas." She moved closer to his warmth. If he allowed her close, she would never leave again. "I should have said it before, but I couldn't trust myself enough to be sure. I thought I loved Robert. I was wrong, and I mistrusted myself so much that I almost lost you because of it. I needed to be sure."

"And now?" He looked as if his entire being hung on her answer. "Are you sure now?"

"Sure enough to drag my entire family here to hear me say it." She held his gaze and let him read the truth in her eyes.

"Indeed." Simon crossed his hands on his pommel. "Are we going to dismount at any point? My arse is sore, and I'm hungry."

"Simon!" Adelaide glared at him. "You're ruining this."

Oliver sighed. "He might be ruining it, but I second his complaints."

"For the sake of my brothers' arses, let me make this clear." Madeleine stood with her toes touching Thomas's. "I love you. I love you so much more than any of the feelings I thought I had for Robert. It just took me a while to realize it."

"Enough to marry me?" Thomas slid his hands about her waist and drew her against him. "Enough to marry me and live here with me? Work by my side to make this demesne all it can be?"

Joy bubbled inside, and Madeleine laughed. "Enough for all of that and a herd of children with it."

"A herd?" Up went Thomas's eyebrow. "That's a lot of—"

"All right." Father dismounted. "We all know how children are beget, and I definitely don't want to hear that in connection with my daughter." He drew abreast of them. "I'm entering this dwelling. Somebody needs to find me something to eat and something to drink." He clapped Thomas on the shoulder. "Now is when you kiss the girl."

Madeleine looped her hands about his neck. "What a splendid idea."

"Before we get to that, I think you should know you've been deceived." Thomas tightened his hold on her.

Adelaide went past them into the manor. "I think deceived is a strong word."

"How are you with lied to?" Thomas pinned Adelaide with a hard stare.

She laughed and patted his cheek. "We are relying on you to make her happy enough to forgive us our slight deception."

Madeleine glared at her sister's back. "What deception?"

"It was for your own good." Mother smiled and followed Adelaide into the hall.

Madeleine turned to Thomas. "What deception?"

"I didn't leave Elford because I thought you had left me for another man." He kissed her forehead. "I refused to believe it until you could tell me yourself."

"He really was most insistent." Edward stopped beside them. "And he was losing his mind looking for you. And to be perfectly honest, hampering search efforts in his determination."

"I was not hampering anything." Thomas glared at Edward.

"You were most insistent on doing everything yourself. We're a family, Thomas. We do things as a family." Andrew replaced Edward as Edward drifted indoors. "Father set him a task." Andrew smiled at her. "For Thomas to get his manor in order for you. When you got back, Father did not want you living in squalor."

Oliver, and Simon went past them into the manor.

Simon winked at her. "We also thought he might discover more about Wilfred's whereabouts."

"Bother, bloody Wilfred." Madeleine wanted to get back to the talk of love and forever.

Heather stopped at the door. "Thomas knew he loved you.

We knew Thomas loved you. We also knew you loved Thomas, but we had to be sure you knew you loved him."

"I did. I do," Madeleine shouted to her back. Thomas hadn't left her. He had never lost faith in her. Thomas was not the sort of man to break his word. She should have known him better than that. Fortunately she had a lifetime to do so. "You didn't leave me?"

"Never." Thomas dropped a soft kiss on her mouth. "You are mine. Now." He kissed her again. "And from this day forward. All mine."

If you're a medieval romance fan, check out Sir Arthur's Legacy also by Sarah Edwards.
Or join my newsletter to read the Prequel to The Betrothal Melee, The Marriage Parley for free (links below the Sweet Bea excerpt).

* * *

Sweet Bea, #1 Sir Arthur's Legacy

* * *

Is love sweeter than revenge?

Dreamy, impulsive, and spirited, the Lady Beatrice embarks on a mission to save her family from losing everything. Unfortunately, she chooses as her savior the very man who hates her family the most.

Angry and sworn to vengeance, Garrett will see Sir Arthur pay for destroying his life. He has chosen as his instrument Sir Arthur's youngest daughter, Beatrice.

Both intent on their missions and drawn together by an undeniable attraction, can Sweet Bea teach Garrett that love, not vengeance, is the greatest reward of all?

* * *

Chapter 1

Beatrice had a secret. A secret of the most delicious sort.

She was being wooed. Wooed with honeyed words and sweeter touches. Tingles spread to Beatrice's fingertips, rushed back again, and pooled in her stomach.

Ducking her head, she kept her pace to a saunter. There was nothing amiss with her. No reason for anyone to pause their day and watch her.

Spring filled the air with scents of new grass and wildflowers. The sun beamed from a cloudless arc of blue above her. Birdsong serenaded her as cornflowers merrily bobbed beside the path. Even the insects buzzed encouragement. She was young, she was in love, and the world could not be more perfect.

Garrett. Just his name made her shiver.

* * *

For first dibs on news, deals, and giveaways, and so much more, join the @Home Collective

Or if Facebook is more your thing, join the Sarah Hegger Collective

Anything and everything you need to know on my website http://sarahhegger.com

About the Author

Sarah Edwards is also published under the name Sarah Hegger

Born British and raised in South Africa, Sarah Hegger suffers from an incurable case of wanderlust. Her match? A hot Canadian engineer, whose marriage proposal she accepted six short weeks after they first met. Together they've made homes in seven different cities across three different continents (and back again once or twice). If only it made her multilingual, but the best she can manage is idiosyncratic English, fluent Afrikaans, conversant Russian, pigeon Portuguese, even worse Zulu and enough French to get herself into trouble.

Mimicking her globe trotting adventures, Sarah's career path began as a gainfully employed actress, drifted into public relations, settled a moment in advertising, and eventually took root in the fertile soil of her first love, writing. She also moonlights as a wife and mother. She currently lives in Ottawa, Canada, filling her empty nest with fur babies. Part footloose buccaneer, part quixotic observer of life, Sarah's restless heart is most content when reading or writing books.

f

Praise for Sarah Edwards

Sarah Edwards also writes as Sarah Hegger

Drove All Night
"The classic romance plot is elevated to a modern-day, wholly accessible real-life fairy tale with an excellent mix of romantic elements and spicy sensuality."
Booklife Prize, Critic's Report

Positively Pippa
"This is the type of romance that makes readers fall in love not just with characters, but with authors as well."
Kirkus Review (Starred Review)

"What begins as a simple second-chance romance quickly transforms into a beautiful, frank examination of love, family dynamics, and following one's dreams. Hegger's unflinching, candid portrayal of interpersonal and generational communication elevates the story to the sublime. Shunning clichés and contrived circumstances, she uses realistic, relatable situations to create a world that readers will want to visit time and again."

Publisher's Weekly, Starred Review

Hegger's utterly delightful first Ghost Falls contemporary is what other romance novels want to grow up to be." – Publisher's Weekly, Best Books of 2017

"The very talented Hegger kicks off an enjoyable new series set in the small Utah town of Ghost Falls. This charming and fun-filled book has everything from passion and humor to betrayal and revenge." –
Jill M Smith, RT Books Reviews 2017 – Contemporary Love and Laughter Nominee

Becoming Bella
"Hegger excels at depicting familial relationships and friendships of all kinds, including purely platonic friendships between women and men. Tears, laughter, and a dollop of suspense make a memorable story that readers will want to revisit time and again."
Publisher's Weekly, Starred Review

"...you have a terrific new romance that Hegger fans are going to love. Don't miss out!"
Jill M. Smith – RT Book Reviews

Blatantly Blythe
"Ms. Hegger has delivered another captivating read for this series in this book that was packed with emotion..." Bec, Bookmagic Review, Harlequin Junkie, HJ Recommends.

Nobody's Fool
"Hegger offers a breath of fresh air in the romance genre." – Terri Dukes, RT Book Reviews

Nobody's Princess
"Hegger continues to live up to her rapidly growing reputation

for breathing fresh air into the romance genre." – Terri Dukes, RT Book Reviews

"I have read the entire Willow Park Series. I have loved each of the books ... Nobody's Princess is my favorite of all time." Harlequin Junkie, Top Pick

Also by Sarah Hegger

Sarah Edwards also writes as Sarah Hegger

Urban Fantasy

The Cré-Witch Chronicles

Prequel: Cast In Stone

Vol l: Born In Water

Vol ll: Purged In Fire

Vol III: Raised In Air

Vol IV: Cradled In Earth

Vol V: Joined In Spirit

Sports Romance

Ottawa Titans Series

Roughing

Hooking

Contemporary Romance

Passing Through Series

Drove All Night

Ticket To Ride

Walk On By

Running On Empty

Ghost Falls Series

Positively Pippa

Becoming Bella

Blatantly Blythe

Loving Laura

Hunter Brothers

Nobody's Angel

Nobody's Fool

Nobody's Princess

Medieval Romance

Sir Arthur's Legacy Series

Sweet Bea

My Lady Faye

Conquering William

Defying Roger

Henry's Honor

Love & War Series

The Marriage Parley

The Betrothal Melee

Western Historical Romance

The Soiled Dove Series

Sugar Ellie

Standalone

The Bride Gift

Bad Wolfe On The Rise

Wild Honey